Other Worlds, Other Nightmares

A Collection of Short Stories
By Kevin Mullin

Written Words Publishing LLC
P.O. Box 462622
Aurora, CO 80046
www.writtenwordspublishing.com

Published by Written Words Publishing LLC October 21, 2024.

ISBN: 978-1-961610-20-0 (paperback)
ISBN: 978-1-961610-21-7 (eBook)

Library of Congress Control Number: 2024921417

This is a work of fiction. All events and characters in this story are solely the product of the author's imagination. Any similarities between any characters and situations presented in this story to any individuals living or dead or actual places and situations are pure coincidence.

Cover designed by Written Words Publishing LLC

Manufactured and printed in the United States of America

AMY COLLINS BOOK SERIES

Finding Home (Book 1)
Amy Collins: A Boston Adventure (Book 2)
Amy Collins and the Marsh Matron (Book 3)

OTHER BOOKS BY KEVIN MULLIN

Other Worlds, Other Nightmares
Dagda: House of Horrors

CONTENTS

The Lawton House

When my brother, Sam, came home from the Vietnam War in the summer of 1971, he was not the same. He had sustained a major head wound and had to have a steel plate inserted just above his right eye, so we expected him to be different. He survived an explosion that killed four other soldiers instantly, but Sam was lucky, even though the shrapnel grazed his head and left him in a coma for weeks. Another unit of soldiers found him and their medic kept him alive long enough for the evacuation helicopter to bring him to the closest hospital where the Army doctors saved his life.

Normally, such a head wound could have caused all kinds of hardships, but Sam seemed to be unscathed. None of the doctors knew him before the injury so they didn't notice how his personality changed. His outlook on life was less casual and unconcerned. I noticed, after his medical discharge, he started to take pride in his appearance. He threw away his jeans and old t-shirts and replaced them with dark slacks and button-down shirts. And although he never wore a tie, he always affixed a tie pin to his lapel. Shaped like a dragon, it sparkled with tiny sapphires. He told me they were real, but I wouldn't know a real sapphire from the cheapest fake.

He wore that pin every day, on every shirt. He never left home without securing it to his collar. Some of his old friends and acquaintances occasionally made fun of him because it looked like a woman's broach. Certainly, it was uncommon for a man to wear something like that, but Sam laughed off any negative comments.

"A real good buddy gave me this pin," he said to me. "He told me it would bring me good luck every day I wear it. And let me tell you something: it kept me alive when the shell hit."

"Wouldn't it have been better luck not to get wounded in the first place?" I was skeptical.

"I wanted to come home, anyway," he shrugged. "But yeah, a regular discharge would have been more convenient."

Home was different for Sam after he returned. He turned twenty-one and the Army and the war hardened something in him. The wound and steel plate affected him as well. His friends all grew a few years older in different ways, which made them still fit into their small-town roles. Sam was never going to fit in again and everyone knew it.

In high school, he lived and breathed football. It was his life. Sam and his best friend, Dave Barkley, played the game together for years. Dave manned the quarterback position and was the smartest boy in school. Sam played left tackle and he could have been smart, as our father always told him, but he had no discernable interests in life other than football. He would pick up a book the way a child would pick up a poopy diaper. The quarterback got all kinds of attention and awards. Dave's name headlined the sports page in every Saturday newspaper when they recapped the game highlights. Sam was a good player but anonymous. Most linemen rarely get their name in the papers, and Sam was no exception, though I genuinely believe he didn't care. Dave also got straight A's and was the class valedictorian. Sam got all C's, thanks to the coach's influence. He received one trophy in his senior year as 'Best Team Player.' although he didn't display it anywhere. He said it was nothing more than a participation award. No big deal.

They joined the Army together instead of going to college. Everyone thought they made a strange decision, especially since Dave received more than a few scholarship offers from some excellent universities. After his father died, he decided to see the world before committing to a career. He easily talked Sam into going with him. Since none of the college scouts even looked at him, Sam decided he had nothing better to do and he needed to make a life for himself. Sam came home with his wound. Dave came home in a box.

Maybe because of the steel plate in his head, Sam lost all interest he had in his old life. He didn't even watch football anymore. His enthusiasm for work became nonexistent, so our uncle hired him to be a night watchman for his closed and deteriorating sawmill. Abandoned buildings draw high school kids and homeless folks faster than free beer at a frat party, he told us. Lawyers love it when the kids fall and hurt themselves. Suing people brings in big money for those who don't like to work. All the adults in our life figured that since 'poor Sam' was virtually unemployable, this would be a good job for him.

Was it ever. He discovered the joy of reading at that job. He began making up for twenty-one years of not studying anything. He devoured books. Real ones, by famous authors. Gone were the comics and girlie magazines he

3

collected before the Army. Nonfiction became his new favorite. He had a passion for science and unsolved mysteries. And we lived near Nueville, the home of Louisiana's strangest occurrences, disappearances, swamp lights, UFOs, unknown creatures, and anything else supernatural. When he wasn't reading, he visited old houses, fetid lakes and who knows what else.

His favorite subject involved the scientist Dr. Scott Montgomery and his theories on interdimensional physics. Very few people study or even remember Montgomery today. Nobody assigns or reads his papers or books anymore. He was the personification of the fictional 'mad scientist.' People associated him with Nicola Tesla, who many people believe was the smartest man of the 20th century. He may have been. All I can say for sure is that he had a lot of competition.

Sam loved to talk about Montgomery, his new hero and the first man he admired not associated with football. He played the central role in the Lawton House Mystery, sometimes referred to as the Halloween murders. No matter what it's called, there is no evidence that murder occurred there that night. Nobody recovered any bodies, anyway. That's what makes it a mystery.

Fifty miles east of us, the Lawton House, a two-story plantation home, rose ominously from the ground, barely visible from State Highway 190. To most people, it was just an old house with a large fence topped with razor wire that the locals avoided. But on nights with no moon ("New moon," Sam would correct me), people told stories of lights that turn on and off, blinking crazily for all the wee hours before going dark again. Sometimes, people would set up cameras and film these occurrences. The 'true' haunted house shows still love to broadcast those grainy old videos.

That is why people say the Lawton House is haunted and why the fence needs to be so sturdy. Haunted houses attract strange people, some destructive but mostly dumb. The kind of fools who break inside and get themselves hurt or killed and then sue the owners for their own stupidity. And they usually win. Maybe they aren't as stupid as everyone thinks.

Nobody knew exactly what happened there on that mysterious night, other than it must have been bad. Since Sam read so many articles on the subject, he created a timeline of events.

What is known is that, like most terrible events, it started out with the best of intentions. Martin Holmes, who married Maria Lawton, the oldest Lawton daughter, owned the place in 1921, the year of the Halloween party. Maria disappeared the year before and nobody ever saw her again.

The doomed costume party happened on Halloween. The invitations included instructions which clearly stated that only those who came to the door dressed as supernatural beings would gain entrance. Demons, devils, monsters, and vampires entered with no questions asked. The ushers rejected all the pirates, princesses, cowboys, and Indians, even if they had an invitation. No second chances. Rules are rules.

Martin Holmes, by all accounts, was an occult enthusiast of the worst kind: he had lots of money. He hired Montgomery to create a Halloween atmosphere, which inspired the scientist to concoct an 'energy interceptor,' a simple generator adapted to capture and direct invisible cosmic forces to suit his needs. He wanted to blur the lines of our reality with another dimension.

His experiments and studies in galactic forces and interdimensional energy drew great debates in the colleges and universities of his era. Today, he is a forgotten man. Even though no one ever disproved any of his ideas, the scientists and scholars never pursued them.

"These forces he harnessed are intense," Sam explained to me one day. "But most of us are unaware of them. Just envision a hurricane with eighty-mile winds. Buckets of rain. Thunder and lightning. Just inches away from us. But we aren't even aware of it because we're in a nice dry house with thick walls protecting us.

"Montgomery had the idea that he could force a small hole through the barriers that separate us from other dimensions and allow us to glimpse multiple worlds. Just think of a television. A click of the button changes the channel. He wanted to do that with reality.

"But the energy field itself could be dark. That's why the guests had to dress up as evil things. It would help enhance the energy flow. Montgomery would harvest that power and channel it into a powerful field and bathe the guests in this dark energy, just enough to momentarily transform them into whatever beast they imitated. The effect would only last for a moment or two and then he would shut it off."

"Why would anyone want to go to a party like that?" I asked.

"No one told them what the plan was. It was all going to be a surprise."

He told me more about that party as time went on. Some of the information was new to me. Out of fifty invited guests who entered the house, only four came out alive. Martin Holmes was not one.

"You see, Montgomery left early that night. All he did was set up the equipment and leave before sundown, as he had another important business venture in Baton Rouge.

He gave Holmes strict instructions on how to operate his machine before driving away. Evidently, he told Holmes to turn the power level to a certain point, but Holmes wanted to see more and cranked it to a higher level. According to Montgomery, Holmes took the energy level to a point of no return. Even after Holmes shut down the machine, the guests didn't transform back to their original selves.

"Montgomery was called to testify later that week in the inquest, but his testimony was permanently sealed."

"What happened to the four survivors?" I asked.

"They were committed to a private asylum where all kinds of doctors and specialists examined them. They couldn't help them, mind you, they only studied them."

"Why was that?"

He shrugged, "Officially, they came out of the house with serious burns and the doctors used an experimental treatment on them. That's what the government said, anyway. Montgomery's machine blew up and everyone else burned to death, their bodies charred beyond recognition. That's why the funerals were all closed-casket. Other people said there were no bodies and they buried empty coffins."

"Oh," I said. "And unofficially?"

"There was no fire. The house doesn't even remotely look charred or burnt. The guests all went mad and killed each other after Holmes released the energy and the transformations took place. He must have permanently transformed them into the creatures they dressed up as that night. Human souls. Monster bodies. And that's what they were for the rest of their short lives. And the bodies in the house were unrecognizable. The officials identified the victims by their costumes or driver's licenses. Only the government officials actually saw anything. And their reports are still sealed, even though it was over fifty years ago."

The Lawton House remained his favorite subject whenever we got together. I always felt it was a harmless obsession of a wounded veteran and nothing would come of it. But I was wrong.

He knocked on my door one morning after he got off work. "You'll never guess who I had coffee with yesterday morning," he said, his eyes wide with excitement.

I looked at the clock as it chimed five o'clock in the morning, then glared at him.

"Niles Warden," he said triumphantly.

"Who?"

"The caretaker of the Lawton House. You know, ever since the night of the party, the owners never let anyone on the property. Just a housekeeper and caretaker for the land. And they can't be on the property until the sun is completely up and gone before dusk. Once, he got involved in a project and lost track of the time and started hearing a voice from the house calling him and he hightailed it out of there. So, I just happened to be in the neighborhood and ran into him."

"The Lawton House is over fifty miles from here. You didn't 'happen' to be there, you made a concerted effort to get there."

"Whatever, the point is that there's nobody there all night. And you know what else? There's a basement. That's where Montgomery set up his cosmic generator."

"Really?" I was skeptical. "Nobody builds basements in Louisiana. We build houses on pilons to keep them above the water. A basement would be a wet, moldy mess that would collapse on itself."

"Montgomery invented a special formula he mixed into

the concrete to seal out water. It had some kind of super small conductors imbedded in the mix and, when the generator was on, it sent electro-static waves throughout the basement, keeping the floor and walls dry. He was able to convert the water back into oxygen and hydrogen. No moisture."

"Oh," I replied, unsure if he was serious or pulling off an elaborate joke.

"We'll recognize the basement door because it's at the end of a galley style hall with pentagrams and other occult symbols painted on it to help with the dimensional transfer."

"Some effect. Did he get the idea from an old vampire movie?"

He shrugged.

"So, according to what the police leaked out to the public, before Montgomery left for Baton Rouge he set up the equipment and gave Holmes instructions on how to work it. When to turn it on, don't touch the settings and make sure it doesn't overheat from the influx of all that cosmic energy, which is what he thought happened. But we'll never know. They couldn't find the machine. Or the basement.

"Which brings me to the point of my visit. We're going to see the house tonight. Remember Niles, the caretaker? He told me that Montgomery left a whole bunch of notebooks in the basement that night. He wanted to keep them near the generator so they'd be available right away for him to notate the results."

I liked Sam better when he was virtually illiterate.

"You know that when Tesla died, the FBI ransacked his apartment and stole boxes and boxes of notes. The same thing happened in 1950 when Montgomery died. If we can find any of his research papers, we can auction them off and be rich beyond our wildest dreams."

"You want us to break into a haunted house?"

"Absolutely not, and it's not haunted, just abandoned. Niles told me the combination to the gate's keypad and where they hide the housekey. It's under a flowerpot on the porch."

"Why is he giving you all this information?" I asked.

"We're giving him a cut of the fortune we're going to make."

"Why doesn't he get it himself? It doesn't sound like he even needs us. And he can just get the notes in the daytime. Nobody will ever suspect him."

He shrugged, "If he sells the notes, people will say he stole them and he'll lose his job and they'll arrest him for stealing and burglary. He needs to be above suspicion."

"Me, too. I don't want to get involved in this," I said firmly. "Obviously, this is illegal and I want no part of it."

"Yes, you do," he replied softly while taking off his dragon pin. He held it to the light and the little jewels flashed at me a few times.

"You don't care about breaking a couple of little, unimportant laws. You want to do this, don't you? You'll have a good time with me."

I nodded. I had a complete change of mind. I just knew this would be a fun adventure.

We arrived at the Lawton House just past midnight on a dark moonless evening with only pale blue stars above us. The gate opened on the first try and we parked under a gigantic live oak tree with high spreading branches. After I turned off the headlights, the night was so black we could barely see the ominous outline of the old mansion.

"I don't know about this," I said doubtfully.

"Relax," he reassured. "This won't be a problem. We only need to find the basement and get the notebooks. We'll be in and out in no time."

Thick autumn mist covered the ground almost to our knees. Our cheap plastic flashlights created eerie, shadowy creatures that rose above us momentarily until the wind quickly dissolved them back into formless vapor. It was unnerving. I wished somebody had at least left on the porch light.

Sam carried a pick and small spade and I had twenty feet of rope coiled around my shoulder. I understood the rope. The stairs are so old they might be unsafe. But the digging equipment? We wouldn't know where to dig and if Holmes buried the notes, they'd be rotten, moldy and useless. But Sam insisted.

The key was right where the caretaker said it would be and the door opened with a high-pitched groan. Even though there were no lights on inside, we could see. All the rooms glowed from a soft blue mist, providing us with an eerie illumination.

"Well, that's handy, if creepy," Sam commented as we turned off our flashlights. "At least we can save our batteries."

We looked around. The door entered the kitchen where everything looked as neat as a pin. The housekeeper wiped down and polished the table earlier. The sink was spotless. But then, why would it be any other way? The housekeeper cleaned daily and no one lived there.

Each wall held a door.

All doors lead to the kitchen, I remembered hearing my mother say when I was a child.

The electric lights suddenly turned on and my musings stopped. We both blinked as the bright lights overwhelmed our pupils. Screams erupted from everywhere, some were howls of agony. Pathetic screeches of sheer terror attacked our ears. I imagined seeing some kind of creature, too hairy and deformed to be human, running toward us but something even more hideous caught it. Something with horns and razor-sharp fangs. This demonic thing grabbed its deformed prey with little effort and chewed it to death while the victim expired after emitting a few pathetic whimpers. The demonic fiend looked right at us, unaware that we were there and proceeded to drag its bleeding victim away from the door.

The lights disappeared, replaced by the unearthly blue glow.

"I'll wait for you in the car," I said quietly and turned to leave but Sam positioned himself between me and the door, holding up his flickering dragon broach.

"You want to see this through," he said. "Don't you?"

I nodded. My fear vanished. We continued.

"Good. I need you to help me get everything out of the basement."

We explored the dining room to our left. The table was meticulously set with highly polished silverware. White cloth napkins shaped like boats claimed the center of each China plate. Crystal wine glasses and water goblets finished each setting. A white tablecloth hung down elegantly, not quite touching the eight empty chairs. It was set up beautifully. And it was for no one.

Several portraits from the 17th and 18th century hung high. Long dead patriarchs from the Lawton family sneered at us with stern, unsmiling faces. We walked through the room, careful not to touch anything, since it felt like we were walking through a museum.

Another door to our right opened into a wide, open

room that I guessed was the living room or entertainment area. It was large, with a few couches and chairs pushed back against the wall. The front door stood locked and bolted. A polished and empty bar was in one corner and a small makeshift stage was in the other. More old pictures filled the walls. This time, mature, middle-aged women with severe features glared at us. The wives.

"This is where everyone was dancing when the party began," Sam told me.

I already figured out that much. We walked across the room, where another doorway beckoned, our shoes clicking on the floor and echoing through the house.

Once again, the lights came on. The shrieks filled our ears. A woman dressed in a pastel green fairy costume was crawling off the stage, blood pouring out of a fatal gouge. A beast-like man with a bull's head stood over her, blood and gore dripping from his horns. His head was down. He was going to attack her again.

He started his fatal charge when the lights blinked out and we plunged back into the darkness. I was thankful that blue glow illuminated nothing more of that scene. I was also glad the floor was well polished and I could find no trace of blood anywhere.

We walked through the other door and back into the kitchen. To our left was the back door we came in from. To our right was a small aisle with cabinets on both sides. Beautiful China place settings gleamed at us from one side while crystal glassware and table centerpieces sparkled on the other. An oak door was at the end.

"Was all this here when we came in?" I asked.

"Must have been," he shrugged. "I didn't see it either."

"I really don't think these notes are worth being in here," I complained. But when I turned to him all I saw was that damn dragon pin, flashing and sparkling, filling the lost confidence back into my terrified soul.

"I believe we're safe, don't you?" he asked quietly.

"We're safe," I agreed, although every instinct I had said otherwise.

"This way," he said and we headed to the door at the end of the aisle.

At first glance, it appeared to be a short distance but, by the time we got to the end, it seemed like we walked at least a hundred yards. Two more portraits flanked the door on either wall. A hauntingly beautiful woman in her wedding dress smiled sadly at me. Something in those warm blue eyes made me feel guilty I invaded her home. The matrimonial arch stood behind her and she clutched a bouquet of red roses in her outstretched hand, showing off a very large diamond ring. Her earrings seemed cut to match it. A bronze label affixed to the frame read: Maria Lawton, 1890.

Across from her, another likeness hung. I would have originally assumed the second painting was the groom, but it was not. A matronly woman of middle age sat straight up and primly in a pastel green blouse that reached the bottom of the frame. Ice cold blue eyes stared, filled with contempt. Her hands sat below the picture frame, most likely clasped together in her unseen lap, possibly holding something. A kitten, maybe. Her expression was haughty and confident, without a trace of humor. She carried herself as though she were royalty. I found it odd that she didn't wear any jewelry. I read the label on this one: Maria Holmes, 1920.

Dark shades of brown and gray made up the background showing nothing except her. She was not an unattractive woman who noticeably maintained her grace and poise as time stole her youth and beauty. She certainly had no use for vanity.

"She aged well," Sam said clinically from behind me.

"Did she die that night?"

"She disappeared the year before. Probably not long after she sat for the painting." He glanced at the image for a moment, "Nice brushwork. Let's go."

I nodded and turned to the basement door. It had faded traces of pentagrams and other disturbing symbols I didn't recognize. Obviously, somebody washed over them many times but they survived each cleaning. I thought I heard a feminine cough and whirled around. Nothing was there. A small movement caught my eye and I turned toward the later portrait of Maria. She was leaning a bit to the right with her head tilted coquettishly. Her lips had a trace of a knowing smile.

"Let's go," Sam hissed at me. "Something happened and we lost time. It's after three. We only have two hours until sunrise and we've been here almost three hours doing absolutely nothing. We must leave before Niles catches us."

"Why's that? Doesn't he know we're already here?"

"It's okay as long as we're gone before he gets here. He has orders to detain or shoot all trespassers when he catches them, especially treasure hunters."

"And that's just what we are," I mused, losing my cool a bit. "Treasure hunters."

"We're archaeologists. We just don't go so far back to find things. Point is: we don't want to get shot."

"Why didn't you tell me any of this before we came here?" I growled at him.

"You wouldn't have come."

"Let's just go," I said while shaking my head and silently disowning him forever.

He nodded and opened the door. A rickety looking staircase greeted us with dusty steps running steeply down and out of sight. The mysterious blue glow didn't provide light down there.

Our flashlights cut through the dark. At first, I really didn't want to go down, but I dutifully followed my brother. It wasn't long before he found the light switch and dimly lit up the room. Why would anybody put the basement light switch at the bottom of the stairs?

We stood on a rough-hewn pine floor. Some boxes guarded the corners, filled with old photographs of long dead and forgotten people. Some looked like they were set on tin. One photo caught my eye and I showed it to Sam.

It was a picture of the older Maria lying naked on a stone altar. A hooded man stood above her holding a ceremonial knife high over his head. Two giant snakes coiled around his legs, staring at the helpless woman, who seemed drugged and confused. I hoped the serpents were decorative. But I knew they were real.

Sam dropped the photos back in the box and shone his light on the ceiling. A heavy metal hook screwed into the support beam hung down. Right below it, a trapdoor lurked.

"We're here," Sam said excitedly. "This is where they lowered the generator down into the basement by using a pulley system. That's what's left of it."

We quickly opened the trapdoor and let it fall with a bang. We waited a bit until the echoes died down. The noise didn't seem to disturb anything and we aimed our flashlights down into a subcellar. No stairs or ladder waited for us to climb down.

The generator dominated one corner, dusty but intact. Obviously, it didn't explode that night. Made of slowly rusting steel, it filled the area, an ominous reminder of the dangers of scientific discovery. Dust, grime and cobwebs covered it in a gray shroud of filth. In the other corner was a decayed trunk with a broken and rusty hasp.

However, the actual floor captured my gaze. Piles of old bones and skulls covered it, chewed and pocked, broken and ground down. We stared at gnawed ribs, scattered throughout what could only be described as a tomb. So those coffins from the funeral were empty after all. Nobody ever found the bodies of these poor souls.

While I stared at this ghastly sight, Sam tied the rope in a loop and caught the hook with it. I reluctantly tied the other end to the trapdoor latch, which still looked firm and solid.

"Pull me up when I'm done," he said and started to lower himself down.

He landed with a crunch on some poor victim's scattered knuckles. He bent over and picked up one of the skulls and lifted it up to show me. It was large and had impossibly huge eye sockets. Curved horns rose menacingly from its crown.

"What was it?" I asked dreading the answer.

"It was born a man," he replied. "Dr. Montgomery's machine obviously worked. Whoever he was, he wound up transformed unwillingly into his costume. Maybe he was a minotaur. Or the devil."

"Just make sure that contraption is off."

He laughed, "No lights, no motor humming. It's off. Right now, I just want to find his notes. We can come back for his generator later."

"Yes, you can," I muttered. "Just hurry up and see what's in the chest."

He trotted across the floor, oblivious to the disgusting

crunch when he stomped on the bones. A clanging noise rang up as he flipped the broken hasp to the floor and a hideous low groan sent shivers up my spine as he opened the chest and pushed the lid back until it thudded to the floor. He shined his light into the box but all I saw was black. Blacker than the night. But this black was moving.

Horrid things came swarming out of the opening. Grotesque creatures. They looked like large spiders with black sacks attached to their loathsome hairy backs. And they were fast, crawling over Sam in a heartbeat. He was brushing them off his clothes and stomping them as he retreated to the rope. Then they must have started biting him. He screamed in pure agony and continued to fight and stomp, dropping his light to the floor. For a moment, I wanted to shimmy down the rope to help him, but I already knew it was too late.

The beasts slurped his blood and bit again. The sacks on their back were filling with Sam's blood. He soon fell to the ground, his screams turning into sobs. Finally, silence. The only noise was those things eating.

I heard sounds near me and turned my light to the walls. They were climbing swiftly up the rope to the opening, coming for me. One large creature was almost to the top. Menacing green eyes protruded from its black head as it quickened its pace. It was staring at me with pure hatred. Or maybe hunger.

It was my turn to scream. Turning tail like the coward I freely admit that I am, I retreated up the stairs as quickly as I could. When I got back into the house, I slammed the door behind me and leaned back, catching my breath.

I glanced around. The portrait of the young woman still stared ahead but the older version transformed completely. Her head turned to face me and she looked down at me with a malignant smirk. Sam's dragon pin glittered on her collar.

I pressed against the wall and slowly sidestepped past her. And then she moved. I saw her, only pigment and paint, reach down below the frame and triumphantly hold up a yellow skull. A rusting steel plate was above the right eye, mocking me. The woman held it near her lips and licked it with a long green tongue.

I froze at the sight, even though I heard those spider things biting at the door trying to reach me. I could only stare at the woman.

"Run," a female voice called from behind me.

That broke the spell of terror that held me. I turned around to see the young Maria nodding her head toward the exit.

I ran down the long hall and through the kitchen. I hurried out the door and to the car. I didn't even notice that dawn replaced the black of night. The clouds I could see through the tops of the pines were bright red and orange. I hopped in my car as fast as possible and sped down the driveway to the gate.

Someone already opened it, but a beat-up old Ford pickup was blocking my escape. A middle-aged man wearing a beat-up cowboy hat was getting out from the driver's side and waved me down. I had no choice but to stop.

"I have to get out of here," I shrieked breathlessly as I rolled down the window. "Those things killed my brother. They're after me, now."

"Nothing's chasing you, son," he said calmly, ignoring my hysteria. "Just look around. Nothing's there. It's daylight."

I looked around in the dim morning light and checked

all three mirrors. He was right. There was nothing there. I escaped that nightmare house.

"Your brother was in there?" he asked gently.

I nodded. I was afraid to speak because I might start crying.

"You know," he slowly went on, "I've worked here for almost twenty years. Maybe ten or twelve times each year one of you explorer types sneak in. I can always tell. The car's there, but they aren't. You're the only one who went in there during the night and came out. The others?"

He shrugged indifferently.

"Nobody knows. We just tow away their cars. Sometimes, there's a report about a stolen car or a missing person, but usually not. It doesn't matter, they weren't supposed to be there."

"What's going to happen?"

He shrugged, "I knew there'd be a break-in soon. I assume you're Sam's brother?"

I nodded and he looked away for a minute.

"The other day he came into the café where I eat breakfast. I didn't want to tell him anything, but he had that Toltec talisman. A dragon with muti-colored jewels. When he held it to the light, I couldn't help but tell him everything he wanted to know. The combination. Where we put the key. I didn't want to, mind you, but I did."

"So, you're saying that those times when I wanted to leave, his little dragon pin kept me there?"

"I imagine so," he said thoughtfully. "So, Sam brought it into the house with him?"

"He did. I wanted to leave. Never wanted to come here in the first place, but he kept sparkling it at me and I always did what he wanted."

"So, now she has it?"

I nodded miserably.

"That's bad," he said sadly. "With that charm, she just might be able to call you back. Convince you it's safe to return. But it won't be. You never want to go into the place again."

"I know. But what should I do?" I was getting frantic.

"Drive," he said with a shrug. "Drive far away and don't ever come back. And don't tell anyone where you're going or where you end up. Don't even write your family a letter. It won't be Sam that disappeared. It'll be both of you. You might stand a chance if she can't find you."

That was twenty-five years ago, and I drove long and far, just like he told me. I drove until I ran out of money for gas. I found a job here in Lincoln. I got married and have a family. After my youngest left for college, I started to have nightmares.

I relive the events of that night. They start with me entering that house again. I dream of that party that started off so well but ended so badly. I have visions of men and women trapped in strange bodies and killed. I see bones and spiders. To this day, I can hear Sam screaming while those things ate him alive.

But mostly, I dream of Maria. She comes to me, wearing that pastel green outfit. She flashes that dragon pin in the light, making it glitter and sparkle.

"Come home," she calls to me gently.

PRISCILLA

Although Priscilla Hobbs was not a pretty girl, she was not unattractive by any means. She filled out her jeans and blouse well enough to draw appreciative glances. Sadly, her face lacked anything to make it appealing. Her gray eyes situated themselves much too close together, which made her long and hooked nose more prominent. It curled in so far that it almost pointed to her thin, colorless lips. Her teeth were crooked with a prominent overbite. If all that wasn't bad enough, fiery red acne ravaged her skin, leaving deep pock marks on her cheeks and forehead.

In high school, the boys graduated from calling her 'pizza face' to 'crater head.' Some of the girls did too. She ignored them as best she could but would go to her room and cry every day after the bus dropped her off. Her one small victory was that they never saw the tears they caused. She never gave them the satisfaction of knowing how much they hurt her.

Things became unbearable in her junior year. That was when her father discovered she became a young woman, almost fully developed. When he started touching and kissing her neck, she always pulled away and ran to her room. His laugh and mean taunts always followed her.

"Come on, Prissy," he called through the door once. "You know no one else wants you. Not with that face."

Her mother was no help. She was always too sick with hangovers in the mornings to hear anything and passed out drunk on the couch when she got home from school.

Priscilla usually stayed inside the building after school so she could be alone while she waited for the bus to arrive. Then she'd run out to catch it, being the last one to get on. She could avoid a lot of misery that way.

One day, she saw old Mr. Mannix, her science teacher, sitting at his desk alone, grading papers. She decided to confide in him about what was going on in her life. He was an adult. Maybe he had some helpful advice for her.

"You know, in my day," he said after listening sympathetically, "it was easy for a girl to quit school and leave home, even without a job or prospects. Just get married. Of course, it's more successful when the husband works and doesn't drink."

"Wouldn't a girl have to be pretty for that to work?" she whined morosely. "I think another requirement would be that the man needs to be blind. At least for it to work for me."

"Don't sell yourself short," Mannix replied. "He wouldn't have to be blind at all, just not as superficial as so many of the young men of today are."

"How would I find a boy like that?" she asked hopefully.

"A young man who is employed, doesn't drink, and is trustworthy and loyal? As it so happens, I have a nephew."

He certainly did. Mark Conners, his youngest sister's son, was tall, dark and ugly. He was big boned with a round face, an extremely upturned nose and protruding brown eyes. He made her think that maybe his family evolved from frogs instead of primates. She thought they would do well together.

The Conners family was well-known in Indianola Parish. Louisiana had a great many rural areas but not like here. There were only a few gas station/post office combination stores that sold groceries and delivered mail, which were strategically located near the railroad stops and on the crossroads. Residents had to drive to Victorville, the county seat, if they wanted to find clothes or shoes.

Victorville also was home to the high school. The sheriff's office (which used to be a funeral home) was on the main street. A little clinic that called itself a hospital attracted a few patients, though it offered little more than aspirin and Band-Aids. The people with serious illnesses or injuries trekked over to the Neuville hospital, seventy miles away.

The pioneering Conners family became one of the first European settlers in this area of pine and oak forests, swamp, marsh, stagnant ponds, and wetlands. Originally, they owned most of everything here since no one else wanted it. Not even the Native American Malanihanna tribe visited this part of the state.

Pierre Conners, the original patriarch, made a fortune by trapping and selling furs. He found the secret to his success in the land, which he occasionally told to friends and acquaintances. In fact, the land held many mysteries and he knew them all.

He married a young French girl and the Conners family grew large. The children soon married and contributed their own offspring to the expanding family. The true Conners children never welcomed any of their new in-laws since they only married into the family, as opposed to being born into it. Since the family needed the fresh blood to produce a healthy next generation, they tolerated the newcomers and took an interest in them. They even helped them when it was in their own best interests. But they never shared any of Pierre's ancient Conners family secrets.

Despite that, the outsiders who married into the Conners family always considered themselves to be lucky. The family was wealthy and well connected. They always made the right decisions on what to plant, where to fish, and in later times, where to invest. Nobody in their extended 'family' wanted for anything, except maybe love, and love was a luxury anyway.

The family fell on hard times after the depression when Henry Conners, Mark's great grandfather, became a serious Christian. Crops failed. Their investments collapsed. Chickens died. But the Conners family went on. Some remained successful, provided they moved off the original property where Mark lived.

Priscilla met Mark's family not long after their first date and they were pleasant to her, if not exactly warm, but she expected that. She remembered their first date.

"You're so pretty," he said while slathering mayo on his hamburger.

She snorted, "You haven't even looked at my face."

He leered at her bust.

"My eyes haven't got that far up," he said dryly.

She laughed with a deep red blush. She was grateful for the compliment, crude as it was, but offended that he would say something like that, especially in public. It embarrassed her but made her happy and opened a whole kaleidoscope of emotion. She knew it was inappropriate, but she was sixteen and this was her first date. Mark was five years older than her. She didn't want to ruin the night by being a prude. Especially because she knew he was the one for her. He felt the same way and they married seven weeks later.

His family tolerated her at first, as was their family way, but that toleration seemed to decrease with each year. She was the only one to not have a job outside of the house. Cooking, cleaning, killing mosquitos and roaches didn't seem to count as work to them.

But she wasn't married to them. Just Mark. He could be charming to her. He made her feel loved and important. He didn't say anything mean to her about her lack of beauty. Never suggested she should apply her make-up with a trowel. Always searched for nice things and especially complimented her on her figure.

Right before they married, he inherited seventeen acres of property, mostly forest, the rest weeds, with an old house laughingly called *Conners Manor*. At least he called it a house. Originally, a huge manor house loomed over the cotton plantation, but the Union Army torched it during the Civil War. The less fortunate Conners families of the Reconstruction Era built a modest farmhouse over the blackened ashes of the fallen building. It burned down again in 1949 when hard times returned.

This modern *Conners Manor* originated as a chicken shed. Since it had walls and a floor, it was easy to convert into a small frame house. Just add insulation, electricity and plumbing. The family simply evicted the chickens that found a home in an abandoned hovel a little further out into the woods.

Priscilla's new home was certainly not much, but it was hers. She owned it with her husband. And she never invited her father over to visit. Sadly, he never wanted to, but it sounded better the way she phrased it.

Mark was a good husband at first. He had his own cleaning business with several large clients and came home by eight so they could do all the things that married people do. He preferred her to be a stay-at-home wife and, since the idea of getting a job frying potatoes or changing sheets in a cheap motel didn't really appeal to her, she happily agreed. Of course, she had no social life because she never met new people, but socializing was painful before she met Mark anyway. Dropping out of high school to get married seemed to be a good decision.

They never used birth control and wondered when the babies would start arriving. Not that she was in a hurry. The house was not a great place for children. Or adults, by her way of thinking. The windows needed to be reglazed. The rubber molding around the doors had rotted away years ago and insects thought it was their home as well and spent a great deal of time trying to evict the human invaders with their biting and stinging. And it had no interior walls. Just blankets thrown over twine that separated the rooms.

After two years, she began to feel discontented. She was reasonable enough. She was willing to live there. She just wanted walls built. Rooms added on. A serious remodel of the kitchen and bathroom. And modern windows that kept the bugs out. Maybe a fireplace, though with the Conners family's history with fire, she wouldn't insist on that one.

She reasoned that the money was there. She only stayed at home because that's what Mark wanted. He picked up the local library as a client, even though it was so far away. He worked long hours and stayed even later reading the special collection of historical documents. He came home late every evening filled with stories about his family and its history.

It seemed that the Conners family and offshoots in days

past were a little wilder than most people of their era. He also discovered some terrible family secret. Hints of it came out in bits and pieces. Some of the young wives fled the family's lands in terror and refused to return to their husbands. Priscilla assumed it wasn't much more than some distant ancestor married into the wrong race and a little high drama. That's what most such things were. The world was too modern for anything like that to be important anymore. Or so she thought.

Mark came home with more stories of long ago. Adultery. Duels. Murder. Bodies buried in the woods from centuries ago. Indian rituals. Not the Malanihanna, but a tribe that was fierce and feared by all the other native people. On his off days, he explored the woods behind the house for hours at a time.

"What's back there?" Priscilla asked one day.

"Treasure," he replied with a knowing smile.

"Gold?" she asked. "Jewels? Antiques?"

"Even better. History."

She lost interest. History wasn't going to improve her life or remodel the house or get her a car or fix her skin or teeth. But she didn't complain. She had a good, boring life. Maybe his treasure would earn enough to at least install new windows.

One spring day, he came home early in the afternoon. The air was warm and heavy. She had that happy-to-be-alive-and-young feeling and so did he. He kissed her passionately while rubbing and squeezing her rear end with his hands. Then he left her rather breathless and headed for the linen closet, grabbing sheets, pillows and blankets before heading out back toward the woods.

"What are you doing?" she asked, surprised and highly annoyed.

"I'm creating a magical spell for us," he replied. "We're going to be the happiest, luckiest, most blessed couple in the world. I found my treasure and it's all about you. Be patient and give me ten minutes. You'll love me."

"I already do," she said softly, though she wondered why as the door slammed shut behind him.

He was gone for twenty minutes. Enough time for her to fluff her hair, drink a cup of super strong coffee, and brush her teeth and rinse. She wanted to be wide awake and smelling good for him when he returned. He came back home all smiles.

"I have something to show you in the woods," he said.

She sighed. She had already explored the forest they owned and maybe some belonging to the neighbors they never met and she didn't like any of it. The ground was damp and giant spider webs spread from tree to tree, with huge blue spiders perched above, watching her. Mosquitoes attacked her mercilessly out there. They even tried to bite through her blouse and bra until she fled back to the house. At least the insects at home had more class.

"What?" she scoffed. "I'm not going out there ever again. You know what my opinion of your trees is."

"I know exactly what you think of them in summer. Insects and bites, snakes and rats. But this is spring and there's a breeze. It's too early for snakes and too windy for bugs."

"It's still damp and muddy," she protested. "The washer's broken and we wash our clothes at the laundromat, where everybody sees our dirty laundry. I don't want people to see mud all over my panties. What will people say?"

"Easy fix," he grinned while sweeping her into his arms, nibbling at the side of her neck in the process.

29

He was obviously determined to claim his conjugal rights in the wilderness while ignoring her right of refusal. But his lips and mouth felt good and she decided that if he really wanted to go outside with her, she could accommodate him, at least once.

He navigated through knee-high weeds, dyed light brown to announce their long-ago death.

"Why don't we get a tractor to cut down all this grass?"

"Why don't I get sharper teeth to pleasure your neck more?" He pulled her closer to him for a sensual nibble.

She closed her eyes, enjoying his touch and when she opened them, they were there.

"You're kidding," she said flatly as she surveyed the setting.

A circle of small stone pillars, maybe two feet tall encompassed a barren patch of land. Not even a tree leaf or pine needle littered the ground. Mark arranged the blankets and pillows neatly on a raised platform in the center. It reminded her of an exceptionally creepy altar.

Two candelabras with three burning candles bookended the cushions. The candles smelled familiar with a sickening stench of death and decay. A large round pot burning a sweet-smelling incense stood at the foot of the altar, smoke billowing out of its open top. The two scents combined to reek with an intensity that turned her stomach.

He carried her between two of the pillars and instantly she felt the atmosphere change. The air was denser, the temperature warmer. Even the forest changed into something different. Gone were the pine trees, replaced by huge ferns, like none she had ever seen before. They rustled and shook gently, as though something (or someone) was moving close by, watching them.

"No," she said firmly, wiggling free from him and

getting on her feet. "Not here." She looked around. "What is this place?"

He pulled her toward him and she spun away, turning to run but found herself lifted from behind and pushed down on the makeshift bed. He savagely ripped off her blouse as she screamed and scratched him as best she could. He ruined her bra by roughly twisting and tugging at it. She managed to get in a good eye gouge and was satisfied at the sound of his roar of pain.

They were in a stalemate. He could pin her arms back, but she snapped and bit at him when he tried pulling down her shorts. He looked up beyond her and nodded his head. He then forced both of her arms down to the ground while she tried to kick into his groin.

Something slimy but strong grabbed her wrists. They weren't exactly hands. They were too long and thin, with thick, spongy fingers. Whatever they were, they had her arms completely immobilized. She twisted to see who or what his accomplice was but saw nothing.

That gave Mark the advantage he needed. Her fight was over. She felt other of those hand-like things gently caressing her while Mark undressed her. She focused her eyes on the waving green ferns above her while Mark completed the penetration. It hurt at first, but then she just felt him moving inside her. There was no more real pain, but certainly no pleasure. Then it was over and done. Or so she wanted to believe.

The horrible part was coming next. Strong arms and those inhuman hands separated her thighs again. Another weight was on top of her. She heard rhythmic hissing in her ears. She saw nothing, just felt it. She saw Mark slipping back into his clothes, while he watched her suffer with a smirk. He offered her no help. She started crying in frustration and humiliation.

Then it was over. But no, another thing replaced it and the torture went on. And then another thing mounted her. Again and again. The sun hid behind the trees when her ordeal ended, though there was still some light that illuminated the long shadows.

Those things released her wrists and she stumbled up to her shredded clothes. Mark tried to help her, but she shrank away. When he approached again, she hit him with her fist as hard as she could. He looked stunned and angry.

Rhythmic hissing came from behind. She turned, covering herself up with the rags that used to be her clothes. In the dusky half-light, she saw them. The horrors that violated her. They weren't human, but similar, with green skin that seemed to glisten with sweat or oil. Their flattened heads were green, with protruding eyes and elongated jaws, all slightly open, with long thin tongues flicking in and out. These froglike things stared at her blankly, unconcerned about their nakedness or hers. Their arms were much too long for their bodies and ended in hands with very short fingers that had rounded suckers. She only briefly saw their groins and turned away in disgust.

"Prissscilla," she heard them whisper.

A sharp pain pierced the back of her neck. She almost immediately lost all her strength and collapsed to the ground, lying on her back. Mark stood over her with a hypodermic needle in his hand.

She laid there on the ground trying to remember how to use her body to get up and run. Mark was outside that devilish circle whispering to those things, occasionally glancing back at her.

"She's still awake," she distinctly heard him say.

"There was coffee in her breath," came a hissing reply. "It counteracts the relaxant. You must convince her it was all a dream. A nightmare, if you will. When she awakens, she must not believe it happened. She's not prepared for us yet."

She saw Mark nod grimly and he returned to her.

"Prissscilla," she heard the hissing voice again. "It was only a nightmare. Mark got too excited today. That's all it was."

She drifted off to a merciful sleep. But was it really only a dream when Mark picked her up in the blankets and carried her home? Everything was hazy. Reality and darkness flickered like a strobe light in her eyes. She remembered him stumbling and almost falling once but he regained balance and they made it home. She remembered him setting her down in the bed. Washing her. Helping her into a nightgown. Through it all, she heard one word: revenge.

She woke with a start four days later, tired, sore and weak, but conscious. She wondered if it really happened, but she knew it did. She just didn't want to believe her own husband would do such a thing to her. But he did.

Mark was rummaging around in the other room and soon came in with a tray of plain crackers and hot tea.

"You've been very sick these last few days," he said. "And such a high fever. I had a doctor stop by to examine you."

Doctors don't make house calls.

"You haven't had anything solid for four days, so we'll have to go easy for now. A little soup and some starch. You got a mosquito bite in the woods. It may have had encephalitis."

She glared at him.

33

"Well, okay, going out there was a bad idea. I got so excited, I just turned into a beast. I'm sorry. Never again outside. Not only did you get sick, you had some real nightmares. You were quite delirious. Those were terrible dreams, if what you were saying in your sleep was any indication."

She nodded and drank the tea.

"I have some good news," he said, not letting her cold silence stop him. "We won the lottery. Six million dollars after taxes. *Conners Manor* is all yours to redecorate, remodel, tear down, and start again. Blank check. Anything you want."

Revenge.

She nodded glumly and sipped the tea. Mark obviously was going to pretend nothing happened. She decided to pretend she didn't remember. At least for now.

But what did she remember? Was it a real experience or a nightmare? Her neck was still sore and a little swollen. From an injection or a mosquito bite? Maybe it was all a terrible dream. After all, why would her own husband take her to where hideous animals lived and then let them rape her? Maybe she was delirious and it was time to move on. She could forgive him for taking her out in the woods and forcing himself on her like that. And those things? All part of the delirium?

But she knew better.

Mark stayed with her the next day but then went back to work. Even though he expected the lottery money would be in their bank account next week, there were bills due now. She was glad he was gone.

She got up and started looking for her garments from that day to convince herself it was all a dream just like he said. Mark just got too rough and she got sick from a mosquito bite. The laundry pile almost reached the ceiling and the broken washing machine stood there, useless. Her clothes from that day weren't there.

She rummaged through the garbage until she found them. Ripped, shredded, ruined. The wire in her bra twisted itself into a crazy angle. It was useless. She didn't want to touch the blanket he carried her home in, but she did anyway. When she shook it out, she heard a tiny thump as something hit the floor. She found it. Incontrovertible proof that it wasn't a dream. It really did happen. The hypodermic needle stared at her from the faded linoleum. It happened and she remembered it. All that coffee obviously weakened the effects of the drug, just as that thing told Mark.

She never said a word to her husband about her discovery. But she didn't kiss him anymore. She gave one-word responses to all his attempts to start a conversation. She professed she was still weak from the "illness." She pretended everything would be all right when she felt better.

However, within a couple of weeks, she not only didn't feel better, she got worse. Her stomach ached and she lost her appetite. She ate meat sometimes, but most everything else simply disgusted her. Queasiness overtook her at times, especially in the mornings. But she never said a word about it to Mark. What went on in her body was none of his concern anymore.

When the full moon brightened the nights and her period didn't come, she knew she was pregnant. With what? Some kind of hideous half human half…thing. A monster. Just like the man she married.

"Priscilla," Mark called out when he came home one night. "Good news. The lottery money hit the bank. I hope you know what you want."

Revenge.

She allowed him to kiss her, repugnant as it was. He was excited and blabbering about all the investments he was going to make. She dutifully pretended to be excited and joyful at this development.

Mark talked about closing his business and staying home as a wealthy gentleman of leisure. She suggested that he go to college. His love of knowledge would make him a perfect student. He seemed to like that idea and went to the campus to see about registering for classes.

Good, she smiled. She didn't want him at home with her ever again.

While he made arrangements and told his family about their good fortune, she went to the doctor. After patiently listening to him tell her what she already knew, she explained what happened. Not the part with the demons, of course. She said some strangers raped her that day.

"It was nice out and I was only taking a walk on our own property. They were there and when they saw me, they attacked. They were horrible, terrible men. Disgusting pigs. And I don't want this baby."

He was kind and understanding.

"I wish you had gone to the police," he said. "But I can understand your reluctance. Some husbands don't react well to that kind of news."

My husband is responsible for that kind of news.

He gave her an address and she went immediately. It was not one baby. It was four. But the procedure went well. She was tired and achy when it was over, but content. Whatever she had carried did not belong here or anywhere.

She stopped at her parent's house on the way home. Her father was gone, which was good. Her mother passed out on the sofa again, a spilled bottle of rum on the floor next to her. She didn't care. She didn't come for a visit. She went to their bedroom closet and rummaged around until she found what she came for and slipped it into her purse.

When she pulled into the drive and got out of the car, she knew something wasn't right. The air was different. Heavy and dank. Her feet crunched on the gravel, but the sound was duller. Mark stood at the door, waiting for her.

"Prissscilla," came those hissing voices, though she didn't see anything. "Prissscilla, what have you done?"

"You know," she whispered to the voice as Mark ran toward her with furious eyes. She clutched her handbag and waited for the confrontation.

He grabbed her wrist and yanked it toward him while shouting in her face, "What were you thinking? Do you know what you've done?"

"I killed little monsters," she replied calmly, waiting for him to hit her.

But he didn't. She realized that he was afraid to hit her. Those things didn't want her damaged because she was their breeding stock. And her husband was the man who betrayed her into their world.

"What kind of deal did you make with those things?" she asked quietly.

Her own fury was soul deep, but she made every effort to keep it internal. She needed to keep him calm. She needed to know.

"Those *things*, as you call them, are the others. The ancient gods," he yelled. "You were supposed to have their children. Our children. The native peoples did this for centuries. They brought slave girls to them or gave them their wife for an evening like I did. The firstborn children would be theirs, but we will raise some of them. They'll raise the others. Soon, we'll all come together and they save us from ourselves. They'll create a whole new world order. You see, our children will be the dominant species. Mankind will go the way of the neanderthal. The others will be the new gods. We'll be the new royalty. They can bend reality to help their family and friends, and that's us. That's how we won the lottery. That's how the Conners family became so rich and important, until Henry messed it all up.

"The others mated into the native tribes and were almost ready to begin the process, but the plague wiped out their allies. Nobody replaced their friends and the others became weak and forgotten. That is until my ancestors discovered them and began the process again. They're the reason why my ancestors became so successful when we moved here. We shared our women with the gods. Everyone in my family has some of their genes already. They're like cousins to me. Nobody even guessed that the Conners family had divine blood.

"It wasn't so bad, what I did. What you did. Every woman who married into our family did the same thing. And they all raised the children without complaint. Of course, they were under sedation for the conception and deliveries, so they didn't know. That was the family secret.

"And the others were so close to sending over more of my cousins to speed up the process. Then Uncle Henry became a Christian and ended it all. He didn't even tell his children about them. He just took that option away from them. That's when the Conners' fortune changed. That's why we became poor. And none of us even knew we had this choice."

"I didn't know about this choice," she said calmly.

"You're my wife. I make the decisions. I choose," he brushed her off. His voice sounded dreamy and detached when he continued, "They can't leave the circle in their true form, only their children can do that. But they can rule through their children and other family members, like me.

"And it could be you. When you get pregnant again, you'll be family too. Like a lesser wife. They get stronger with every child, you see. Soon they will be able to conquer our whole world through their children and other relatives. When that happens, they'll rule over all of what's left of mankind. They'll be the gods, and we'll be their king and queen, ruling over all the lands."

"If they're the gods, why do they need us to rule?"

"They want the entire world; they'll need people like us to rule our piece of the kingdom in their name."

"Like you?"

"Like *us*. But you killed off their children. Now we're going to go through the whole thing again. I hope you liked it the first time."

"I did with them. Not with you," she spat out.

A chorus of hissing sounds filled her head. She quickly realized that what she was hearing were their thoughts entering her mind through some kind of telepathy. They were all laughing at Mark. They knew what she knew. There would never be a place for Mark in their 'new world order.'

Mark stopped talking and brutally yanked her wrist and roughly dragged her back into the woods. At first, she fought and twisted for her freedom. She scratched and clawed to escape, but his grip just got stronger as she struggled.

Being a practical girl, she decided that she'd rather walk and stay on her feet than have him mercilessly drag her through the high grass on her side or back, so she allowed him to lead her back to the altar. It was bare today. No blankets or pillows covered it this time. The candles and incense were all lit, perfuming the air with their putrid smells. Its builders did not put much effort into constructing it, she observed. It was just an oblong mound of dirt with a slab of white stone topping it.

He pushed her roughly into the circle and grabbed her waist with one hand and held it tight while fumbling to open her blouse with the other. He seemed slower inside that unholy clearing. But so was she. Just like last time, the air was thicker, the trees transformed into ferns, and the world was just…different. And all the noises of the forest disappeared. The mosquitoes weren't just quiet, they were all gone.

"I can do it without your help," she snarled at him while pushing his hands back off her blouse. "Some of my clothes might survive this time."

She shifted her purse from shoulder to shoulder as she stripped in front of him. She knew those things were watching her, so she made a provocative show of throwing her bra and shirt, shoes and socks out beyond the circle, until only her purse provided her with a little cover.

"And now, gentlemen," she yelled while looking around but not seeing anything. "For your viewing pleasure, you can see me apply a little lotion down there to get me ready for you." She turned to Mark and wagged a finger at him, "Not for you. Your touch makes me sick."

Mark turned bright red as more of the hissing laughter came from behind them.

She stepped back past the altar toward the circle's back boundary and unsnapped the purse's hasp. Instead of lotion, she pulled out her father's old revolver, almost laughing at Mark's look of surprise and fear. She wanted to gloat, but she didn't have much time. She didn't know where those things were. She fired. A red stain immediately grew in the middle of Mark's chest and he fell without a sound. No dramatic last words. Good.

She quickly turned and sprinted through the boundary before those things could stop her. The world became normal again. A tree squirrel looked down at her with a curious gaze, as though she just appeared out of nowhere. The friendly Louisiana mosquitos flew back around her immediately, looking for dinner. The pines rustled overheard. The ground was damp and sticky with decaying leaves and needles, but she was safe.

"Prissscilla," they called to her, angry and desperate. But also, somehow loving and kind. Gentle and seductive. She stopped as they filled her head with glorious visions of herself. Beautiful. Rich. Famous. Powerful. Queen Priscilla the Great, ruling over all the lands.

A movement caught her eye. A gecko scurried up the bark of one of the pines. It reminded her of them and she laughed.

"Priscilla the Great, Queen of the lizards," she yelled out mockingly. She carefully circumnavigated the unholy clearing and retrieved her clothes, shaking them out before putting them on while the sun started to set.

They were becoming visible to her. One was right at the boundary, almost on one of the stones. He raised his hands over his head, as though he was clutching an invisible bar. He was naked and crying.

"Prissscilla," he cried out plaintively, "tell us what you want. We need you here with us. We need our children. We should have forced him to tell you about us. They forgot us for so long and we didn't know that things changed. Don't let the world forget us again. We can offer you so much."

The others were coming forward. Not all of them were so miserable. They looked angry. Enraged. Dangerous. Two smaller ones stopped to sniff at Mark's body. Then a few more. Then all of them except the one who was speaking. Soon, they started nipping at the corpse. Then devouring it. They ripped his flesh and bones with lively abandon, as though they hadn't eaten in weeks. Mark's body quickly disappeared, leaving the disgusting sounds of crunching bones echoing in the forest. Soon there was nothing left. She wouldn't miss him.

"Prissscilla," the tall one called out again to her mind, "we only wanted children and you killed them. We can have more. Just tell us: what do you want?"

"Revenge."

"You have it. Your husband is dead and his body gone. All we want is children."

"Not from me."

"Very well. We'll wait for another, more reasonable couple to find our alter. And then we'll start over."

When people of modest means suddenly become multi-millionaires, they sometimes spend their money on bizarre things. The story goes that when Mark and Priscilla Conners won the lottery, he immediately left her and ran off with another woman. He didn't even split the winnings. He only called her to have her send him money when needed. Years after that happened, he apparently never called. Nobody missed him anyway. His interest in studying occult practices made people around him nervous.

Priscilla Connors' first major purchase was a head scratcher to most. She started to remodel the house by installing a brand-new septic tank, even though the old one was still functional. She ordered the workers to dig up a bunch of stones and a large granite slab from the back of the forest she owned. She paid good money to have them all ground into gravel and used it to line her newly installed cesspool. After she had this chore completed to her satisfaction, she began to build an entirely new house.

Millionaires spend their money strangely, sometimes. It didn't really matter, though. Before a year had passed, the stones, gravel and septic tank were all forgotten.

Nelson's Experiment

"Most everything Scott Montgomery theorized was proven not possible," Professor Johns sniffed when the graduate student showed him the old book. "He's been out of print for almost a hundred years. Cosmic rays having any kind of power to somehow create interdimensional portals have always been too science-fiction for us to acknowledge in a scholarly atmosphere. Where did you even get that book?"

Dylan Nelson stoically indulged Johns' supercilious attitude and smiled through the older man's self-importance.

"In the archives section of the physics library. There was supposed to be one in the science library too, but it's been missing for a few decades."

"No doubt," Johns said dryly. "Too many people try reproducing Montgomery's experiments and getting hurt...or killed."

"I think that's because of the lack of safety precautions they used back in those days," Nelson replied. "I imagine the labs back then something out of those old Frankenstein movies. No covers or shields, no protective clothing or goggles. Nothing. Just a little accident, that wouldn't even happen today, could maim a man back then and end the experiment. That was science back in those days."

"I wasn't aware you were such an expert on scientific methods of the 1920s. Montgomery was one of those scientists, if we can use that term, who considered himself an explorer, sailing on seas of discovery that no one else knew existed. He always found ignorant patrons who financed his idiotic schemes and it always ended in disaster. There are places in this country that are off limits to regular people to this day because of the toxic contaminations he created."

"I heard," Nelson nodded. "But what I found in here could change the world, if it works right."

"If?"

"It looks good to me. I was reading this one part where he was discussing interdimensional travel using electrochemistry to push the rotating electrons away from the molecular nuclei which forces open the interdimensional portal. The energy source he needed to create was intense."

"I see a toxic waste sight being born in your mind right now. There is no such thing as interdimensional travel. It's a waste of time and energy. I hope you're not planning on your thesis being something like this. If you want the faculty to take you seriously, you need thoughtful and original ideas to present to the world. Anything you borrow from Scott Montgomery will be neither original nor thoughtful."

"Well, no," a discouraged Nelson replied. "It's the energy source I was interested in. He had a method to magnify solar energy and cosmic rays and harness that power to open the portal. If I can harness the power source itself into solar energy for electricity, this country could be energy independent for generations. It would have to be small scale at first, of course. But with future adjustment and ideas from other scientists like us, who knows what we can accomplish?"

"And how do you propose to make this work?"

"Well, the book presents the theory that the light rays can be magnified in a chamber that's filled with mirrors that rotate at high speed, which produces the excess heat and energy needed to open the portal. We could use that power for popular consumption instead. The cost of electricity could go down to nothing, if we have even a tiny bit of sunlight."

"Do what you want on your own time. Don't let it interfere with your *real* research. And don't even think of using university equipment for your little fun. Always remember: if you don't take yourself seriously, neither will we. Or anyone else."

Nelson left the meeting not exactly angry but irritated. He understood the professor wanted what he considered the best for the student, but the system itself was unfair. Why should all these old people in power get to decide what he could and couldn't do? What was serious and what wasn't? He understood the essence of Johns' argument: I have the authority to decide what you do and do not do as long as you're here.

He understood it was a problem grad-students had ever since the university system was born. He was also self-aware enough to believe that if he were in the older man's shoes, he would probably use his power the same way. After all, what good is power if you don't lord it over someone?

"How did it go?" Andy O'Brian asked when Nelson returned to their little office.

They were research assistants—paid errand runners who found books and articles for the professors to use. Sometimes, they had to write brief synopsizes of other scholar's articles for the professors to comment on in their own publications. O'Brian already figured out that most of the faculty was more interested in getting something or anything in print than actually doing research or teaching. The university system was built on the *publish or perish* philosophy.

"He thought it was a dumb idea. Don't expect any credit for it, don't pursue it on university time and don't use our equipment. Just what we expected."

"I wouldn't worry about it," O'Brian encouraged him. "If I understood you correctly, we can't use university time and equipment. We can pretend we're doing something they approved back a while ago. Most of the stuff we can get online and we can borrow some of the components at the end of the semester and put them back when the next one starts."

"They do inventory at the end of the semester."

"Who do you think is running the inventory team?"

The two research assistants smiled.

The house they rented with four other budding scientific geniuses had an unused garage, mostly filled with the landlord's junk. A large skylight dominated the roof and in daytime, they never needed to turn on the lights.

"You can move it but don't break it," he told them gruffly as they all signed the lease.

They decided the time came for them to move it. They needed room for an over-sized refrigerator, a control panel, a monitoring screen, and two computers with multiple screens. They spent every waking moment in a constant state of excitement as they read Montgomery's instructions and improvised modern digital equipment for the antique motors and panels he used back in the 1920s.

The inevitable noise they continuously made did not go unnoticed. Four unimpressed heads popped into their makeshift laboratory to see what kind of contraption the young men were making and if they were safe.

As the questions poured in and the answers flowed out, three of their roommates went back to their own projects, mainly video games. Oddly enough, the fourth tenant, Anne Conners, a mere undergraduate, showed great interest in their project and stayed in the room with them, only leaving to fetch a tool or a drink when requested.

Anne was a nondescript girl, pretty in an unremarkable way, with not-blonde, not-brown hair tied back in a bland ponytail, and almost colorless blue eyes. But she was pleasant enough, though she majored in ecology, which guaranteed she would be no significant help in the project. But her enthusiasm at the very thought of an energy source putting an end to coal and natural gas power plants made her happy and she grew to love being in the room with her two newfound heroes.

"So, this Scott Montgomery discovered this power source and never did anything with it?" she asked Nelson one day when O'Brian was in class.

"Nothing would have happened," he replied. "Nicola Tessla was experimenting with a power source using the Earth's own energy so that everyone in the world would have free electricity. Andrew Mellon, the famous banker, destroyed it and it was never attempted again. Once everyone had a free source of power, there would be no profit."

"Profit is everything," she repeated bitterly.

"Well, it's the big motivator."

"What was the point of Montgomery's experiment?"

"He concentrated the power in the chamber and the energy it released would alter the electron rotation. This would spiral the chamber and its occupant into another dimension."

"How did he concentrate it?"

"He used convex mirrors coated in reflective varnish. The light grew brighter and brighter with each rotation of a spinning circular top piece."

"Did it work?"

"I think so. He used his version on a test subject, a homeless world war vet who had nothing to lose. He got in the chamber and never got out, according to some of the witnesses. There was an issue with the experiment: if too much power emanated into the chamber, the subject could simply disintegrate into nothingness as the bonds between the electrons are broken and they go on to attach to other nuclei. Maybe that's what happened. Maybe he transported the subject into another world and Montgomery couldn't bring him back. Maybe, as Montgomery himself stated, the subject never showed up at the lab in the first place and his assistants wanted to steal his discovery."

"What do you think?"

"I think Montgomery was careless, whether in who he chose as helpers or in how he calculated the proper settings. Problem was: there was no record of a veteran disappearing. Was that because Montgomery never did the experiment in the first place? Or was it because he chose a victim nobody would ever miss?"

"That poor man."

"Yeah, well, scientists are always misunderstood."

"I meant the veteran."

"He was brave. He died in the pursuit of knowledge for all mankind. Or he died a forgotten drunk."

"Can you really use this machine to break into another dimension?"

"I suppose, but it's the creation of a sustainable energy source that we're looking to create."

"Is it? I think you're just as brave as that veteran who went exploring a whole new world. You're building this piece of the future, even though the faculty doesn't want you to. The blind men in charge always try to stop the visionaries among us. But you won't let them stop you, will you?"

"Well, no, but stop us from what? Discovering an energy source or proving other dimensions exist and travel between them is possible? Why would they want to stop us from making such a contribution to mankind?"

She linked her arm into his and kissed him. Nelson blushed. It was his first real kiss outside of silly middle school games.

"I think it's wonderful," she snuggled up to him, rubbing his thigh with her hand.

"The experiment?"

"I meant you."

Nelson was done for the night. His concentration was shattered. Anne whispered to him about how tired he looked and it was time for a bit more strenuous activity to clear his mind from all this science. He spent the rest of the night falling in love. They went dancing and enjoyed each other's company, eventually winding up in her bed. His room was too dirty for her to accept.

After he returned home from his classes the next day, he was still distracted by the memory of Anne's touch, her perfume, her breath. He loved waking up with her. He wondered if she was as in love as he was.

O'Brian laughed when he arrived the next evening.

"You picked a bad time to fall in love. You have a lot of class papers to write and exams to take," he smiled. "We're not even a quarter of the way done here and you decide to fall for a girl. Oh well, I suppose if I were here last night and you were in the research lab, it might have been me."

"I doubt it. She was born to be with me."

They spent another night re-creating their experiment from notes and drawings. Dr. Montgomery was not a fearful man. He left no ambiguity in his writings. Every fact was explained in a few words with no doubt of their meaning. He was a man who wanted his successors to know what he did and how it could be done again.

Of course, they were annoyed by distractions. Both O'Brian and Nelson had jobs and their classes demanded time and energy. Anne required attention as well, though she was a distraction from Heaven. Nelson even considered abandoning his experiment to devote his life to her, but she was too interested in the project to accept such a thing.

After he turned in a few mediocre assignments to maintain his good graces within the department, he continued with the interdimensional portal. He was unaware of it by then, but between it and his love for Anne, he had no interest in anything else life had to offer.

The semester finally ended. O'Brian managed to borrow everything else they needed for the break and they continued working. Nelson devoted his life to every page of his precious book and bringing to life Montgomery's wonderful machine.

The first experiment was perfect. Anne came down to

their garage-lab with a kitchen chair, plastic and peeling, with one leg not tightly screwed in. Odd as it may sound, there were six scientists in the house, but none of them were proficient with a screwdriver.

"Think it's ready for a trial run?" Nelson asked.

"Why not?" O'Brian shrugged. "We can use the chair. No one will miss it if it doesn't come back."

Not that it mattered what O'Brian said. It was Nelson's experiment. Although he referred to O'Brian as his partner, Nelson was the one in charge. O'Brian was little more than an assistant. More knowledgeable than Anne, of course, but not as pretty. And Anne meant more to Nelson now. Next to his experiment, she was his everything.

They quickly secured tinted goggles over their eyes and began. Anne's chair fit perfectly. Nelson allowed O'Brian to secure it in the machine under the open skylight to catch the midday sunlight. After they were at a safe distance, he allowed Anne to flip the two toggle switches—one to start the machine and the other to connect it to the computer to monitor the events as it gathered and magnified the light.

The machine's bright top spun slowly at first, but soon so fast it seemed almost invisible. The refrigerator shook slightly as the power gradually filtered down into its structure. An unearthly orange glow shined outwards, bathing them in an unpleasant warmth. Nelson shuddered and noticed his assistants also seemed repulsed as the light filled the room.

Although he wanted to stop the machine, he remembered that Montgomery left it on for a full ten minutes. He had a few more to go, according to his timer. The invading light seemed to make noises that sounded like people whispering and hissing in a foreign language. Shadows of daylight swirled in front of him. Silhouettes of terrible creatures walked through the room, examining them all, amused at what they saw.

One, human in shape, tall and thin, seemed to try to touch his beloved Anne. He tried to go to her, to save her from that thing, but he felt held back, as though his arms were pinned. His feet moved, but he only slid on the floor, never leaving his place. Anne's attacker seemed to caress her. Nelson could see her shiver, he hoped with disgust, but her face indicated pleasure. He watched as the thing bent down and gently kissed the lips of the woman he loved. And he could do nothing to help her.

He regained control of his arms when the timer rang and turned off the first switch to the power. They all watched the light-shadow creatures vanish and the orange glowing brightness fade back into the chamber. Anne fell in his arms in less than a heartbeat. Nelson felt himself shaking.

"You two all right?" O'Brian asked. "Maybe we didn't seal the chamber as well as we should have. It got shockingly bright in here."

"Didn't you see anything?" Nelson was amazed.

Anne fainted at that moment and he had to tend to her until she regained consciousness.

"Light," his assistant shrugged as he opened the chamber door. "Look at this."

The refrigerator stood there empty.

"We did it," Nelson yelled in excitement.

Anne stirred in his arms and he gently set her on her feet.

"Where is it?" Anne asked weakly as her senses quickly returned.

"Here," O'Brian said smugly and he switched off the other toggle.

As the computer ordered the top to stop spinning and gathering sunlight, the room grew silent. The empty refrigerator slowly darkened, filling itself with impossibly dark shadows. Soon, the shadows swirled around and dissipated, leaving behind the chair.

All three of them were excited, stomping and prancing throughout the room. Nelson grabbed the chair and tested it. Wherever it went, no damage was done to it. It was like nothing had happened to it at all.

"Just think," O'Brian stopped, "what we can do now. With some minor adjustments, this could be like the transporters in those old science fiction TV shows. We can beam across the world instead of flying. Maybe even be able to go to the moon and back."

"Or maybe to another dimension," Anne added, her green eyes shining with enthusiasm. "That's what Dr. Montgomery built it for."

Nelson turned his surprise to her. This was the first time she mentioned interdimensional travel seriously. Her dark blonde hair framed her delicately chiseled face and his heart thumped once, out of rhythm. Was it because he was happy at her new enthusiasm or because he just discovered that she was so attractive.

How did he ever think she was bland and nondescript? If it weren't for the fact that he knew her for almost a year, he would have confessed it was love at first sight.

"You alright?" O'Brian asked from behind them, breaking the spell.

"I just noticed that Anne is the most beautiful girl in the world."

"Oh," O'Brian replied, confused, as he inspected her and obviously found her wanting.

"Can you clean up here while I take my gorgeous assistant to dinner?"

"What's going to happen now?" she asked at the sandwich shop they frequented.

"We'll eat, go back home, and instead of you going to your room and me to mine, I'd think it'll be better for us to be together in my room. You fainted and I should stay with you to make sure there's no adverse residual effects from the experiment. It's the sort of thing that people in love do."

He hoped he sounded confident. He never propositioned a girl before, but he wanted her badly tonight.

"Not likely," she teased him with a seductive smile. "I've seen your room. You'll have to spend the night with me. And clean your place up tomorrow."

"What's going to happen now?" she asked as she lay next to him, stoking his thigh.

He stared at the ceiling with glazed eyes.

"We'll try again," he said, leaning over to kiss her.

"I mean with the experiment."

"I love experimenting with biology."

"So do I, but I meant with the portal."

"We'll try again, but we need to stand back and get some kind of protective cover. When all the light poured out, I saw it completely surround you, like it was somehow enveloping you, kissing you."

"Really," she replied, her green eyes deep in thought. "I did feel warmer around my face for a moment or two. I thought I saw it swirling all around you, now that you mention it. I never felt a kiss though."

"That's because it was keeping me away from you. I felt it behind me, like it had me in some kind of a wrestling hold," he said ruefully.

"I didn't see anything like that."

"I wonder what O'Brian saw," he said drowsily.

"Probably just light. I think he was monitoring the controls and didn't pay too much attention. Besides, if you came over from another dimension, would you be interested in him?"

He chuckled and pulled her on top of him.

They tried another experiment with the portal the next day, only this time with a wicker cage holding an imprisoned cricket. The results were spectacular. The cricket came back alive and vigorous, at least as far as they could tell, none of them being experts on insect health.

The next day, they bought a white rat from a pet store. He was alert, quick on his feet and never stayed still, always flitting about, curious about his new surroundings.

"It's so cute," Anne exclaimed when it scurried in front of her brown eyes.

Her hair had darkened as well. It was brunette, a soft brown color with red highlights. Her face was a little fuller and softer.

Why is she not a movie star, Nelson wondered. His dream-filled eyes followed her as she darted in and out of the lab cooing at the lab rat.

"Don't get attached," O'Brian warned her. "A mammal is way more complicated than an insect and a whole lot more bad things can happen when we start the experiment."

"Nothing will happen," she replied defiantly. "It's too adorable for that."

"Somehow," O'Brian muttered, "I don't think the laws of physics take that into consideration."

Anne flipped the two switches on and they watched as

the machine hummed to life. Slowly, the orange light seeped into the lab. O'Brian was oblivious to it, but Anne was fascinated by the obscure shapes and shades of color that formed figures for brief moments before they transformed into other forms.

Nelson observed that the light did seem to be attracted to Anne, bathing her in an eerie glow as it danced around her, almost as though the light was performing some kind of ritual. He felt its unholy warmth on his skin and shivered, despite the heat. O'Brian was positioned just beyond the reach of the orange glow. Nelson knew instinctively that if the light wanted to flow into O'Brian, it could. His partner just didn't seem to attract it.

The rat survived the portal. He appeared to be lethargic and tired. He didn't object when Anne picked him up and put him down in the cage. His dull eyes blinked occasionally, but he took no interest in anything else that day.

"Maybe interdimensional travel is stressful and takes a lot out of you," he shrugged to Anne after they went back to her room. "Maybe we need a whole lot more sex so when I go over, we're content until I get recovered and ready again."

"Maybe we need a whole lot less in case you don't get recovered and ready."

"Do you want me to go to a strange new world sexually unfulfilled?"

"You're going on the next trial?" She lifted herself on an elbow. "Are you sure that's safe? I thought you needed more animal trials. O'Brian was talking about setting up cameras on the next run. I thought we were buying a rabbit tomorrow."

"No, none of that. We don't have the budget and

O'Brian wants to start writing the paper. He thinks that not only will we be shoo-ins for our master's degrees, we may also win a Nobel Prize. How many scientists can you think of who got a Nobel Prize before their Ph.D.?"

"I'm not sure this is a good idea," O'Brian told him the next morning. "We have enough data to turn the academic world on its ear. We already proved Scott Montgomery was a genius after all. The power source we created will be able to convert the whole world into using our patented, almost free electricity. And the potential to transport cargo and people is unapparelled.

"We can put our findings out there and have every university in the country try to replicate our results. We need to get out of the lab and get to the patent office. Write our papers. Make our names known in this world. Don't you see, Nelson? We don't need to take any more risks now. What more is left for us to prove?"

"Somebody will be the first man to travel from one dimension to another. Everyone's heard of Leif Ericson, Christopher Columbus, Chuck Yaeger, John Glenn, Neil Armstrong. Soon, there'll be a whole new scientific frontier opening for mankind. And Dylan Nelson will the first man to walk through it. The Nelson Experiment will be talked about and studied until the end of civilization. And we three partners will be rich beyond our wildest dreams. To hell with people like Dr. Johns. They're small thinkers who resent visionaries like us."

"Why is it the Nelson Experiment and not the Nelson-O'Brian Experiment?"

"Because I'm the one who thought up the whole plan."

"Wasn't Scott Montgomery the one who thought it up?"

"I'm the one who thought up the idea of following his ideas. His works have laid in obscurity for a century. It's time to prove to the world what an open-minded scientist can accomplish."

"But—"

Anne put his hand on his shoulder.

"His blood is up on this one. Let's just let him go. He wants the fame and fortune and someone needs to stay behind to work the equipment."

"But what about safety? Shouldn't we run another test?" he asked, obviously hurt and confused.

"We should. Do you want to tell him?"

She walked up to Nelson and buried her head in his chest. He gazed down into her charcoal gray eyes with his own and smiled as he stroked her coal black hair.

"This research needs to go on. Nothing will go wrong, you'll see."

She smiled as she gazed back at him with her sparkling, laughing eyes.

"I know, my love," she answered. "It will all go according to our plan. I have no doubt about that. The whole university will be talking about the Nelson Experiment for years."

She backed away with her hand holding his until just their fingertips touched for a moment, then she spun away to the panel while O'Brian did the final safety check. After his assistant's nod, Nelson entered the chamber and closed the door behind him. He heard O'Brian seal the door shut and he suddenly wondered whether he should have left a will.

The thought faded as the top above him started its rotation, slowly at first, then faster until it was invisible. The air was warm and heavy and he sank to his knees, using the wall as a support as the blinding light bathed him in its unnatural warmth.

Slowly, the warmth faded, along with all feeling. He was there, but he wasn't. He wanted to panic but his emotions were gone. They should have made calculations based on his human weight. Just because it worked on a rat didn't mean it had to work on a man.

He was disintegrating. The electrons were separating too far from the atomic nuclei. Soon, he would vanish forever. How stupid. And he was leaving behind Anne, his raven-haired beauty, or brunette, or blonde. With her black eyes, or were they brown? Green?

The feeling vanished as the top stopped spinning. The light faded into shadow as his eyes adjusted to the gloom. He was still sealed in the chamber. He waited as long as he could in the stale air. He expected black shadows to form around him as O'Brian turned off the second toggle, but nothing was happening.

He pressed against the chamber door and it opened easily. Surprised, he climbed out and stood up, stretching to regain his circulation. The empty lab stood before him. Neither O'Brian nor Anne greeted him. He walked to the control panel to find it destroyed, as though it exploded from the inside out.

A crinkling sound, almost musical, found his ears and he glanced up to see the last pieces of the old refrigerator-chamber tumble to the floor. The garage was a disaster of shattered equipment and half burned papers scattered everywhere.

Was there an explosion? he asked himself as he stepped into the house. It was unharmed by whatever happened in the garage but it was still different.

The hall slanted upwards at an odd tilt, steep and

curved, the carpet shimmered as the orange light reflected off it. A quick search out the window showed him the bright sun, orange and angry in the sky. Tiny, yet powerful. The walls throbbed in an eerie pulse, the booming sound slowing down with each minute. It was his heartbeat, he realized. The pounding of his heart reflected in the wall.

"Dylan," Anne's voice called from behind him.

He turned to her but recoiled when she stood in his view. Her face was almost the same as before, but different. Her skin's texture was soft and fluid, like butter almost melted in a dish. It constantly changed as though he was viewing her through a distorted mirror. Her hair also changed colors from black to white and everything in between. Her eyes shone as bright as the orange sun, though muted behind ever-changing colors.

"You did it, my love," she smiled at him with sinister glee. "You made it home."

"Home?" he gulped.

She touched his hand with hers, but he felt nothing. He realized instantly that her body was made of light and not matter.

"Your new home. Your research was correct. Now you can continue your experiments with us for the rest of your life."

Other beings stepped into his view. Like Anne, their bodies fluctuated every second into something new and different, yet enough remained to recognize them as individuals. He involuntarily shivered when these creatures smiled at him, welcoming him to their world.

"Yes, Nelson," one stood behind Anne, caressing her breasts with both hands while she purred and leaned back into him, caressing his jaw with one fluid hand. "We welcome you here. The last specimen we had died of old age and war wounds many years ago. You are our only living specimen and you can continue your pursuit of knowledge with us. Forever."

"But…O'Brian should be returning me back home."

"Oh no, my love," the Anne creature said as she disengaged from the other one. "One dimension isn't all that different than another. That lab was destroyed, just like this one. You're in your new home now."

"But Anne?"

"When you performed your first experiment, I was able to deposit my essence into your female, displacing her soul."

"You killed her?" his blood chilled.

"No, but she died in the process and I replaced her with my essence. It's science, after all. Everybody makes sacrifices in the name of science, not only you. She was just one of many. After I removed her soul from our body, I was able to adjust your equipment so that you would come here to my home. My essence left her body to come back with you and here we are. Together again. Of course, you are still made of your matter and we are made of light so we can never touch each other again."

"But I loved…Anne." He couldn't find the words. Everything was destroyed and he couldn't go back?

"You needed my help to get here. She was pretty, I suppose, but she didn't know the science. And you never seemed to understand that some places in the dimensional spectrum are dangerous, filled with monstrous creatures with no souls. Things that would eat you without a second thought. Your whole experiment was terribly dangerous, especially if you opened a portal and couldn't secure it. Your government classified all Mongomery's notes and destroyed his equipment, though some sanctioned researchers still experiment with his ideas. But they are too cautious to achieve results. Not results like yours.

"When we became aware of you, we decided to help you. You were about to make a fatal error and land in a deadly world of predatory creatures. I was able to adjust your equipment so that you would come here to my home. My essence came back with you and here we are."

"But O'Brian—"

"Poor O'Brian," she said with mocking sympathy. "His calculations sent too much power into your machine. You two really should have done a safety check. The whole lab exploded and he died. His body, and Anne's, will soon be found. The authorities will condemn the building and confiscate anything they can salvage. You were lost in the experiment and your body will never be found. You'll be presumed disintegrated and dead. After all, no one could have survived that explosion.

"He was riding on your coattails, you know. He had nothing to offer but he was going to get half of your credit. That was so wrong and we wanted you with us. We had no use for him and couldn't let him live. He might help another bold young scientist like yourself. So, I took the liberty of disabling your device, which caused the explosion. That way, we can be together, just you and me."

"Why? You said it yourself, we can't even touch."

"On your world, why do you have zoos?"

He winced. He left his world to be a trained seal?

"But the police, the university, they'll keep looking for me."

She sighed as she strode toward him and indicated to him to turn around and view the wreckage of his lab.

"Look at all that junk. And two dead bodies as well. They don't know that your experiment worked and now you live here with your kind. Our kind. And no one will ever rebuild your experiment after a disaster like that."

"You mean I can't go back. Ever."

"Oh, Nelson," she laughed. "Why would you want to go back there, when you can stay with us…forever?"

PALADINE

Centered in north central Phoenix is the Paladine neighborhood. It stands bordered by Monet Avenue to the north and Renoir Drive on the south, between Watercress and Golden Lilly to the east and west. Its construction started right after World War II when people didn't mind that all the houses looked the same. It saved money. The builders didn't care about style and the buyers just wanted their own house.

As the new owners moved in, they planted trees, most of which died immediately. They painted, built additions, constructed walls, and added decorative windmills and other things to make their home look unique and individual. Some planted grass but none ever grew. Soon, the whole development had matching gravel yards. A few lucky owners coaxed lantana, cactus and agaves to grow, but most accepted the fact that living plants didn't thrive here.

The original owner of the land was Jack Jenson. He owned a huge swarth of acres just outside of city limits and had a gigantic citrus orchard. In springtime, the honeyed smell of orange blossoms dominated the air. But not in this one area. Nothing grew here for him. When the developer approached him with the idea to put a neighborhood of wall-to-wall houses and offered him a generous price, he quickly accepted.

Construction started in 1946 and the homes sold fast. By 1948, two hundred and twelve 1,300 square feet homes were purchased, most of them before the workers completed the buildings. After the war, people discovered the swamp cooler, which added water to the air and circulated it, making the desert summers bearable, provided people stayed inside. The city of Phoenix grew and the population climbed higher after air conditioning became commonplace. With growth came demand for larger houses, which made Paladine less desirable as time progressed.

Ralph Bunker's parents bought one of the first homes built in Paladine just before he was born in 1947 and that is where he spent his childhood. His family lived in Paladine longer than anyone else. Most people moved in for a few years and left for bigger houses in nicer neighborhoods. Paladine was ideal for first-time home buyers to buy, build up equity and move on as their families grew. That was the official story, anyway.

Another reason so few people stayed was the uneasy feeling in the air, especially at night. Most everybody felt as though something evil hovered over them, just out of sight, stalking them. Few people went out for evening strolls. Fewer left their dogs out at night. The inconsiderate ones who let their cats out rarely saw their feline friends again.

An old man lived alone on Jenson Street and he bothered no one. In fact, he occasionally hired one or two local boys to pick the weeds in his yard. He rarely hired the same boy twice because red ants thrived and swarmed there. They were aggressive and their bite was painful.

Ralph lived through it. He bought some gloves, a kneeling pad and a few cans of Raid. The old man laughed when he saw his supplies.

"Now that's the way to tackle your problems," he smiled.

Ralph became his regular landscaper from then on. Two hours of work turned into five dollars. A good deal in those days, for sure. One particularly hot morning, after Ralph finished, the old man invited him in for iced tea.

Lots of dust greeted him. The dirt on the tables and bookcases looked thick enough to fill a flowerpot. But Ralph marveled at the amount of books in the collection. The house looked like the public library and Ralph loved reading. Most boys read a lot over the summer as it was too hot to do much else. Phoenix was scorching in the summer sun and they couldn't watch television because their mothers were always watching soap operas while ironing or cooking.

"So, what's your name, son," the old man asked him and nodded in approval and told him his address.

Ralph was amazed.

"Why? Everyone plasters the family name on their mailboxes. Not hard to get to know your neighbors that way. Basic logic. My father was an expert on that sort of thing. You may have heard of him. Scott Montgomery."

"No, sir. I'm sorry, but I haven't."

"Oh, well," he laughed. "Fame is fleeting. Let me introduce myself. I am Howard Montgomery."

They shook hands and had a pleasant talk. Ralph went home with a borrowed book: *Inner Dimensions and What Dwells Within* by Scott Montgomery.

And so, a friendship was born. Ralph spent most of his

afternoons visiting Howard. He read more books and they discussed them over iced tea. Those were pleasant visits. They got him away from his father and four sisters. His mother didn't annoy him, but the rest of the household did. His sisters' only hobbies were to get him in trouble and embarrass him in school. That would bring him to his father's attention, and his father liked to criticize everything he did.

But Howard only encouraged him. By the time he graduated high school, Howard tutored him in inter-dimensional forces and cosmic physics to the point where he became somewhat of an expert. Too bad there wasn't much demand for such knowledge.

Howard was different at night. He was one of the few residents who would take long midnight walks. He walked out to Renoir Drive and south. Where he went afterwards was unknown. It was rumored that he picked up an occasional prostitute. Or maybe did drug deals. Or who knows what. He was very unfriendly to anyone who tried to stop and talk to him.

When Ralph graduated, he joined the Army before they could draft him and went to Vietnam. Howard encouraged his continued education and the GI Bill would do wonders for him. And he was lucky enough to never see combat because he was assigned to a support duty.

By 1968, after he was discharged and returned home, he found a job at a gas station and made just enough to move out on his own and stay fed. Going to college was a dream of his so he took advantage of the GI Bill and signed up for evening courses.

Howard died in 1972 and willed his house to Ralph. He quickly moved in and made the necessary changes to make it his own home, but he kept Howard's things. He started wearing Howard's clothes. He also hired the occasional schoolboy to do the lawn work. He also took long solitary walks, even though he had a car.

As time went on, he started using the word 'we' when speaking of himself and his solitary household. He never married. He occasionally invited a girl over for dinner, but nothing came of his advances. The neighbors eventually spotted him driving home with known prostitutes. If his sisters ever visited him, no one knew about it. He was destined to be a lonely man.

As before mentioned, Phoenix grew exponentially due to the availability of air conditioning. The city planners allowed the developers to destroy the surrounding citrus groves as a sacrifice to growth and progress. Newer homes competed for residents. Paladine saw more homeowners move out and choose to rent their property for what they could get. Others sold for a loss. Everyone knew it was only a matter of time before the inevitable decline would make their neighborhood dangerous and unlivable. Paladine's time was over and the development was doomed to be a slum.

A new class of residents moved in and out through the years. Police cars were regular visitors to Paladine now. Drug users littered Monat Avenue. Soon, they started breaking into homes. Addicts destroyed the houses they invaded to steal the appliances and copper wiring in the walls. Some of the rougher kids held wild parties in the abandoned buildings before they trashed them. Eventually, the distraught owners of over fifty houses nailed plywood to the windows to keep the trespassers out while they tried to sell the almost useless property. The banks took over some properties but abandoned them to the rats and drug addicts. Nobody cared about Paladine.

It became one of the more dangerous places in the city. The Kings claimed most of those places. They were a notoriously violent gang of Los Angles cast outs who claimed ownership of everything around them. More than a few bodies littered the streets of Paladine. Several times, Ralph called the police to have one removed, though he never saw what happened.

Through it all, Ralph lived his lonely life. He inherited a nice sum of money when his parents died. He quit his job, kept his house up to the old standards and employed young boys to pick weeds. He didn't care that his neighbors were no longer white. He found it sad that the neighborhood became so blighted, but there was nothing he could do about it. He continued to make his solitary walks at night, remembering what it was like in his childhood.

He usually left after midnight. He was a familiar sight to the drug dealers and gangbangers who were his new neighbors. Some suggested they should beat him up to get him out of the 'hood,' but wiser heads always prevailed. He wasn't hurting anyone and he kept his mouth shut. Unneeded police activity wasn't desirable. But two days after his seventieth birthday, an incident occurred on Jenson Street.

"Hey, old man," two Kings shouted at him just as he started his walk.

He turned to face them. They were very young. One was maybe twelve, the other closer to sixteen. The older one had good genes. He was already past six feet tall and weighed at least two hundred pounds. His face was damaged, scarred from what must have been a vicious knife attack. He carried a wicked looking Bowie knife in one hand. The little one looked like a typical adolescent, except for his hate filled eyes. He simply exuded anger.

"I don't know if you know it yet, but this here's a toll road," the scarred one said.

"Yeah," the angry one echoed. "No white guys in this 'hood. You want to stay, you gotta pay."

"Pay?" Ralph asked, suppressing a smile. "I've lived here forever. Never had to pay before."

The knife was at his throat.

"You do now, old man," the little one said. "Go live with all the other crackers. You stay, you pay."

"Fifty dollars if you stay," the other one grinned.

"If you insist," Ralph said deferentially, gently guiding the knife away from his neck.

He looked at them again. They both wore gold chains. The older one had a large ring with at least one large diamond set in a black background.

"But, you see," Ralph went on smoothly, "I don't carry that kind of cash on me. We'll have to go to my house so I can get it for you. It's in the safe."

"You know," Scarface sneered. "It'll be more if we have to walk with you."

"I can get it and come back."

They both scoffed out laughs.

"You got it backwards, old man," Scarface jeered at him. "We ain't dumb. You are. Let's go."

So, they walked back to Ralph's home. They passed by the house he originally grew up in, which was little more than a shell with plywood pulled loose so the addicts could use it as a shelter. A little further down, they reached Ralph's little palace. At least it looked majestic compared to what surrounded it.

The door opened quietly. Ralph maintained his house well. It was a good habit to get into, he remembered his father advising him when he inherited it. He recalled how much he resented his father in high school and how he came to love the man after he returned from the war.

An old lamp brightened the room at the click of the switch. The living room had old furniture that dated back to the forties. The upholstery faded, but Ralph refused to trade it in for the modern junk he knew wouldn't even last a year.

"You live here?" the young one said contemptuously. "It looks like a second-rate museum."

"To each his own," Ralph replied easily. "I've lived in this house for forty-five years and in Paladine my whole life. Never saw a need to change anything. I wouldn't mind changing the neighborhood though."

"Make it all white again," Scarface said. "Never going to happen."

Ralph shrugged. "Let's go get you your money."

With that, he led then down the hall to his little guest room and opened the door, reaching in to turn on the light. They gasped when they saw what awaited them. Piles of jewels. Gold and silver coins, necklaces, bracelets, rings, armbands, broaches, pins, and gold chains piled up at least four feet high. Above the glorious treasure was an open safe, overflowing with the promised paper bills. And thousands of paper dollars sat on top of it.

The two thieves looked at each other for a moment and ran through the plunder toward the cash, stopping to pick up some jewels and stuffing them in their pockets. Ralph quietly closed the door while they laughed with joy at their find.

These two nameless thugs tried to make their way closer to the safe, which obviously had more than fifty dollars in it, but found their feet were somehow frozen.

"What the hell…," Scarface muttered while looking down.

The treasure they were standing in had fused together, as though it somehow melted. The younger one was already untying his shoe as he tried to free himself from it when a whirlwind of dusty air blew around them, rising to the ceiling, forming the shape of an ethereal dragon. Second by second, it materialized into a sold being. It was not a lovable dragon from a movie or cartoon. It had no scales or smooth skin. It was a large serpent with golden feathers and a nasty looking beak instead of fangs. Two large wings flapped languidly at its sides, helping it keep balance as it looked down at the unfortunate thieves.

They heard a voice in their heads saying, "My servant has done unusually well tonight. He usually finds me decaying husks of humanity to feed on. The diseased. Drug addicts. Whores. Drunks. Those who are already dying and tasteless. But what does he offer me tonight? Two fine specimens of humanity. Young. Hardy. Bodies not destroyed by their own vices. You two will taste so good and that makes me happy."

"Like hell," Scarface screamed at the worm and dropped his knife to pull out a .38 semi-automatic.

He started firing at the dragon, hitting it with almost every shot. The monster seemed startled at first, then angry.

"You come into my house and attack me? Let me show you what a real attack looks like."

With a swift strike, the beak clamped onto and ripped off Scarface's arm. The gun fell harmlessly in the treasure while Scarface screamed in fear and agony as he and the youngster hood watched the snake flip his appendage into the air and swallow it.

Both thugs were screaming and crying out for mercy.

The young one got out of his shoes and ran to the door to escape, but Ralph locked it from the hall. His only way out was through the winged serpent. He slowly turned around with his tear-stained face to watch the thing pull Scarface out of the bejeweled trap, leaving his knees and feet stuck in the goo that used to be treasure. The now legless Scarface was no longer screaming but sobbing in fear as the monster flipped him into the air and caught him in that loathsome beak. The little one could hear the crunching of bones as the beast crushed and swallowed his friend. He turned back to the door and started pounding on it.

"Let me out. Oh, please. Mister. open the door!"

He kept pounding on it, but the door did not budge and Ralph wasn't answering. If the boy thought of it, he would have realized he broke one hand already, but he was too panicked to notice the pain.

He heard flapping behind him and turned to see that horrid beak swoop down on him. He felt pain as the beak crushed his chest with a crunching sound. He was vaguely aware that it flipped him up high up into the air and caught him. That beak ripped him in half before he slipped away into darkness. The chewing of his flesh was the last thing he heard.

After he brushed his teeth and washed up for bed, Ralph opened the door to the guest room. All was as it should be. The jewels were there, the money untouched. There wasn't a trace of either mugger.

"They certainly sounded mean and intimidating when I met them," he said to the empty room, "But they sure didn't stay tough for long."

He heard a contented squawk reply.

Sculpture and Witchcraft

It was a simple gas station, built back in the Roaring Twenties, right in front of the Keaton River. It had two bays with hydraulic lifts and four state-of-the-art gas pumps. They would be valuable antiques today, if they still existed. Their squared bodies were crowned with a circular top that made them look like stationary robots. Bright orange cursive lettering that advertised Griffon Gas ran down each pump's curvature from top to bottom. Connected to the garage was a tiny general store that sold soda, candy and cheap souvenirs for the occasional tourists who stopped by to use the restrooms and fill their thirsty cars with premium gas.

The station, store, pumps, and grounds were always clean and polished. Mr. Dormer, the owner, believed the station was an extension of his personality and a reflection of him. So, he, his wife and four children were constantly searching the premises for dirt, grime, oil, weeds, or stains of any kind to do battle with and eliminate them without a trace. The farmers and bargemen who lived nearby always found their way to Griffon Station in their spare time to have a cola or sandwich, fresh and handmade by Mrs. Dormer and always served with a smile.

Mr. Dormer needed his children to keep the garage up

to his very high standards. The customers kept him busy working on cars and pumping gas. The children needed to do everything else to maintain the family business. Although he would be surprised if anyone told him that his two older sons and two younger daughters never really thought of him as a loving father, no one else in town would be. Many of his customers shook their heads sadly when they saw his daughters scrubbing oil stains off the asphalt in front of the pumps to make his gas station the cleanest in the parish.

To his family, he was only a taskmaster who loved to watch them work for free and hated to spend any money so they could enjoy the fun things life had to offer. A clean garage and home were all they needed to be content, he firmly believed. It never occurred to him that cleanliness, although next to godliness, was not the same as love. Such a lack of awareness would eventually cost him his life.

The depression caught the Dormers off-guard, like so many others in the parish. The children, who rarely wore new clothes or had new toys or anything else, received even less. But with some careful planning, the family made it through the worst of the hard times. Eight small hands doing free labor made all the difference in keeping the business running.

Disaster struck in 1938 and no one could have predicted that such a small thing (monumental in the eyes of a child) would have changed the course of the family's history. But it did, and that is where their story truly begins.

Raffy, short for Raphael, was a happy little dog. He didn't resemble any breed. He was just a dog. He couldn't hunt, fish or herd. The family didn't have anything for him to do except keep the girls occupied. The boys were almost adults and didn't play with dogs anymore. Raffy knew the

Dormers were his family and he loved all of them, but he really belonged to Estelle, the older daughter.

She was a precocious ten-year old tomboy with short hair and brown eyes. Obviously, since she was a girl who was four years younger than Tom and six years younger than Dale, her brothers had little to do with her. The girls from school frowned at her overalls and lack of curls. They couldn't understand how she could live without a doll to fuss over and nurture. Emily Harris even offered her one of her own so she could play games like House, Hopscotch and pretending they were adults with the other girls. Estelle politely refused the doll. Emily and the other girls condemned the nonconformist to a childhood of having no real friends, except for Karen.

At eight, Karen idolized her older sister, but still liked her own little 'Dolly.' And so, during the long days of summer, when they could get away from the garage for a bit, the four of them—Estelle, Karen, Raffy, and Dolly— wandered through the lush green meadows and dense forests of central Louisiana. They explored old, abandoned houses and barns. They hunted for old arrowheads or spent bullet casings. They laughed and hugged each other. Estelle even hugged Dolly, though she thought that was a complete waste of a perfectly good cuddle.

The old Miller place was a favorite haunt of theirs, especially since the Millers no longer lived there. That family left about five years earlier, after the bank foreclosed on them. Lightning struck the house soon after and because nobody heard the strike or saw the flames, it burned to the ground. All that remained were a few singed boards that fed colonies of termites.

"Maybe we can find something valuable," Estelle told Karen. "Let's look around. Maybe there's some old coins that spilled out of their pockets when they left, or a piece of silverware. You never know."

And so, they searched. Karen didn't really know what they were looking for, but she was happy to be doing something with her sister. So, she scavenged the area, finding nothing. She wandered a bit further out. An old fallen tree wasn't too far away and she headed for it, thinking she could climb on top to better see treasure.

A brown streak of fur darted in front of her at the same time a lightning blur of color struck out at her ankle. Raffy yelped in pain while Karen watched in horror as a copperhead snake slithered away through the tall grass. Estelle was there in a heartbeat and picked up the whimpering dog.

They ran like the wind home. Estelle stumbled a bit on the concrete stairs that led up to the back porch but determinedly kept going.

"There's nothing we can do for him except make him comfortable," their mother said sadly. She made a warm mustard poultice and placed it on his wound, "But at least we know this wonderful dog saved your sister. He'll always be a hero to us."

"No," Estelle cried, along with Karen. "There has to be something we can do."

"Well, there isn't," Mrs. Dormer said flatly. "And I have to start dinner."

The screen door slammed shut behind the girls as they looked for someone more sympathetic to help them. Mrs. Dormer looked up, visibly angry, and called out through the window screen. Karen stopped and came back but Estelle must not have heard her.

Three blocks later, Estelle was at the garage, begging Mr. Dormer to help her. He stopped working on someone's car for a few seconds to glare at her, then turned back to his job.

"I'm busy," he said curtly. "I've got an oil change and tune-up on the lifts and Mama Rochelle there needs to have her list picked out and paid for. All this came in after I sent the boys home and I need to do it before I close today."

Estelle turned and saw an ancient wagon parked to the side with a tired looking old horse standing in front of it. Mama Rochelle, a black woman, sat on the bench watching her. Her middle-aged face was unsmiling as Estelle pleaded for help for her dog.

"But Raffy was bit by a poisonous snake," she wailed. "He saved Karen's life by jumping in front of her like he did. He deserves at least some care."

"Estelle," her father said in that quiet and fierce you-could-get-a-whupping tone of voice, "I am indeed sorry. He's a hero dog, but at the end of the day, he's a dog. And I'm not the only garage in town."

He turned away from her tear-stained face.

"Bring the animal here," a voice commanded. Mama Rochelle's expression seemed fierce, but she spoke with a soft and comforting voice.

Estelle complied as her father turned back to her for a second. He was going to stop his daughter, but the store phone rang and he had to answer it.

"Put the animal in the back of the cart with the bite on top."

When they arranged Raffy perfectly, the woman grabbed her leather handbag, got down from her perch and examined the wound.

"Copperhead," she pronounced, as if Estelle didn't already know. "Very bad for such a small thing."

She reached inside her purse and pulled out an aged,

stained vial with some red powder.

"Get me some water," she commanded.

Estelle hesitated. Mr. Dormer always told her to keep a distance from black people.

"Do you want the dog to live or not?" the woman snapped at her.

With a quick nod, Estelle ran to the pump and filled a glass to the rim. She hurried back to the wagon.

Mama Rochelle poured some of the water into the vial and shook it until the fluid inside was a reddish color that sparkled like glitter in the afternoon sun.

"Help the dog on his hind legs."

With little effort, Estelle got Raffy to stand. His sad eyes looked into hers, as though he was saying goodbye. Her eyes were tearing up again.

"Stop that nonsense," Mama Rochelle rebuked. "I need you to pull the mouth open."

She followed the instructions. The older woman took the stoper out of the vial, poured the fluid down the dog's throat, then held his mouth shut until she was satisfied that Raffy swallowed the medicine.

"He will be sick for a week," she pronounced. "Then his strength will come back. He will live."

Indeed, he was already twisting a bit in her arms, indicating he wanted her to let him down. Estelle put him on the ground and he laid down at her feet.

"Oh, thank you," Estelle cried tears of happiness this time. "What can I do to thank you?"

"You? Nothing," the old woman said harshly, but then softened a bit. "No, something. Here is my list and here is ten dollars. Go fetch my groceries. You know my money can go through your door, but I can't."

Estelle took the list and turned to go into the store. A

Whites Only sign she never really paid attention to seemed to grow larger, blocking everything else out of her vision. Then it was normal again. The sign was prominent, but not large at all.

Estelle turned to the old woman for a second, but Mama Rochelle's eyes were staring into the trees, not seeing her at all. The girl quickly ran into the store and filled the list, putting an extra can of tuna in the bag for her.

"I'm sorry," she said as she snugged the groceries into the back of the wagon while Raffy watched.

"Nothing for you to be sorry about," the old woman said imperiously. "You didn't create the world. You're like me. We just live in it."

With that, she flicked the reins and the horse trotted off. She returned occasionally for more groceries and Estelle always made sure she was the one who carried the items to her cart.

One day, Mama Rochelle came with a painted clay alligator for Estelle.

"Made it myself from river clay," she said. "Made it for you. Baked it in my old cauldron at home. Pretty, isn't it?"

"Yes, it is," Estelle said dutifully.

She thought it was ugly, because alligators all have evil looking eyes. God may have made all the animals, but Estelle still believed the devil snuck in one night to make alligators and mosquitos.

"You lie," Mama Rochelle laughed. "But you watch. You will be very glad one day. It can protect you from hurt. You can use it only once."

"Use it?"

"You'll know what to do."

"You make other statues like these?" Estelle asked.

"At least two a week. The arthritis bothers me when I make more."

"What do you do with them?"

"I sell them. Some folks say I have a real talent for them."

"I think so. Maybe we can sell some in the store for you."

"Your parents won't allow it."

"I can try," Estelle said confidently.

She enlisted Karen's aid in trying to get Mama Rochelle's clay pieces in the store to sell on consignment, but both her parents adamantly refused. The girls showed their father piece after piece. All realistic, handmade, pieces of Louisiana culture. All rejected. The Dormers would not sell artwork made by a black woman.

One day, they showed him a turtle with its head stretched out like it almost had a fish. Unfortunately, he was talking to Mrs. McHindly. All the girls in town called her Mrs. McHiney because she wiggled her hiney so much when she walked in front of any man. Estelle didn't understand why the adult women in town gossiped about her with such hatred. She always found the woman to be kind enough to her and Karen. Mrs. McHiney seemed to be a cruel nickname.

"Oh, how precious," Mrs. McHindly cooed when Estelle presented it to their father. "It looks so real."

"It does," Karen nodded enthusiastically. "We've been trying to get Father to sell them in the store, but he won't."

"Why not?" Mrs. McHindly asked while holding the figurine up to look at its underside. "This is so good. It looks just like the turtles in the zoo."

"Mama Rochelle made it."

"It was made by a black woman?"

The father nodded solemnly while Mrs. McHindly paled.

"Oh, dear," she said and gave it back to Karen. "I have to go wash up now."

She headed for the ladies' room, in a hurry, unaware she just lost the respect of two little girls.

"You see her reaction. She's washing her hands now and all she did was touch it. That's why I won't sell anything from her," their father sternly said to them. "No one wants to pick up anything after a black person handled it. She needs to sell it to her own kind."

That incident defeated the girls. Karen was even crying. She understood the rules of segregation, but this was simply unjust. Estelle was disappointed but understood now. Nothing Mama Rochelle made would sell but she still wanted her friend to know that she tried to help her. They marched back with a healthy Raffy at their heels.

"That's alright, my dears," Mama Rochelle soothed as she wrapped up the turtle in muslin. "Nothing to feel bad about. In fact," she pulled out two muslin bundles that were maybe six inches long each, "these are for you because you are kind and try to do the right thing. Use them well."

She snapped the reins and the horse moved along as the girls unwrapped their presents. Two black snakes with extra-long fangs greeted them with pitted eyes. Karen almost dropped hers.

"It's awful. I don't want it."

"It's not awful. She does swamp things. Can I have yours?"

Karen gladly gave her the snake. Estelle put them both in her apron pocket. They would go along nicely with her alligator at home.

Use them well. Use them for what?

83

The family's division of labor was simple enough. The boys handled the oil changes and cleaning around the garage and parking lot. Karen wiped down the counters and dusted the shelves. Estelle washed the windows and mopped the floors. She rotated the chores daily. Today was the floor.

When the boys and Karen left, she filled the mop bucket. After she shut off the water, she locked the front door and sat down to remove her shoes, opened a cold bottle of cola, and started stuffing peanuts down the throat of the bottle. Peanuts always tasted better in cola.

"Are they all gone?" Mrs. McHindly asked from outside.

Estelle instinctively hunched down. No telling what juicy details she might hear. She heard the lock rattle.

"Yep," her father's voice replied. If a voice could leer, his just did.

"Let's get that skinny dip in while there's still some sun," that home wrecker said next.

Estelle stared after them, appalled. Her father and that woman? Her mother would be so humiliated. Estelle's shock turned to anger as she heard them walk toward the river together.

She quietly rushed to the back door and looked out the storm window. Mrs. McHindly was leaning a hand on her father's chest as she balanced a foot in the air to slip her shoes off while her father was pulling off his oily shirt. Soon, they were both stark naked and playing with each other. Estelle watched them cavort in the muddy water, aghast, but still curious enough to watch. Were they just going to skinny dip or do something else? It looked like her father was trying to gently ease her to the ground, but with a laugh, Mrs. McHindly broke his grasp and ran into the river, her backside wiggling like two molds of Jell-O.

They were together, their bodies swallowed by the dark water. Good! She didn't want to see any more of them. She backed away, wondering what to do. Her apron snagged on one of the shelves and she felt the edge of the figurines in the apron's pocket as they pressed against her thigh.

She pulled them out thoughtfully. *Use them well.* If she thought about it, she wouldn't have done it, but sometimes a child's brain reacts first and thinks later.

"And that's what causes regret. Action first, thought second," she heard Pastor O'Rourke's voice from a not so long-ago sermon.

To be fair, Estelle didn't know what would happen anyway. Perhaps she wouldn't have done it if she did. Perhaps.

She quietly slipped out the door. Her father was nibbling on Mrs. McHindly's neck, his face turned away from her. Mrs. McHindly pulled her back onto her father's shoulder, her closed eyes pointing to the sky. She exhaled sharply with what sounded like a small moan combined with a heavy sigh. They never noticed Estelle sneaking down to the river's edge.

The lapping water gently whooshed by her, almost noiselessly as she submerged her two toys in the dark water. She crawled back a step and watched them for a moment. Then back up at the two adulterers. Then back down.

The clay snakes were growing. Their tails were twitching, slowly at first, then a bit faster as the rest of their bodies twisted with life. They were soon over four feet long, swimming in circles around each other.

This was a bad time to be playing with them, Estelle thought, but she didn't want to reach into the water to retrieve them. They were real. They were thick. And they were cottonmouths. They stuck their heads out of the water and opened their mouths, revealing their white maws, then swam over to the lovebirds as Estelle hid behind some Iris plants and watched.

The illicit lovers didn't see the deadly serpents approaching them. Her father was oblivious to everything else in the world expect Mrs. McHindly. He had her backside in both hands and lifted her out of the water so he could nibble on her breast. She wasn't just moaning now; she was practically screaming.

"Ow, hey," her father yelled, dropping her and looking down and around to his lower back.

"What?" she fumed.

"I think I got bit by a snake."

"What? Oh my God, it's too early for them."

"Yeah? Well, we better get out of here and I gotta get to a doctor. Look."

He turned his back to her to show the twin puncture wounds on the top of his backside.

"Hurry," she screamed, leaving him behind as she scurried out toward her clothes.

He was not far behind when he yelped again. He looked down at his hip. Estelle could see the viper easily swim away.

"Well, just get out of there," the woman cried out.

She was out of the water and hurrying to her pile of clothes. Just as she reached her panties, the second snake aimed a lightning-fast strike right into her left eye. She grabbed her wounded face with a scream of pain and fear, while falling over backwards. She rolled over on her stomach and tried to pull up on her feet, her whole backside in view for Estelle to see, not that she wanted to.

She was now the perfect target for her enemy. The snake struck again with a perfectly aimed bite right on the mid portion of her right cheek. The poor woman was crying in agony and begging it to stop while she fell on her stomach, crying softly, her volume getting softer each second.

Estelle turned her attention to her father. He was out of the river, trying to reach the almost still form on the ground. Another strike hit his calf. He still had enough fight in him to reach down and grab the serpent with his hand and smash it down hard on the water a few times. He didn't notice the other one swimming at him as he threw his first adversary far downstream. He fell to his knees in defeat just as the other moccasin struck his crotch.

He screamed at the top of his lungs and ripped the beast away, along with part of his scrotum. His glazed eyes glanced down at the still body of his girlfriend. Then he saw Estelle step out from behind the Iris.

"Estelle?"

He fell forward into the water. A small amount of bubbles rose from beneath him. Then a few more. Then nothing.

Estelle walked over to the river's edge. Her father looked ridiculous, face down with his naked butt in the air. The water was too shallow for him to float away. She wished she could feel bad for him, but the first thought she had was: *I can do something else with my life besides clean, dust and mop the garage.*

In fact, that seemed to be the first thing everyone else in the family thought when they heard the news. Nobody shed a tear for the man and woman who died of snake bites while in the process of committing adultery. No one from school even mentioned it to her face, although she could hear the gossip when people thought she was not listening.

A few of the more practical sort thought the widow and widower should start to date each other, but there was no love there and many children. They both reasonably figured they experienced enough love and its consequences. After the dry-eyed funeral, Mama Rochelle stopped by the store and Estelle came out to greet her.

"Sign still there," the old woman said.

"Mama says we'll lose too much business if we take it down. I don't have control over it."

The woman nodded.

"You used your snakes. They won't be any good no more."

"I figured. I wish you had told me about them. I wouldn't have done it."

"Perhaps not then. But you want to live a life. Ain't no kind of life just going to school and working in a shop. And when you got out of school, it'd just be the store. He wasn't going to let you get away when you work for free. It'd be a big fight. Getting your freedom always is. And you don't know how to fight. You just obey.

"And you knew what they'd do. You wouldn't have put them in the water if you didn't. You'd have just slunk away home and cried in your pillow."

Estelle had no answer for that.

"Come to my place. I will teach you how to mold your own animals. How to shape your own destiny."

"Mama would never let me—"

"Then let her live your life for you," the old woman sneered and pulled away.

The next Thursday, after dinner, Estelle went to her room and crawled out the window, landing onto the soft ground. It didn't take long to get to the road and find someone to tell her where Mama Rochelle lived.

Her first lesson was simple. She took a pail and filled it with mud from the riverbank. It was too wet. She had to get another. It was too dry.

"This is a joke, isn't it?" Estelle exclaimed. "You're just sending me back and forth until I give up. Aren't you?"

"Why would I do that? I'm wasting my time to have you waste yours? That don't make no sense. You have more time than I do. Here. I'll go with and show you what you should already know."

She picked up her cane and hobbled in front of the girl to show her where to get the best mud. Estelle soon filled it to the brim and hauled it back to the old woman's shack. Estelle's first artistic creation was a worm. Mama Rochelle nodded her approval and molded a bird, making sure the girl saw and understood the technique.

The next week, Estelle showed up again. It only took one trip to the riverbank. When she returned, a black man was in the house. She waited at the screen door, out of sight. But she could hear.

"I don't know what to do," the man said. "My little Bella is all I have left. I can't lose her, not like this."

"No, Buell Carter, you can't. It won't happen. I have vowed to never help a fool with the *Hai-Tak-Koo* arts. And you are a fool to be dealing with Robert Freeman. A *fool*."

"I know, Mama Rochelle. I wish I were smarter."

"Smart? Smart got nothing to do with it. You are weak. You gamble until you owe more than your life is worth. So, now what? Your daughter goes to marry Robert Freeman. You out of debt. But why should she pay for you, Buell Carter? If it was just someone killing you, I could live with it. But the girl? Does she deserve a fate worse than death because of you?

"I will help you. Permanent help. You be here tomorrow. My apprentice and I will make your solution. You will have no more problems. Now go."

"Thank you, M—"

"Go!"

The front screen door slammed and Estelle heard footsteps fade toward the road. Mama Rochelle smiled at her when she came in.

"Tonight, we will make something special."

They poured the clay on the table and the old woman soon opened a drawer and came to the table with an old can filled with blue dust.

"From Kheliesis," she told her apprentice in a conspiratorial whisper. Of course, that meant nothing to Estelle.

The old woman smiled, "Kheliesis is another existence. A world beyond ours. There, magic rules, not science. Supernatural creatures live there with the people. Do you know what the Djinn is?"

Estelle shook her head no.

"Like the genie in the bottle. Only real. A Djinn is powerful and evil. He is the enemy of the people of Kheliesis. His magic is the most powerful of all the demons. When the Djinn dies, his body fades to this powder. It is the essence of magic. We call this figurine a Djinn-fury. It allows the Djinn to still do it's evil and, at the same time, it hands out poetic justice."

She sprinkled a liberal amount of the blue powder into the mud and the two of them kneaded it into the clay until it was completely mixed.

"You do know what the *loup-garou* is, don't you?"

Estelle shook her head no.

"Half man, half wolf. Neither one though. Something completely different. Something to solve problems with."

Together, they shaped the clay into a big blob, then the old woman slowly molded an animal snout with extra-long fangs. The body was manly and powerful. A small knife carved claws into the large paws. It looked like a nightmare. Estelle shuddered her approval.

"Go home now while I heat it up. Keep low and quiet. We will see the result of our work tomorrow when the moon is full. Stay away for at least a week."

She heard the news on the bus. Some kind of swamp monster killed five men from the colored area of the parish. Whatever it was, it was something big. The creature mangled and mutilated the bodies beyond recognition. On the bus ride home, she heard the names. Three she never heard before. Two she knew: Robert Freeman and Buell Carter.

"Why did so many have to die when we only wanted to hurt Robert Freeman?" Estelle asked as she put the werewolf figurine in her bag to sell. It would never come to life again. Might as well see if they could make some money from it.

"Buell Carter? If he got himself into that mess once, he will again. Well, would have."

"But the other three?"

"Hang out with bad men, bad things happen. If those men been at home with their wives and families, where they belong, they would still be alive now."

And so, for the next five years things went on. Estelle snuck out of her room every Thursday and no one at home noticed. Karen had her friends. Tom and Dale discovered girls. Mama discovered gin.

Estelle became quite a proficient sculptor in her own right. She made all the reptiles the swamp was known for and moved up to mammals. She took the figurines to the store and people purchased them. She sold Mama Rochelle's as well. No had to know the black woman made them. The tourists bought enough to justify the space. Estelle's name was on all of them, but she split the money with the older woman.

They had a special bond, this white teenager and old black woman. They were friends and family. Neither one cared about what the world thought of that. Then, in 1944, it all fell apart. Paul Heatherton destroyed it, as far as Estelle was concerned, but Mama Rochelle assigned all the blame on Estelle.

"Why do you hang out with that black woman?" Paul asked her one day while waiting for the school bus. He was always nice to her, ever since first grade, even though he came from the right side of town where all the houses were perfect and everyone had enough money.

"She's my friend. She taught me how to make those figurines we sell to the tourists. I'm still learning, in fact. She's going to start teaching me how to mold birds soon. It's nice to do something besides stand behind the counter doing boring homework."

"What about your Ma and sister?" he asked.

She shrugged, "Ma works till school's out then I stay till eight and close and lock up the store. Karen works the weekends."

"I never see any cars there when I drive by. Maybe you should reopen the gas pumps."

The pumps and garage were not in use anymore. Her brothers enlisted in the military and were fighting in the war. Her mother drank herself in a stupor every night. The house stank of gin. Sometimes of vomit. Karen did her best, but the house was declining almost as fast as the store.

"Mama don't want to do that. She'd rather too little business instead of too much."

"But if there aren't any customers, wouldn't it be better to close earlier?"

"Don't say that," she exclaimed. "I like some time for myself."

And less time at home.

"Well, can I stop by when you're working and visit? Keep you company?"

"I'd like that."

Visiting soon became rides home. He asked her out a few times and the other girls considered them to be a couple, or so she thought. He had a Ford Deluxe and they drove everywhere. Although it was a convertible, he always kept the top up. Too much rain in Louisiana. They went roller skating. Then to the movies. And from there, parking down Lover's Lane. After so many years of neglect and indifference from the father who should have loved her, Estelle had a spiritual, emotional and physical connection with the man she loved. It was the happiest time of her life.

But the happiness was short lived.

"Looks like you got yourself knocked up," her Mama said one morning while she watched Estelle throw up. Her voice was mean, although her face showed some concern. "You know what you're going to do? I've been planning to live happy and free without no kids when you graduate. You can stay here until it's born. But it can't. An adult decision leads to adult consequences."

She took a long swig of gin, then her eyes bored in to her.

"Don't think you're getting out of your shift tonight, or

any other shift. You live here, you work."

Karen gave her all the support she could, but a fourteen-year-old girl could only be so useful.

"Marry you?" Paul said, his voice mocking. "I'm only sixteen. I have a life of my own. And a baby just doesn't fit into it."

And neither do you.

He didn't say it, but he didn't need to. She was on her own. She thought about an abortion but rejected it. Not every girl survived that procedure. Besides, she kind of liked the idea of being a mother.

She made the decision that changed the course of history two days later. Paul was walking down the hall with Cindy Harman, his arm firmly around her waist. Cindy smiled at her with an evil leer. And as they walked by, she waved her promise ring almost in Estelle's face. Paul never gave her a ring at all. Behind them, Penny Fowler and Mary Granger, Cindy's two best friends, smirked at her. The laughter rang out after they all passed her.

It didn't matter, Estelle thought bitterly. A ring is only worth what you put into it. Cindy can find out about it on her own and nurture her own bitterness. Estelle had plenty of her own to deal with right now.

"Well, I haven't seen you in a while, now," Mama Rochelle exclaimed when she showed up at the shack the next Thursday, "I thought you was done with me."

"Never," Estelle said, looking down. "It's just that I met a boy…and—"

She started crying. Mama Rochelle listened with great patience and whispered comforting shushes. It was the only empathy Estelle got. After a cup of tea, the older woman decided Estelle should go back to sculpting.

"But only clay. Don't go thinking about getting no

revenge. Justified, but the Djinn-fury isn't for lovers that don't love. It's to do bad things to make the world a better place to be."

Things went well that evening. Estelle learned to make a hawk, though it looked more like an opossum with wings. They laughed and wet the clay down and put it in a bucket.

Mama Rochelle had to use the restroom, which for her was an old outhouse. While she was gone, Estelle went to the drawer and filled an old perfume bottle with the magic blue powder. When the old woman came back, it was too late to make another attempt at a figurine, so they had another cup of tea and Estelle went home.

The next morning, she told her mother that she was no longer going to go to school. Everyone knew about her condition, thanks to Cindy. A high school degree was just a piece of paper anyway. Her mother nodded and Estelle worked all day at the store while her mother stayed at home, drinking gin and reliving her life, the way it should have been.

Just as well. Estelle went to the riverside and gathered up a fine batch of mud and put it on the back porch to let dry. By ten that morning, business slowed down to a crawl and she started kneading the blue powder into the clay. After she was satisfied the mixture was perfect, the comic book vendor came in and filled the rack.

Underneath the *Archie* magazines was a superhero battling what looked like some kind of demon. Seven eyes were staring at a guy in a red costume. The creature had blue skin and red eyes, flashing with hatred. Its nose was a long, deadly looking horn, which matched two more that were curled behind its floppy ears. Impossibly long fangs sneered out at the little human character and a forked tongue hung out of the hellish mouth. Its hands were claws of razor-sharp steel and a barbed tail twisted behind it.

Estelle stared at it for a few minutes, then stared down at the bewitched clay. One more glance at the magazine, then her mouth twisted into an evil grin and she nodded. She stared at the comic book as she molded her image. It went in the oven that night.

"Paul and Cindy weren't in school today," Karen told her the next day.

"Oh?" Estelle feigned indifference.

"Do you think they eloped?"

"That would be nice," Estelle said quietly. "But probably not. They're probably still at Lover's Lane. I'm sure Paul wants to do to her what he did to me. Then find another one."

Karen nodded, obviously at a loss for words. The sisters worked the store full time now. Estelle worked all day and Karen from the time the bus let her off after school. Their mother handled the books early in the mornings, then went home with a fresh bottle. Just as well. Neither girl really desired her company.

"Oh, my Lord," Karen came in the next day, jumping and dancing with excitement. "You were so right."

"What?" Estelle asked, confused at her entrance.

"They found Paul and Cindy on Lover's Lane. Someone killed them. Doris Fleming says that new rookie cop threw up when he saw the bodies. Whoever did it, ripped them apart in pieces."

"Couldn't have happened to a nicer couple."

Although Karen wasn't expecting anything close to grief, her sister's indifference chilled her. She went back to the walk-in refrigerator and started stocking the soft drinks. She felt warmer in the cooler than she did near her sister today.

When Karen was safely out of sight, Estelle circled around the store, looking for the now de-witched figurine. She could not find it. Did it remain at the murder scene? The Djinn-furies were always supposed to come back to their creator after the magic left them. Where was it? Did it go back to Mama Rochelle? Estelle would have to face the older woman's wrath, if so. But then, after some logical thought, Estelle knew Mama Rochelle would find out what happened sooner or later.

"How could you have done such a thing?" Mama Rochelle yelled at her. "I trusted you. I let you into my house. I taught you how to use your hands to create art. And this is how you repay me?"

Estelle just hung her head low. There was nothing to say. Mama Rochelle started screaming at her the moment she let her into the shack.

"I knew the moment I heard they were dead what you did. I checked my drawer," the old woman calmed down for a bit. "You put too much blue powder in whatever you created. You used enough to bring it to life and keep it alive forever. That's why it didn't come back. It's not finished killing things. And it won't go away the normal way. We're going to find it and kill it. You and me. Now, what did you make?"

Estelle tried to describe it but wound up going to the store and fetching back one of the comics. The old woman shook her head when she saw it.

"Not even real," she said sadly shaking her head. "What you have released."

Before she could duck, Mama Rochelle raised her walking stick high and swatted her shoulder, near her neck. Estelle cried out in shock and pain, waving her hands over her head to shield herself from another blow. But the old woman seemed satisfied now.

"Why would you make such a thing?"

"I wanted them to pay. I wanted—"

"Revenge. Didn't I tell you this magic wasn't for something so childish and petty?"

Estelle nodded miserably.

"Our only chance is for me to create something worse. Now, go bring me some mud."

The old woman created something unimaginable. A nightmare in clay. It reminded Estelle of a spider with long tentacles hanging back from its face. The eight legs all ended in needle-sharp points. When she was satisfied with her work, she took out a salve and rubbed it on the tentacles and feet.

"Snake venom," she said to her disgraced apprentice. "Now, go home. We can't do no more tonight. Whatever happens, happens. Tomorrow will tell if we did good enough."

There was no home to go to. The house had an ominous darkness to it. No lights were on. *Karen should still be up,* Estelle thought with a moment of panic, even if Mama drank herself stupid. She hurried up the stairs.

There was no door anymore. It laid inside the living room completely pulled off the frame including the hinges. Estelle listened for a moment then quietly entered, listening for any hostile sound. All she heard was lots of buzzing. When she was satisfied the noise was harmless, just some flies, she clicked the light and screamed.

Broken pieces of furniture lay strewn all over the floor, almost down to sawdust. Stuffing from the pillows was everywhere. Her mother's head lay in the middle of the room. Estelle creeped up against the sink and moved past the gory scene, looking for Karen. She found her when she got a view of the living room. Her right arm and leg were on one side of the room. The rest of her was on the other. Estelle ran.

"You're a mighty luck girl, getting home when you did," the deputy told her later. "Any sooner and you'd have been gone too."

Mama Rochelle was there by now, leaning on her walking stick, looking old and frail.

"You can't go home, but this here woman says you can spend the evening with her if you want, or we can clear out a cell and make it good and comfortable until better arrangements can be made."

"I'll go with her," Estelle heard herself say, but she didn't feel like she really said it.

The doctor gave her a drought to make her sleep and she bedded down on the living room couch while Mama Rochelle hovered over until she was satisfied she would sleep.

"Are you happy you got your revenge?" were her last words that night.

"No," she replied. "I wish I never did it. I wish I..." And she slept.

She was woozy when she woke up. Mama Rochelle insisted she drink some tea. The hot beverage made her feel better.

"Another family was killed last night."

Estelle cried.

"Penny Fowler and Mary Granger were at the Fowler's house. They said it looked like a slaughterhouse. They all died. Just like your family. The thing you called up is still getting revenge for you. Everyone you've ever been mad at in your life is going to die now. I assume you knew the victims."

Estelle nodded. "But Karen?"

"You must have been mad at her at least once. It knows. The thing is yours. It's like a son to you. You created it. Shaped it. Brought it to life. It's trying to make you happy now. It's getting revenge for you against everyone you were ever mad at, no matter how much you forgave them, no matter how long ago. Even if you don't want revenge anymore, it will get it for you. That's why you don't unleash these things for petty reasons. The *Hai-Tak-Koo* remembers everything about you. It knows what you've done and will never forgive you. It will destroy you if you ever use it again or tell anyone about it. You must keep it out of your life."

"I don't want to use it ever again. I wish I never heard of it."

Mama Rochelle's face twisted into a stoney stare.

"Your son is sleeping after his kill. He will rise tonight."

She held up the spidery abomination she created.

"We can only hope we can defeat it when it wakes up."

They waited in silence. The old woman stared at Estelle impassively, but the girl could feel the older woman's anger. She felt ashamed in the morning, but by evening, her shame started to turn into resentment. Then anger. Mama Rochelle could feel the anger. It was good.

When the shadows were long, they walked to the river and set the spider-demon into the water. It started to grow immediately. Estelle stood for a moment to watch it transform into a living thing, but Mama Rochelle grabbed her by the elbow and they went back inside.

Within minutes, they heard a high-pitched roar coming from the woods. The trees swayed as though an elephant was running through them. The spider demon, by now eight feet tall and twelve feet long, raised its two front legs waving its forearms.

"Tick-click-click-bick-glick-tick," its noise answered the creature in the woods.

The high-pitched bellow called again and the spider-thing sped into the trees. Within minutes, the two creatures found each other. Screams and clicking noises erupted in a loud and eerie cacophony. The high-pitched voice was obviously in pain and panic. Then the clicking noises got louder. Loud clangs that sounded like steel rods snapping in two filled the night as the two things struggled.

Then it was quiet. The spider thing crawled back to the yard. Its tentacles were gone and its torso was missing four of its six limbs, obviously ripped out during the struggle. It crawled on its front two legs into the yard, where it fell on its back. The appendages twitched in the air, but the women both knew it was dead.

"Your beast came to kill me," Mama Rochelle said softly. "It knew you were mad at me and its only purpose in life is to avenge you. That was why it was coming here."

More noise came from the forest as Estelle's mortally wounded demon burst out of the trees. The spider gouged out five of its eyes and destroyed the unicorn tusk as well as its left curved ram's horn. One of the spider's missing legs impaled his left flank. It fell to its right side with its arm stretched toward the door.

"Looks like your Djinn-fury was successful," the old woman whispered to her. "Go to your creature. Give him comfort."

The thought horrified Estelle.

"What?"

"It's the right thing to do. You are his mother as surely as the baby in your belly. You created him. Everything he did was for you. Didn't you create him for revenge? How was he to know you wanted revenge against only two people? He thinks he was a faithful son. Don't let him die alone."

After a gentle push, Estelle opened the screen and slowly walked to the dying creature. One of the fading eyes saw her and brightened a bit.

"Mama," it cried out in a heartbreaking moan.

Estelle hurried over to it and stoked its one horn.

"Baby," she cooed to it, tears streaming down her face.

It put a hand on her lap and croaked out, "Mama," one last time. Its life faded away and it shrank down to a broken clay sculpture.

Seven years later, Estelle Dormer Roberts walked out to her swimming pool in Los Angeles. Life was good to her after she left Louisiana. The sheriff gave her some forged documents stating she had married Paul Heatherton, along with a copy of his death certificate. Her brothers ceded the property to her and there was no other inheritance. She sold it to the parish for half of what it was worth. The gas station became a sheriff's office. She left the house she grew up in, never to return, and caught a bus for California. The only thing she took were some clothes and the first figurine, the alligator, that Mama Rochelle made for her, hidden in an old cheap jewelry box.

In the big city, she met and married Donald Roberts. He was a Hollywood scriptwriter who made a good enough living. She was content. She had two children now. Johnny and Baby Rochelle, though she was now five and not a baby.

The sun felt warm on her face as she drifted idly in the cool water on an inflated pool mattress. A gin fizz helped her to relax. She soon was asleep. It was a perfect day for an afternoon nap. She slept through Johnny and Rochelle coming home and didn't hear their conversation.

"Mommy has an alligator in her room," Rochelle told her older brother.

"Yeah, right," Johnny didn't care. *Gavin The Goose* was coming on in a few minutes.

"She does. I found it while playing dress up yesterday. I'll show you."

In a few minutes, she was back. Johnny looked at it.

"It looks pretty cool," he admitted. He was especially impressed with the sharp, perfectly formed teeth that peeked out of the half open mouth.

"It looks real. I bet it floats. It'll be a great bathtub toy," Rochelle told him.

"Too heavy to float," Johnny said after considering its weight.

"Let's see."

The little girl ran to the backyard and plopped it into the shallow end of the pool. It sank to the bottom.

"Told you so," Johnny said.

Rochelle was starting to wade into the water to retrieve it.

"Leave it," he said. "And don't wake Mother up. You know how she gets when she drinks gin."

The little girl nodded and they ran in to watch *Gavin the Goose* together. The show was so enthralling that they didn't hear a loud splash or a muffled whimper come out of the backyard.

When they got hungry for dinner, the children went out to wake their mother. They screamed at the sight of her mangled body, submerged near the bottom of the pool's now red water. Parts of the pool mattress floated over her; others sank to the bottom. And the little toy alligator was floating near the pool's edge, its mouth shut tight.

The Finger Lake Kelpie

The duckweed actually looked pretty floating on the pond's surface. *But it has to go*, Wayne Cox thought as he hauled his long, curved water rake from his beat-up old Ford truck. No telling if there were snakes hunting fish beneath the green leaves. He didn't want to find out the hard way.

"This'll only take a minute, Brandy," he called out to his girlfriend who was sitting on the truck's tailgate.

She glanced his way for a second while rolling her eyes in impatience and continued to file her nails with such speed and force that she appeared to hate her fingers. Her dark expression said it all. She was almost ready to explode.

"I would hope so," she called back in a cold voice. "You've been here a dozen times without me. I don't know why you dragged me here today. I'm half bored, half disappointed, half resentful, and more than half angry. And I hate bugs."

She swatted a brave horsefly that landed on her arm and shoed it away when it came back for a second round. Wayne knew if the breeze died down, a few mosquitos

104

would also be hovering around her looking for an afternoon snack.

"That's more than two hundred percent," Wayne laughed back at her, oblivious to her words. "It's a good thing you're not majoring in math or science."

"I'm smart enough to know that I happen to be twice the woman you deserve," she shot back at him. "And since I'm majoring in 17th Century English Literature, I don't need math or science. All I need is the brainpower to read Shakespeare and Marlowe and understand it. And if you read some of the more important things life has to offer, you would know better than to take your lovely, talented and unappreciated girlfriend out in the middle of the swamp for a day of togetherness. Some date."

She lowered her voice in an unflattering imitation of his own, "'We'll get out of the city and commune with nature. We'll have a romantic Cajun lunch and go dancing in a club. It'll just be you and me for the whole day.'"

"Well, we're out of the city and communing with nature," he responded good naturedly. "And it's just the two of us—"

"No, it's not," she screamed in fear and frustration as a dragonfly landed on her head briefly. "Every insect in the country is here with us. And they're hungry."

"But we're not," Wayne called back sweetly. "We had a nice romantic lunch."

"Don't you dare tell me that you think *Fat Jack's* is a highly regarded 'romantic' restaurant," she huffed back at him. "It's about as romantic as a gas station."

"I don't know," he replied smoothly. "They have some really nice food in gas stations these days and they all have Ethyl waiting there for us, so you better be nice."

"Nobody calls premium gas 'Ethyl' anymore. And

you're changing the subject. You promised me a romantic evening and you took me here to look at plants. You don't know the first thing about having a romantic evening."

He smiled, unmindful of her tone and body language, "I'm pretty sure I said romantic evening *after* I do some research. Besides, we're communing with nature as we speak. You knew I had to get some botanical samples from the water out here. I was shocked when you agreed to come with me. And I love that you're here. I love you more than any water plant you can name."

He almost smiled when he saw her face turn red and her hands transform into fists.

"But you know that when a man's writing his dissertation, all those professors demand absolute perfection. And really, if you think about it now, wouldn't you rather marry Dr. Wayne Cox instead of Mr. Wayne Cox? Now, why don't you come over and join me? It's better than just sitting there."

She was sulking over there, which didn't really bother him. He adored sneaking an occasional peak as she pouted in her adorable and sexy way. He loved pretending to be oblivious to her frustration when she made such a melodramatic point of snubbing him like he didn't exist, but furtively glanced his way to make sure he knew she was ignoring him. But he knew better than to say this out loud. He could finish up his work out here while she was quietly angry. She could be a major distraction when she was in one of her rages and started screaming at him.

"Besides, they were playing *Brown Eyed Girl*, at *Fat Jack's*. I know that's your favorite. So, it's not that bad. Come and join me."

Brandy sighed. Some choice. Watch the grass grow while sitting on the metal tailgate, which was starting to hurt her backside, or watch it grow close up. She hopped off and slammed the hatch shut to show her disgust. But he was walking back to the pond with that rake, ignoring her dramatic effort. Now, she was even more upset.

Here she was, a nineteen-year-old raving beauty with dark brown hair she spent almost an hour this morning curling to look perfect for him. She always applied eyeshadow and mascara discreetly to those big chocolate brown eyes, her best feature (which was why *Brown Eyed Girl* was her favorite song). And she always took all the time she needed to make sure nobody could see her eyeshadow or blush. The whole point of make-up was to make others believe all her beauty was natural. She did not want to look overdone. Even though she had to take time to get it right, she did it for him.

She wore a lowcut blouse tied below her breasts to help push them up for the best view of her cleavage for him. Her bare midriff legally exposed all the skin possible without looking desperate for him. Her shorts were so tight they hurt, all to show off her fantastic ass for him. She made sure not even a hint of hair lurked on her legs or armpits for him. And what was he doing? Looking at pond scum, weeds and slime. She wondered if she'd look better to him covered in algae with a water lily in her mouth.

Granted, he was beginning to write his dissertation for a PhD in botany and that required him to do a copious amount of research, which took up most of his days and nights. In fact, that was why they weren't married already. It was abundantly clear to them both that he couldn't give that damn dissertation the attention it needed if he spent all his time with her. That made her want to scream, even though she found his general sense of brilliance to be quite attractive.

With a sigh, she followed him to the small body of water. She was his girl and she knew if he couldn't really see her as the most attractive woman he ever saw, he couldn't see any other woman in that way either. In thirty years, she supposed, that would work in her favor.

Yes, she sighed again, he was her man, even if sometimes she didn't want him. Maybe romance was overrated. Wayne was going to be a limnologist, a scientist who studied lakes and the plants and animals that made them their home. She figured a job like that would be high paying. After all, not many people could stand the boredom involved in studying dirty water filled with slime and fish shit. There had to be more lakes and ponds in Louisiana than there were limnologists in the whole world, and even if that wasn't true, there were lakes in other states.

This pond was called Lake Ramgot. Why it had a 't' at the end was a mystery. It was pronounced ram-go. Wayne explained to her that it was technically a pond because it was so shallow that the light reached all the way to the bottom in a murky sort of way. It was one of Louisiana's finger lakes, so called because of the native Malika tribe's legend that a great Earth god rose from the swampy ground and pushed himself up to fight a ferocious enemy. The finger lakes were the indentations of his fingers as they sank into the earth from his weight.

The native people avoided all the finger lakes and the surrounding woods. The fish tasted bad and there were all kinds of strange stories about the area. Bad things happened to people foolish enough to go there. Nameless and undescribed creatures lurked out of sight, waiting to hunt and kill those unwary people foolish enough to explore near the edges.

"Hey, Brandy," he called. "Take a look at this."

She trotted up next to him and stared into the dark water. Green, slimy looking water plants swayed in the water, tenuously attached to the pond's mucky shores. Parts of the pond's dark muddy sides contrasted with them.

"What?" she asked, trying to be interested, but failing. "The muddy banks look cleaner than the plants?"

"No," he said a bit impatiently. "Look at the way the plant life is shaped."

The green edges curved in and out a bit, but Brandy supposed she didn't have the right kind of imagination. She shrugged.

"Sorry, I didn't do well as a little girl seeing shapes in clouds either. They were just blobs of white on the blue."

"That's okay. But see," he gestured again. "Right there. It looks like you."

That got her attention and she looked again, focusing all her attention on the steep bank he indicated. She supposed that maybe the coon weed and green slimy stuff did form into a curvy sort of shape, if she viewed it from the right angle. She tilted her head and squinted a bit while shading her eyes from the sun's glare.

The way the weeds bound themselves together did look a little bit like a woman's body, she conceded silently. Thin waist, jutting hips, smooth thighs, symmetrical breasts. Even a head with hair which could have passed for curls. This form attached itself to the bank by what might be arms, but they weren't clearly visible. Neither were the feet.

"Well, that's downright insulting," she said with a huff, flinging her head back so she could feel her hair whipping her neck and shoulders. "You really have to use your imagination to think that thing resembles a woman at all. But then you say, 'Brandy, you look just like that clump of rotting vegetation.'

"Well, I have two things to say to you. One: I don't look all green and slimy like that and I'm sorry you think I do. Two: if that's what you find attractive, go get it."

She pushed him toward the edge, but didn't have the strength to make him fall into the water. He glared at her, confused. She stared right back at him, getting angrier.

"I work like a slave to be attractive and sexy so you'll be proud to be with me. And what do you do? What's my reward? You take me out to the middle of a stinking swamp to watch you study a bunch of green slime. And you don't look at me at all the whole time we're here. I'm the only woman around for miles and miles and what do you do? You go ogling some nasty smelly weeds. Nobody else pays any attention to me in college anymore because they think I'm taken. The only cuddling I'm getting out here is from mosquitos and flies and you just told me I look like green slime."

That wasn't true. There was enough of a breeze to keep the mosquitos parked somewhere since they never flew when the wind was blowing. She knew that, but she liked the way it added drama to her harangue as she vented at him. Besides, the wind didn't drive the flies off.

"Now, that's not fair," he said crestfallen. "I compared the botany to you, not you to the botanical growth. Besides, you look much sexier than the coon weed and algae. Don't be angry."

He reached for her, but she pushed away, her anger unabated by his pitiful response.

"I'm supposed to look better than coon weed and algae. There shouldn't even be a comparison. Listen, I can't do this. The fact that I have to explain it to you is totally depressing. I want to go home and maybe attract a man who knows what to do with a woman. And that will never be you. Just get me out of here, now."

She regretted those words instantly. She wanted to get the upper hand and go home to make out with him. She did not want to end their entire relationship.

"Okay," he said, obviously intimidated by her righteous wrath. "I'll get my equipment and we'll go have fun. I won't take you anywhere near a lake again."

"Excuse me," she responded, making a show of forcing herself to calm down. "I like lakes. But I like the ones I can swim in. No sane person would come to this one to swim in. There are probably a thousand snakes in there just waiting to bite anyone they see."

He was gathering up his rakes and pincers and whatever other tools he had while she spoke. He stepped over several jars of water and algae and other green slimy things on his way back to the truck.

She did not go too far, after all. She was relieved and triumphant because she just definitively defined her role as the dominant partner in their relationship.

"These ponds are too small to be able to provide enough food for that many snakes," he pointed out in a sad attempt to save face. "It would take a sizable amount of water. Maybe a bayou with lots a stagnant water."

She took a deep breath and held it, nose to the sky in a truly awe-inspiring melodramatic pose of maintaining her patience while she tried not to laugh.

"I'll put the tools away and come back for the water samples," he said, his back slumping a bit in defeat.

She triumphantly suppressed a smile. That was total annihilation. Her feminine wiles completely overwhelmed his pathetic male defenses. She was so happy she spent so much time practicing that I-am-trying-to-be patient-but it-is-really-an-effort pose. He didn't even know what hit him.

She remembered her mother's advice she heard so many times while growing up.

Victory in love, victory in marriage, victory in life.

Words to memorize. And her mother ruled the roost with an iron hand. Her father never argued with her. In fact, he hardly ever spoke to her mother. He was there to provide for them and take orders. And he did that so well for many years until, one day, he left. Her mother never forgave him for that. Even though, obviously, the desertion didn't bother her too much, she still refused to let Brandy have any contact with him ever again. Then she remarried and started the process all over again.

Soon that lifestyle would all be hers, although she knew that, occasionally, Wayne would have to win a battle. A small one here and there. Maybe her father would have stayed if he didn't lose every single argument. Once she was married to Wayne with children, she didn't want him to desert her unless she wanted him to leave.

Who knows? Maybe she would. Her mother always reminded her that she loved playdough when she was young and then outgrew it. It's the same thing with a man, she sagely advised her daughter.

"The woman is the artist," her mother said. "The family is the clay. There comes a point when the sculpture is finished. Then it's time to create another masterpiece."

She shook the thought out of her head. If Wayne was going to require years of effort, she wouldn't let him go. Some things are too good to just throw away. Heck, she still had some of her old Barbie dolls sitting in the closet.

She watched Wayne coming back from the truck to retrieve another load. The mason jars were only quart size. She knew she could help him with the water, but she wanted to bask in the glory of her victory for a few more minutes.

She glanced over at the weed-woman again. It seemed to be even more human now when she squinted her eyes a little bit and used her imagination. It seemed to have moved away from the edge, giving it a rounded, even more human appearance. The head had more of a face. The tendrils somehow caught some small, brown, twiggy looking things. They looked like closed eyes, complete with lashes and brows and two well-formed lips below a protruding bulge that she thought looked like a nose. A small, dimpled chin connected itself below and she could see a well-formed neck now.

The slimy looking weeds that formed the hair did remind her of her own locks and curls and approximated her own hair's length. The form bobbed up and down in the water as the wind pushed small waves to and fro. The jiggly parts moved like a dancer. She wondered why the water wasn't slowly dissolving it back into its separate parts.

Wayne's cell phone went off and she heard him answer it. She glanced over, annoyed. It was his mentor, getting an update on his research. She decided to let him talk. Many young girls lost their prey when they exercised their control too many times over every little thing. She was a woman and knew better. He could have his little conversation as long as it didn't last too long.

She pulled out her compact and inspected her make-up. She looked perfect. Nice red lips, a little color on the cheeks and a dab of shadow to bring out those chocolate eyes. When he came back for the water samples, she'd help him and walk next to him with a snuggle or two. That would make him forget he lost big-time in the battle for dominance in their relationship. Winning was important, her mother told her, but gloating would turn it all into ashes.

She snapped the mirror shut and walked back to the pond's edge, so he wouldn't think she was eavesdropping on his conversation. She didn't want to appear pushy or nosy, after all. She stepped over the long tentacles of duck weed that Wayne pulled out and glanced at her "rival" again.

It was uncanny. She could see the woman in it now without having to use her imagination. A sexy woman, at that. And the face was fully formed, or so it seemed. Brandy stared at it for a second. It had a long nose and the closed eyes absolutely had long lashes. The mouth was cruel and wrinkles of weeds covered what would have been the face. *It was an old woman's head on a young girl's body,* she thought. Wayne would never compare it to her now. It was ugly and almost scary.

And then it opened its eyes and stared at her with green orbs that shined with pure hatred. The lips parted, showing nasty looking sharp, serrated fangs, not even remotely human. It reminded her of a piranha, only grinning at her.

Brandy gasped and turned to run. She stepped on something and looked down to see the duck weed wrapped itself around her shoe while she was staring at the thing in the water. She tried to shake her foot free, but tendril after tendril grabbed her feet and calves, pulling her off her feet. She landed on her back and had the wind knocked out of her. The strong wires of plant stems yanked and pulled her toward the water while she grabbed ahold of the land weeds and grass around her to no avail. She tried to yell to Wayne for help, but more weeds jammed into her mouth.

More of the tendrils wrapped around her waist and shoulders, dragging her to the water's edge and underwater.

She continued screaming through her vegetative gag as loud as she could but stopped when her head went under and the vegetation spewed itself from her mouth. She clamped her mouth shut as the cords turned her around to face that hideous plant-demon. She wanted to scream, to free herself, to swim back to the surface. Anything to get away from this nightmare. But she was helpless. Her limbs were immobilized by too many plants and weeds for her to count.

She was now staring at the thing while more and more underwater vines attacked her face, pushing her cheek, pulling her lips and forcing her mouth open. Her struggles were getting weaker. She needed to breathe but she couldn't because she was underwater. Soon, the pressure was too much and the plant things eventually pried open her lips and jaw.

The plant-demon opened her mouth at the same time and a spew of green slime vomited past her tongue and down her throat. The green algae and river plankton swarmed past her defenses and streamed into the back of her throat, oozing through her sinuses, down her throat, into her lungs and stomach. There was nothing more for Brandy to do except retch, swallow and die.

She could feel herself, but she could not move. The weeds and vines quickly disentangled from her and started floating harmlessly away while the water gently suspended her body just beneath the surface. The vegetation that once looked dimly like a woman's body carved from various plants no longer existed. All was the way it was supposed to be.

"Brandy," she vaguely heard Wayne call out, but he was far away and on the surface. She shouldn't have been able to hear him anyway.

When Wayne heard Brandy scream, he quickly threw the phone down and hurried over to the pond. She was floating in the water, facedown and lifeless when he arrived. His heart skipped a beat and he ran to the water, stopping only long enough to kick off his shoes so they wouldn't drag him down, and jumped in. The weeds floated around him, touching him, sliding over him, but he paid them no attention while he grabbed Brandy and dragged her ashore.

First, he laid her on her side and pushed out as much water as he could. When she didn't respond, he turned her over and performed mouth to mouth resuscitation while pressing on her stomach area.

A huge amount of mucky water spilled out of her mouth and he turned her on her side until it was cleared out. More breathing into her, more clearing out pond water. He tried again and again to revive her as the adrenalin pouring into his blood gave him the necessary strength.

Finally, she convulsed and started choking in air on her own. She vomited out huge amounts of green water. When she was done, he helped her to the truck. She sat on the tailgate and he covered her with a blanket while she shivered and stared at the ground.

"Oh, Brandy," he whispered. "I'm so sorry. What happened? How did you fall into the lake?"

She shook her head.

"Are you alright? You ready to go?"

He didn't quite understand what she said. It sounded like, "Laght jore garou deign."

The words chilled his soul. He knew she was not making sounds. She was speaking in a language he didn't understand.

"Let's go," he soothed. "We'll stop at a twenty-four-hour care and get you looked at, okay?"

She nodded then shivered for a bit before standing up and dropping the blanket. She wasn't trembling anymore and obviously regained her strength.

"No," she said in a sweet, somewhat stilted voice. "I don't need or want anything but you. I was being so unreasonable, wasn't I? It may have been so important to me a few minutes ago, but no, after all that, I realize I was being foolish. You have plants and water to study and here I am vocalizing foolish discontent."

Vocalizing foolish discontent? Brandy never spoke like that. Nobody he knew spoke like that.

"How are you supposed to know what I want if I don't tell you?" she continued apologetically. "And do you know what I have always wanted, from the very first moment I saw you? I want you, Wayne Cox. Because of all the humans I have ever encountered, you are the one who I love. And I won't let anybody get in my way to keep you. You'll be my consort and we'll be together forever. Do you understand that?"

"Well," Wayne said, somewhat confused at the word 'consort,' another term he never heard Brandy use, "I think I do. But right now, I think we must get you to a doctor to make sure you're all right. Maybe you hit your head on something. You seem to be so different."

Not as shallow as you usually are. And more than a little bit unnerving.

He went on, "I want to make sure you're all right, okay? You're all that matters right now."

She coolly stared deep into his eyes and smiled, as though she was studying his mind or soul.

Wayne began to surmise this was not the same girl who fell into the lake. Something about her was unfamiliar. He felt a little unnerved by how she watched him. He gazed into her eyes. They somehow changed as well, but he couldn't place how. In fact, Brandy seemed like a completely different person. If Wayne was a bit more of an observant man, he would have known something was very wrong. But his scientific mind could only presume she was reacting to her near death.

Her cool gaze turned into a conspiratorial leer.

"You know what they say when you fall off a horse? Get back on it or you'll never ride again," she said coyly. "I think we should take a swim together. The best way to study a lake is to get in it. Don't you think? We should take a nice little dip together. Just you and me."

She untied her blouse, pulled it off, stood up, and stripped down to the skin.

"My clothes are wet," she whispered in his ear. "So are yours. They need to dry for a bit before we get in the truck."

He nodded, almost in shock.

"Are you finally beginning to see me?" she asked, continuing to leer at him while she reached over and started to unbutton his shirt.

Wayne nodded, as he began to strip his wet clothes off. Her recovery from her scare was obvious. The fright of almost drowning must have aroused her something fierce. No sense in wasting a moment like this by insisting he take her to a doctor when she was obviously fully recovered. And naked.

She touched him.

"I guess coming that close to death just got me thinking. I want you. From the first time you came to visit me here, I wanted you. Forever."

"The first time I visited you here?" Wayne was confused, but her touch captured his attention. He could wonder about it later.

She kissed him and wrestled him to the ground. Their sounds of love echoed in the trees and bounced off the water's surface. After they completed their magic moment, she stood up sensually and smiled down at him while he stared at her silently, hypnotized by her beauty and appeal.

"What are you looking at," she asked coyly as she thrust her hands into her hair and threw her brown mane back, making sure she was displaying herself to him with a sexy, self-assured poise. "Are you happy with me?"

"I am," Wayne replied, also standing.

He reached for her and gently held her close, gazing intently into her enlarged pupils.

"You know something? I never noticed your eyes before. How beautiful and green."

She smiled, "Let's go for that swim. Together this time. There's a lot more for you to discover."

The Vampire Princess of Kheliesis

Freddy Wells could recognize a terrible day when he saw one and today would be one. He knew it from the moment he woke up. It was one of those sneaky bad days where everything went by as normal as possible, but the awkward feeling just became more intense as the expected events, whatever they were, continued to not happen. So far, things seemed normal enough for him to leave the house as soon as possible and get away from his father. Big Jake Wells came home mean and drunk last night, which meant his mood would be hateful and vindictive when he and his hangover got up. Everyone in the house always tried to be somewhere other than home on a day like this.

At least Freddy had a good excuse to leave early: he had his own business. Last year, he bought a dozen chickens and started selling eggs. Soon, his flock grew to over two hundred hens and a dozen roosters. They resided in a nice coop he built himself. He was proud of his handywork, even though his father told him it was just like Freddy—a big piece of shit. But it held chickens and Freddy managed to sell enough eggs at the farmer's market to make a small profit. Half of it went to Big Jake in the form of room and board, but he earned enough to drop out of high school. Before he died, Uncle Sherman gave him an old pick-up truck to help with the deliveries. It got him and his eggs to his clients. That was a good enough start to keep Freddy happy and optimistic.

Ultimately, he wanted to move out of his father's house and get off his land, but his chickens all lived there. Big Jake already told him if he was old enough to leave home at 16, he was old enough to take his business with him. For that, Freddy would need to buy a place with some land. No bank lends that kind of money to a 16-year-old, especially in 1936, with a depression still in effect.

His older brother, Little Jake, was staring out the kitchen window. He worked on an oil rig near Shreveport but was off for the week.

"Going to Neuville today?" Little Jake asked as Freddy futilely searched for something to munch on for breakfast. Something was in the oven, but it was cooking.

"Every Monday, Wednesday and Friday, Mr. Hartnett buys most of my eggs, you know. That's why I spend so much time packing them for him."

"Oh," Little Jake smiled, "I thought you just liked to get out of the house and away from…" He indicated upstairs where their father was sleeping off his booze.

"That too," Freddy conceded.

"Well, I think you're doing good. Keep saving money, don't buy stupid things, you'll be on your own in no time."

Little Jake took a sip of hot coffee, Louisiana style, thick and strong.

"Let's hope so. Living with him is so hard sometimes. The man just doesn't like me."

"He loves you. He loves all of us. He just worries and gets upset. The depression hit him the hardest. He's the breadwinner and for a long time we didn't know what our next meal would be or if we'd get one. That tore him up."

"Hmm," Freddy responded. "He didn't seem any better before the depression, at least to me. Besides, I was content with fish, if we caught enough anyway."

Freddy contemplated his older brother. Although everyone called him 'Little Jake,' he stood a full half foot taller than their father. His clipped brown hair was in a flat-top style and his chiseled features reminded Freddy of Spencer Tracy. Little Jake must have favored their mother. Freddy was more like Big Jake, who only earned the nickname 'Big' after his oldest son was born. Today, big meant older, not larger. Freddy resembled Big Jake more than Little Jake ever would. They were both short and dumpy. Big Jake was totally bald and Freddy found his hair abandoning his head in large numbers.

Their three sisters were still asleep. They all had their father's features as well but with more hair. They adored Little Jake, were afraid of Big Jake and tended to forget Freddy was also their brother. That was okay with Freddy. They only spied on him and told tales to Big Jake, which usually earned him a beating. Freddy had to admit, though, that when he started giving his father money every week, the hostility faded a bit.

"You give him money now," Little Jake explained. "If you leave, your room and board go with you. He doesn't want to give you an incentive to move out."

"How about an incentive to stay?"

"He can't. His pride's too strong to tell you he needs you."

"Well, I got to go," Freddy said and opened the door. "It's an hour to get there, half hour to unload and tally, an hour to get back. Might take longer to get home if it rains."

"If?" Little Jake laughed. "You are the eternal optimist."

"I am," Freddy grinned. "The longer gone, the less time with—"

He nodded upstairs.

"Here, catch," his brother threw him a hot biscuit, fresh from the oven.

Freddy had to juggle it to avoid burning his fingers and started nibbling at it on the way to his car. He was glad he loaded the twelve dozen eggs last night and tied them down snuggly under a burlap tarp. He would have to drive slowly. The hard dirt road was always a little slippery when it rained and the bridge over Banshee Creek had no guard rails. More than one car slid off the side and into the water during a storm. Freddy wanted to get to the train station in Neuville on time and at least get back across the bridge before the deluge came.

The transaction went smoothly. *Mr. Hartnett was a good customer*, Freddy thought to himself. He met Freddy at the station to buy eggs at three cents each. That way, Freddy cut a few miles off his driving time. They completed the transaction at noon without any rain instigated delays. Maybe today wouldn't be so bad after all.

Mr. Hartnett gave him five dollars that day, more than he needed to. Even so, Freddy's profit was minimal, between feed, gas and his father's fee for room and board. It didn't matter. He knew to always allow a hen or two to hatch a brood to increase his flock. Maybe it would grow to the point where he would be one of Mr. Hartnett's major suppliers. As for now, he was lucky his client even spoke to him.

By the time they completed the transaction, lightning bolts flashed through the clouds, though the water stayed put long enough for Freddy to get back on the road. As soon as the cobblestone street transitioned to hard dirt, the water poured down, almost as though the sky waited for that moment before it released what seemed like a lake onto the land. Freddy turned on his wipers, though they didn't help much with the heavy rain.

He had to drive slowly because the windshield fogged up, limiting his visibility. He thought about turning back to town, but he had nowhere to go and nobody to talk to in Neuville. There was nothing for him at home either, but at least it was dry. He continued with the rain hitting his hood and bouncing back up, obscuring his vision, sometimes completely. More than once, he had to stop to get his bearings. The last thing he wanted to do was drive off the road. The ditch was low and filled with water. A disaster like that would completely ruin the truck and leave him stranded, provided he survived.

He drove past a driveway overgrown with grass and thorns that made him shiver. The feeling that something bad was going to happen returned, stronger than ever. He was near the old Forrest place, once a beautiful home he visited a few times in his childhood. It had been abandoned to the swamp about ten years before when Crispen Forrest murdered his family and hung himself. He almost forgot about it and its grisly history. He sped past the Forrest driveway until it was out of sight without even noticing his increased speed.

He continued down Route 57 in the ferocious thunderstorm. The bridge over Banshee Creek washed away and the road barricades blocked his path. Now the bad part of the day was starting. He had to turn around on a dirt road without sliding down into the drainage ditch, which now looked like a raging river. Then he had to retrace his path back down Route 57 and return to Neuville so he could take the 190 to Long Street and make it home that way. That option added nearly two hours to his drive because he had to go in the opposite direction on another dirt road in the pouring rain. Sadly, his only other choice was an overnight sleep in his truck since the Wells farm lay well off the beaten path and only a few roads could get him home. His father liked to tell people they lived halfway between Neuville and hell. Freddy snorted. As if Neuville was all that great a destination in the first place. Oh well, at least he made his delivery.

His plans changed when he saw a giant pine tree stretched across the road. It was too big for him to push aside and the truck couldn't drive over it. He was stuck between a washed-out bridge and a roadblock on a dirt road in a massive thunderstorm. Freddy thought briefly about going back to the Forrest house but rejected the idea. He wanted to stay on the road for now. It was safer.

However, the truck was already sinking in the quagmire that used to be a road. The tires spun and squealed as he applied his foot to the gas pedal, but there was no traction at all. His poor truck was useless and he could feel it sinking in a little deeper. He got out to inspect it. The mud was up to the axle. He wasn't going anywhere now.

He had two choices. He could stay in the truck and hope it didn't sink below the doors, which would trap him inside until Lord knows when, or get out and find shelter. The old Forrest house had a covered front porch that would keep any more rain from falling on him. And it was only a small distance behind him. He had his rain slicker over his head as he stepped out of the truck but hesitated until he felt his feet sinking in the gooey mud. As he pulled each shoe up, listening to the slurping sound of the ground as it tried to suck him down to a muddy death, he made his decision. He

125

found himself walking toward the Forrest place.

The rain seemed to let up when he left the truck behind. It was still coming down, but it was quite a bit lighter, although the clouds, if anything, got darker. He slowly made his way down the road and soon turned on what used to be the driveway. The grass and weeds felt firmer under his weight as he walked comfortably down the path. The trees stood tall and thick around him, dripping with the cold rainwater.

He began to think he lost his way. The house used to be visible from the road and he didn't remember the entrance drive being so long, but he reminded himself that it was over ten years since his family visited here. Silver droplets of water covered the grass, shaking loose on his shoes as he progressed down the path. The water drenched his pants near the hems and was invading his shoes, soaking his socks.

Maybe I should have stayed in the truck after all. At least I'd be dry.

The house appeared to his right, almost like it materialized out of the mist and rain. It was mostly the way he remembered it. The forest dutifully cleared away into a square meadow of tall weeds and young pine trees. Nature was trying to reclaim its ground.

Freddy vaguely remembered fragments of the Forrest family tragedy. Crispen Forrest was a family friend. He stood tall with light blond hair that seemed almost white. He claimed to be a displaced Count from Ukraine. Nobody really believed him though. He spoke with no discernable accent and he knew how to work with tools too well to be royalty. He built the two-story house, complete with a formal living room large enough to have parties and dance. His four daughters each had their own room on the second floor, a luxury unknown since the antebellum days gone by.

His wife, Gretchen, was almost as tall as he was with a graceful, if unapproachable, demeanor. She wore her golden tresses curled and pinned with elegant hair combs shaped like red dragons. Freddy didn't really remember the daughters that much. Ten years ago, he was only six and all he knew was that they went to the same church.

The Forrest family invited the Wells family over to their house on several occasions. Freddy played mostly with Sarah, the youngest daughter, who was two years older than him. Rhianon and Gwyneth sometimes joined them, but mostly went their own way. They were entering their teenage years and had eyes only for Little Jake. Little Jake, on the other hand, only saw Guinevere, the oldest daughter, who seemed to generate at least some interest back. She was polite, but at 17, she saw the 16-year-old Jake for what he was: an uneducated common man with no prospects. Guinevere was not going to settle for anything less than a man of her own class.

Then, on a cold winter's night, Crispen went berserk and killed his wife and children. He just marched them out to the backyard and hacked them to pieces with an axe, leaving the gory bodies in pools of blood, except Guinevere. Once he was done hacking his children's bodies, he turned his attention to his oldest daughter. He apparently raped the poor child many times and whatever else he did to her left her body drained of blood. No cuts or gashes were visible and people could only speculate about what happened to her vital fluids. Did he drink her blood? Pour it down the drain? Whatever he did, after he was satisfied with his hellish deeds, he hanged himself on the front porch.

"Too bad he didn't hang himself first," Freddy

remembered hearing his father say to someone during the funeral. Nobody disagreed with that sentiment.

Big Jake never spoke about the Forrests after it happened. Nobody did. Freddy sometimes wondered if all the adults knew something about it but never told anyone. The murders and suicide alone were enough to keep Freddy away from the house. Oddly enough, most of the other church members didn't even remember how to get to the house. They recalled the family and events, but not where they lived. Freddy only remembered it because something, he didn't know what, jogged his memory as he drove by.

The house was larger than his home, but not by that much, considering there were five bedrooms and a living room large enough to use as a dance floor. But then, it was two stories, which meant it was like two whole houses built on top of each other. It was in fine shape considering its ten-year abandonment. Thick coats of plywood protected the windows and doors from the elements, but the gutters were collapsing and the green paint faded into gray as the years cracked and peeled it. The roof seemed almost perfect, with each piece of galvanized tin firmly in place, at least from Freddy's view. It was a forlorn and lonely house without a family anymore. Freddy could almost feel its sadness.

Beyond the house was the lopsided old barn, which needed a lot of work. The wood slats were slipping free, leaving behind angles of shadow. A decayed door lay on the ground waiting to be reattached to the wall. One rusty hinge barely held up the other one.

Freddy almost smiled as he surveyed the scene. He could repair the barn and convert it into a chicken coop. It would be even better than the one at home. The house might take more effort, but he could do it. He knew it. It was now just a matter of getting the property in his name. How could he have ever thought that today would be a bad day?

The raindrops were getting bigger and they were coming down hard. The tin roof held firm during the onslaught, but the noise was deafening. Freddy trotted up the stoop to the front porch of his new house. Well, maybe not his yet, but in his 16-year-old mind, it was just a matter of time. Obviously, nobody wanted to live here and he needed a place to stay with a shelter for his chickens. His business suddenly became viable. All he had to do was get title to an abandoned property. Granted, he didn't know the first thing about getting that done, but he figured Little Jake could help him with the details.

The porch was a simple rectangle with a door on the long side, which entered the living room, and another on the end going into the kitchen. The wall slats held firm. Freddy couldn't even see any warping. He went to the plywood covering above the living room door and tugged on it, not expecting much give, however, to his surprise, the wood easily pulled back. It took a little effort, but Freddy managed to get the plywood lowered down to the porch.

While he clapped his hands to get the dust off, he noticed the key sitting on the threshold. *That seemed logical,* he thought. The key had to be somewhere in case the current owners needed to get in.

No, it doesn't make any sense at all.

A forceful gust of wind blew the rain onto the porch, spraying the floorboards near him and made him more wet. The water was blowing almost completely sideways and the wind pushed him into the door. He didn't need any more time to think. He reached down and picked up the key. It was the old-fashioned kind that had two rectangular bits to fit into the lock and a fleur-de-lis handle. Very old, almost like a movie prop, not that he was able to see movies very often, times being what they were.

He started to insert the key into the lock when a bolt of thunder, louder than a shotgun blast, pounded the sky. The whole house shook from the terrible force. Freddy turned around in shock, but what greeted him was an even bigger surprise.

Crispen Forrest was hanging from the nearest porch beam, twisting in the heavy wind. His hands tied behind his back; he was slowly turning to face young Freddy. The head twisted at an impossible angle and his eyes were open, staring down to the ground. But when they were face to face, the corpse's eyes shifted to stare into Freddy's own.

He screamed in terror and started to run, but an impossibly strong wind blew him back into the door. His foot sank into something and he looked down to see what it was. A nail from the plywood dug into his shoe, missing his foot, but it certainly came close. Crispen was gone when he turned around. The wind died out. The rain slowed to a sprinkle. A little afternoon sun was peeking out. The worst of the storm was over.

Why were his hands tied behind his back if he hanged himself? It's just my imagination. I didn't see it at all. I'm scaring myself. I should go back to the truck. I should just pick up this plywood and realign the nails to the holes and tap it back together and leave. No one will know I was ever here.

I'll know, he replied to the thought, *I had a chance to at least see what my dream looks like and ran away because I saw shadows in the rain. If I can put the plywood back now, I can explore a little. I never saw the upstairs bedrooms. Crispen wouldn't let any of the boys upstairs in the girls' rooms. I didn't understand then, but I do now. Might as well see what I couldn't see then. If I don't break anything, no one will know I was ever here.*

With that, he reinserted the key and turned it until he heard a loud click. The doorknob twisted slowly in his hand, as though another hand was resisting him from within. He reasserted his grip and tried again, satisfied that he loosened the bolt from its years of immobility and rust. The bottom of the wood dragged on the threshold until it freed itself and opened wide with a loud, high-pitched groan. He tried to close the door tight behind him, but the wood was too swollen to completely shut again. He would put a greater effort into it when it was time to leave.

The living room seemed larger than it should be. The fireplace stood to his right, centered in the wall opposite him. The interior entrance to the kitchen was almost next to it, opposite the staircase. Old furniture, covered in sheets, sat in ghostly silence. The firewood stand contained an abundance of dry, ready to burn logs and kindling.

Freddy moved slowly across the floor to the kitchen. An arched entryway, no door attached, allowed him to see the room as he approached. If any member of the Forrest family put up a struggle, it was here. Pots and pans littered the floor and the cabinet doors were all open. Dust and spider webs covered the countertops. To his left was the bathroom, complete with toilet and sink, oh so modern back then, with its door standing ajar. Again, nothing but years of dusty neglect was visible, along with quite a few rat droppings.

Another bolt of thunder rattled the house, followed by more driving rain pounding on the tin roof. It was getting dark. Was it evening or just more dark clouds blocking out the sun? A childhood memory of a long ago visit flashed through his mind. He went to the far kitchen cabinet and bent down. He retrieved a nice sized hurricane lamp filled with kerosene and a handful of dry matches. The light made the shadows dance until he put the lantern on the counter long enough to check his watch—five-thirty. It was late, the sun was either down or close to it. He couldn't just steal the lamp and walk back to his truck. Even if he could, the rain might start again and douse the flame. It was too wet and slippery to be walking in the night anyway.

Obviously, he should have stayed in the truck no matter how deep it sank into the mud. Now, he was stuck in an abandoned house filled with spiders and rats and who knows what else. He made a bad decision to go exploring and here was where he would spend the night.

He figured he might as well see the rest of the house. Maybe Crispen kept a strongbox loaded with cash that everyone missed when they boarded the place up. He also wanted to see the girls' bedrooms upstairs. He wanted to remember them all. He didn't know what he would find there other than the little girls' toys and things. Why would anything up there interest him at all, after so many years?

Nothing did. A few dresses and gowns hung in the closets, covered in dust. Small little moths greeted him along with a few dolls with lonely eyes that stared at him, recording his every move. He remembered Sarah's toy birdcage, now smashed into pieces on the floor. Nothing else seemed familiar in any of the rooms.

Guinevere's chamber was less childish. She obviously outgrew dolls and stuffed animals. Her room had bottles of dried-up potions, perfume, most likely, other make-up items, ruined through time. Her diary lay on her dresser, closed. He thought about reading the last few pages to see if she left a clue about her fate that night, but shrugged, deciding to let her have her privacy.

It would be ghoulish to read it now, he thought.

It never occurred to him how strange it was that the investigators never found, read or confiscated it. In fact, if he were a bit more experienced in life, he would have wondered why anything was still there at all. It seemed that the police didn't find or touch anything. They certainly didn't preserve the clues they did manage to find.

The master bedroom was a mess. The bed lay broken with the mattress slashed in dozens of places. The stuffing and feathers were scattered throughout the room, mostly on the floor, though some pieces rested on the broken furniture. The dresser drawers also littered the floor; their contents strewn everywhere. Crispen must have been looking for something when his rage began.

A white, formal coat hung in the closet with ribbons and medals still attached to the breast. An old-fashioned sword, bent almost to a 'U' shape was under a pile of Gretchen's clothes, all ripped to pieces. More moths fluttered upwards when he tapped the pile with his foot.

He felt both ashamed and guilty about disturbing the scene. It wasn't his house yet and he knew he really shouldn't be here. He turned and walked out of the room, closing the door behind him. A loud cough sounded from behind it. A man's cough.

"Who's there?" Freddy yelled out in alarm.

If someone caught him trespassing, he might as well give himself up. He opened the door again, but the room was empty. It must have been a partially muffled boom of thunder. Even so, he scurried down the stairs with the intention of running back to the truck. It didn't matter to him anymore if it was night or not. This place was eerie and it frightened him. He no longer intended to buy it.

The front door opened easily. Too easy. The wind blew it right into his face and the whipping rain saturated him by the time he pressed the swollen wood up against the frame and pounded it as close to shut as possible. The blinding rain drenched the porch entirely. He couldn't see the stairs or yard. It was no longer even remotely possible for him to return to his truck. Not in weather like this.

Maybe if I just stay right here in the front room and stay quiet with the door closed, nothing will happen.

He squeaked over to the chimney, worked open the flue and set a few logs of wood on the rack. After a light dose of kerosene, he soon had a small fire going. At least he could get dry by morning. When he was satisfied with the flames, he stood up. A small pillowcase slipped off a mirror that hung above the mantle. He must have jarred it loose while he built the fire, though he had no idea of doing so.

He remembered that mirror from the few times he visited as a child. It had a blue tint to it. It still did. It was high enough that it would require some effort to secure the cloth back to its original position. He could wait until the morning, after the fire smoldered out. He shook a dust cover off a chair and slapped the pillows to shake out the lint and any other things and sat down, stretching his legs out toward the heat of the fire.

About half an inch of water dribbled into his boots during his trek here so he pulled them off and shook them out the front door. The rain and wind died down a bit, but the angry clouds still threatened and a loud boom of thunder shook the floor beneath him. The fire was quite hot when he got back to his chair and he placed his drenched boots a safe distance in front of it for them to dry. His socks came off next and he hung them on a couple of protruding nails from the mantle. *Probably where the girls hung their Christmas stockings*, he thought sadly.

He gently placed another log on the fire and sat back

down in the chair, wishing he had some hot coffee and a few biscuits. The fire's hypnotic flames provided all the entertainment he needed or was going to get. He dozed off after a while and when he woke up, he checked the time. It was just after nine p.m.

He tossed some more fuel onto the fire but by ten o'clock, the flames were low again. Another log brightened the room. He checked his socks and nodded with contentment. They were dry enough, but he turned them around for more heat. After he yanked them up and pulled his pants cuffs free, he checked his boots. They were drier but still wet on the inside. He turned them so the other side would absorb the fire's warmth.

As he sank back down into the musty smelling chair, he noticed movement. The fire was still burning, but what he saw was above the mantle in the mirror. He stared into it, but nothing was different, unless it was slightly bluer. Maybe the fire's glow created an illusion of movement.

He could see the stairs from the angle he had. They almost glowed in the reflection. But the glow seemed to flicker toward the top of his vision, as though there might be a small flame on the second floor. Freddy felt a bit of panic at that. Did he leave the lamp upstairs? No. Could some kerosene have dripped out from the lantern's well and somehow caught on fire? No. He would have felt it while he was carrying it and he would have smelled the fuel oil as well.

He sighed. He would have to go upstairs and see what it was. He stood up and turned toward the steps, but there was no flickering. The house was as dark as could be. Almost against his will, he focused back onto the mirror.

The flicker was more prominent. The top step reflected a soft blue-green. The source of the light was closer now.

The light was brighter. He jerked his head back to the stairs again. All dark. No light. No flicker. No movement.

Freddy slid over to the fireplace and slipped his almost dry socks on. He struggled with his boots because wet boots aren't exactly easy for anyone to get into. He kept darting his eyes between the stairs and mirror. The staircase remained as dark as ever. Someone or something was visible in the mirror. It was a girl or was once a girl. She wore a long diaphanous gown, flowing to her ankles and white slippers. She was maybe four steps down the case and the glow from her light danced on its sheer material. She still wasn't there when he glanced back at the stairs.

He stomped his foot hard into the boot. His toes were crooked but that didn't matter right now. He fumbled for the mate and pushed and pulled his foot into the shrunken leather, all while watching the creature's approach.

Her waist was visible, all white and frilly. Another step down and he saw her elbows, bent while she held her candle. Another step revealed the candle's tiny flame and her delicate hands. One held the metal base and the other shielded the delicate flame from the draft of her movement. It obviously provided her enough light to guide her down the case without needing to use the railing. Her neck and shoulders appeared after the next step down. Blonde hair rested in clumps of curls on her collar.

Mrs. Forrest?

It was the wrong hair style, but right color. Freddy only saw her hair in a bun and had no idea how long it was. He didn't want to see her anyway. From what he remembered overhearing, Crispen hacked everyone's faces and bodies to pieces. Even if he didn't, it was ten years ago. He wouldn't remember what she looked like after all that time anyway, even if her face was whole.

A quick stomp on the floor and the second boot was on, the toes just as crooked as his first foot. He stretched them out as best he could while tensing his muscles to sprint away from this place. But he wanted to see her face before he ran back into the night. He wanted to know who or what he was running from.

Logic told him that nothing in the house could really hurt him. Nothing was here. The stairs were empty in the real world. The woman was only in the mirror. His heart screamed at him to run as fast and as far as possible. He wouldn't have seen any of this if there wasn't something coming down those stairs looking for him.

Her face was visible now that she was on the last stair. He knew who she was. His thoughts of hasty retreat vanished from his mind. He could only stare at her.

"Guinevere Forrest," he said out loud.

The 17-year-old eldest daughter of Crispen and Gretchen Forrest was indeed the ghostly figure in the mirror. Her face was untouched by the violent rage of her father and she looked the same as she did ten years ago. She was beautiful with gray eyes and flowing hair. Skin almost as white as milk glowed with an unwholesome aura. Even so, she was beautiful. When she was alive, Freddy could appreciate her beauty, but he was too young to feel that manly attraction to her. He certainly could now. Her figure was perfect with prominent breasts that stood firm and high and nipples barely visible through the diaphanous material of her gown. She walked as though in a trance, staring straight ahead and ignoring his voice as she floated across the floor to the looking glass.

Freddy backed away, making sure he didn't disturb the vision and make it vanish. She continued to make her way to the mirror and walked through the wall, mantle and fire.

He shook his head for a second and she was there in front of him now, in front of the fire, smiling at him with impossibly white teeth. She was the most beautiful woman he ever saw. He was getting a little uncomfortable below his waist as he realized just how much he wanted her.

"I'm afraid you have the advantage over me, young sir," she smiled as her eyes inspected him from his head down to his dull and dirty boots.

He felt embarrassed. If he knew he was going to meet such a bewitching young woman, he would have worn his Sunday best. He was no longer afraid of her and wondered why he ever was.

Be afraid. Run from this place. Get away from her.

But those thoughts were too deep in his brain to register, though he momentarily began to think that maybe the house cast some kind of spell on him. Everything was wrong. Certainly, a girl ten years dead talking to him just wasn't right. At the very least, he should feel cautious and on edge. But he simply lost all of his fear. She mesmerized him with her beauty as she gazed at him with those liquid gray eyes.

"I heard you call my name when I was walking through the portal," she went on easily with a voice infused with honey. "But I can't say I know your name. It's impolite to leave me in the dark as to whom my own gentleman caller is. Don't you think?"

Portal? Gentleman caller?

Freddy froze in that moment, too stunned to think properly or answer her. The house confused him terribly and he didn't understand what was happening. Could she be real? He hoped so, but he suspected she was part of a wonderful dream. She stared at him with benevolent and smiling eyes as she waited for him to answer.

"Are you not going to tell me?" she asked. Her voice sounded hurt.

She glanced at him with amused eyes.

"Tell you?" he managed to stammer, unsure of what to say or do.

His situation didn't make any sense to him. All he knew was that he wasn't afraid of her, but maybe he should be.

"Your name," she repeated patiently. "You know mine, but I don't know yours."

"Freddy," then he corrected himself as his remaining fear settled down. "I mean Fred. Fred Wells."

She was attractive and he was 16 and wanted to impress her by using his adult name.

"My family visited here a few times years ago. You remember my brother, Little Jake? He was your age and spent all his time with you and the older girls. I played with Sarah. Hide and seek. But that was when—"

He stopped, embarrassed.

"When I was alive?" She smiled, "I am still alive, just different."

She took an exaggerated step back and inspected him again, focusing on the bulge his pants failed to hide.

"Little Freddy Wells," she said in a wondering voice as her eyes moved up and down his body. "Where do the years go? And look at you. You're a man now. A grown-up man, indeed."

Her eyes returned to his belt or rather just below it. When she made eye contact again, she licked her lips and smiled knowingly.

"Poor Freddy, I mean Fred," she smiled knowingly. "You've never been with a woman before, have you?"

"Um…no," he croaked through a dry throat.

How did she know? Was there something obvious

about it? He never thought about it before, but it embarrassed him tonight. He wanted to make up an excuse, but his mind was blank.

"It must be tough," she said sympathetically. "Your father dominated everyone in your family because he was so insecure and everything came easy to Little Jake. Where did that leave you? Right now, your whole world is a farm. And it's not even yours. You had no one to teach you about the delicate things in life. How can you be attractive to a woman with a drunk and mean father who makes you feel useless and no mother to convince you that you're just as good as anyone else? Better than most, I think. Tonight, my gentleman caller, I'll let you be the big man you want to be. You see, I know you went into my room. And I know why."

"I'm sorry. I meant no harm. If I knew——"

She put a finger on his lips.

"You wanted to remember us. You couldn't have known I saw you there. Felt you there might be a better way to say it. I know you saw my diary, but didn't open it, even though you wanted to. I know you wanted to read about my desires and feelings. I thought that was so sweet of you."

Freddy nodded; his throat dry.

"Come upstairs with me, back to my room. It's time for you to understand and celebrate the joy of being a man. And it's time for me to enjoy my place in that celebration. Men and women belong together, you know."

She took his hand and led him up the stairs. As they passed the mirror, Freddy felt a cold blast of foul-smelling wind. He glanced over to the glass. Something stared back at him. Something dark and hairy with long fangs and red eyes that glowed with hate. It was gone in a heartbeat, leaving only the room's reflection behind.

He forgot about that vision almost immediately when she took him by his elbow and cuddled up next to him as they made their way to the bedroom. When she opened the door, the room sparkled at him. Not a trace of dust remained and the room even smelled clean. The furniture covers disappeared and polished wood furniture gleamed in the candlelight. The sheets and blankets on the bed appeared to be freshly laundered.

"How did all this happen?" he asked, dazed.

He felt content because he somehow knew that Guinevere kept the room exactly like this when the Forrest family still lived here. He opened his mouth to ask how she did it but she interrupted before the words came out.

"Don't ask questions now," she laughed as she guided him to the bed. "There'll be time for all that later."

The bed groaned when they sat down facing each other. She smiled and leaned in toward him. He responded and they kissed. It was awkward at first as his nose bumped into hers, but they adjusted. After a moment, while his heart thumped in his chest so loud he thought she could hear it, she snuggled into his shoulder.

"That was your first kiss," she smiled.

He nodded, embarrassed. If it was that obvious, then he wasn't a very good kisser.

"That's okay, we'll try again. Even Cassanova had to learn. Now here, loosen up your chin muscles," she pressed her fingers on his jaw hinge and pressed down with a slight massage. "And don't clench your mouth shut. Relax, pay attention and enjoy. I'm going to show you how I like to be kissed. Then it'll be your turn to kiss me. I prefer the man to take charge of kissing. That's the way it's supposed to be so pay attention and relax."

She pressed her lips against his. Her tongue slowly

licked his upper lip before exploring deeper. She lightly flicked his tongue with hers before tracing his gum line. Then she backed away, scanning his face for his reaction.

He pulled her forward and kissed her back, perhaps a bit more clumsily, but he soon stopped worrying about his technique and started enjoying her mouth. He explored her teeth and rubbed her upper mouth before she started to pull back. He relaxed and started to lean back.

She bit him. His tongue and lip were bleeding. He yanked back with a surprised yelp and look of shock.

"When I pull back, you have to too," she said innocently. "It makes a girl nervous when you refuse to stop. You must remember, we're so much smaller and weaker. When you don't get the idea, that's all we can do."

It didn't make sense to him. He was pulling away from her when she nipped him. She licked her own lips to get the blood off, smiling at him. Then she leaned forward for another kiss. He pulled back. That surprise bite was bad enough and he was still bleeding just a little. But it also unnerved him to see her lick his blood off her own lips. It just wasn't natural.

"Don't pout," she said coyly. "You're still learning. Love isn't love without a surprise or two. Here, you can bite me."

"I don't want to bite you or hurt you," he said petulantly.

"I'm so sorry. I thought you would have liked it. Some people like a little pain in their romance. Let me make it up to you."

They kissed again, pressing their bodies tightly until she separated them. Freddy tasted something in her mouth. It had a slight copper tinge. He recognized it at once. Blood. She bit her own lip and let a few drops of her blood fall into his mouth. He almost pushed her away, but she grabbed his arms with surprising strength and wrapped them around her waist and quickly kissed him again. When he eased back and accepted a few more drops of her blood, she pulled back slightly, gazing at him with love and triumph.

"I wanted to hurt myself because I hurt you," her soft voice cooed. "I will never hurt you again. I only want to make you feel good. Let me prove it."

She stood up and unbuttoned her gown, letting it fall gracefully to the floor in a heap. She smiled at Freddy's expression of amazement and joy.

He stood up beside her, unbuttoning his shirt. Within seconds, they were back on the bed with Guinevere on her back instructing him as he touched and kissed her body all over, from head to thigh. Then she pulled him back on top of her.

"How is all this possible?" he asked when it was over and they were snuggled together on top of the blankets.

"Magic."

He nodded drowsily, "Must be."

He was stroking and squeezing her ass gently until she adjusted herself on her side, her hand reaching down under the blanket.

"Enough rest. Time for another lesson," she said with a laugh, wiggling underneath him as he mounted her again.

He fell asleep after they finished the second time. When he woke up, she was on top of him, her face buried in his neck. Whatever she was doing ached, but it wasn't painful. In fact, he found it almost pleasant. He could have stayed there, but he needed to adjust his weight a little. He gently pushed her up and almost gagged when he saw her bloodstained mouth and chin. His blood. She licked her lips sensuously and laughed softly while daintily wiping the rest of her face with her hand.

"I thought a little love bite might wake you up," she teased. "We don't want you to sleep the night away, my darling. We are lovers and we feast on each other's body. You in your way. I in mine. Isn't that what love's all about? Giving to each other?"

He pulled back to a defensive sitting position, bashing his head against the headboard and holding his wrist in front of his throat. His neck was still bleeding though not very much.

"My God, what are you?" he whispered, too afraid to speak louder.

"I'm Guinevere Forrest. I'm also Guinevere of the Northern Forest. First Princess of the Sixth Family of Kheliesis. Your first girlfriend is royalty. You should bow to show your respect," she said with mock reproachment that turned into a self-conscious laugh when she saw his expression.

He shook his head no while reaching down for his clothes.

"Oh, Fred," she said in a weepy voice with mocking eyes. "Don't you want to spend the rest of your life as the consort to a princess?"

She tilted her head as she looked at him coyly. He shuddered when she smiled. She was a dangerous predator through and through.

"If I tell you who I am, will you love me?" she continued in a contrite voice when she saw that he was disgusted with her.

He nodded while he desperately tried to think. He felt too tired and enervated to respond verbally. She obviously sucked quite a bit of blood from the neck wound, leaving him tired and debilitated. He doubted he could put up much of a fight if she seriously attacked him. Also, part of him didn't want to resist anymore, at least not right now. Somehow, he enjoyed feeding her his life's blood even if he knew he was in danger. She would drain every drop of his blood if she could. But that didn't stop him from wanting her. He had very little mental will or physical strength left to resist her.

She gently reached out and stroked his face from temple to his jaw. He wanted to pull away, but he enjoyed her touch. He should get dressed and run. Maybe just run. But his energy disappeared with his blood. And he was very much in love with his woman who would kill him.

"In Kheliesis, we were royalty. My uncle was the king, nominally king of the entire island, though our control only covered maybe half. His first four brothers were all Dukes—north, south, east, and west. My father was a landless Duke. He was the Duke of the Forest, a polite way of saying he was from an important family, but not important in any other way. And it never mattered. Not to him or any of us. We were all content with what we had in our part of the Island Kingdom.

"Kheliesis is a land of magic, not science. Way back in the dawn of the age of man, The Great Creator separated our worlds. Mankind would destroy itself if it could develop magic and science together. He could not trust mankind with such power. What your world has done with science is truly amazing. What my world has done with magic, the same. Together, we could rule the universe. Or destroy it.

And if you think about it, why have a universe at all if we can't rule it?

"Anyway, it all comes down to who is the most powerful. My uncle was the rightful King of Kheliesis, but there was a pretender. He was a distant cousin from the west, still on the Island of Kheliesis, but far from our civilization and culture. He claimed to have a stronger right to the throne and he gathered vast armies to seize the kingdom. Once it became war, it no longer mattered who had the rightful claim. It came down to who was the better general. Our armies met theirs in three great battles for control. My uncle lost all three, his life in the third one. The remaining generals surrendered and accepted amnesty from the new king. My uncle's opponent, Lord Vidallam the Axeman, became king. The first orders he gave were for the destruction and execution of all the surviving royal families so he could consolidate his control over the people. He wanted no other man to have even a laughable claim to the throne, so he issued an order to exterminate our bloodline. Every man, woman and child related to the old king had to die. There would be no more wars over who was the rightful king.

"Since his armies are immense and merciless, he believes that he is now the rightful ruler of the whole continent. But Kheliesis is a large and vast island. It is a continent as big as Asia. And Vidallam and his followers are warriors. So far, they have conquered every country they invaded, killed all the ruling families, enslaved the survivors, and exterminated any threats. After they consolidated their gains, they went out and conquered again. His army killed and destroyed every possible threat in its path. He spared no one who might be able to help us retake our rightful kingdom. My father and my surviving aunts and uncles all escaped through the portals, along with their families."

"The portals," Freddy whispered, "like the mirror downstairs?"

She nodded while inspecting his eyes. He knew she was only waiting for him to fall back asleep so she could kiss his throat again.

"My father and uncles were organizing a return to Kheliesis to reconquer our land. They used their portals to communicate with each other as they plotted, though they had to be careful. Vidallam also had access and could listen in as they made plans. It would be another long and dreadful war. Hundreds of thousands of souls died in the first war. Hundreds of thousands of souls would die in the next. That is the nature of war.

"I, Guinevere the Foolish, thought I could reach a compromise. If I could convince Vidallam to marry me and make me his queen, then all the families would unite under his rule. After all, we would all be family by marriage. Kheliesis would know peace again. The fighting and killing could stop and we would all be happy. It was a perfect plan.

"When I told my mother about my idea, she slapped my face hard and told me to get that silly idea out of my head. To even think such a thought was a betrayal of my father and family. My uncle was still king and he was the only one to negotiate with Vidallam the Axeman. It was not my place to volunteer to do such a thing. Besides, Vidallam already had a wife, the Dark Queen of Margoth Island. But they never legally married and they had no children together. He could simply put her aside, marry me, and together, we would conquer the rest of the Island Kingdom and unite it with all the people. With me as his queen, providing him heirs and descendants, the Vidallam Dynasty would last forever.

"So, I, Guinevere the Betrayer, went to the mirror and called out to Vidallam and made my proposal. He agreed to it immediately. He needed me to tell him how to get here so he could bring his wedding party and, to my shame and disgrace, I told him where we were and how he could come here. I accomplished my perfect plan. I would be Queen of Kheliesis."

"It didn't go as planned," Freddy said flatly.

He may be uneducated and naïve, but he already knew how this story ended.

"Alas, I, Guinevere the Betrayed, watched the wedding party pour through the mirror. A dozen warriors and the Dark Queen herself, along with her brother, Margustos, the Vampire King. You know what happened. They captured us all. They found my father's ceremonial sword and bent it to a 'V' shape to announce Vidallam's victory. They searched the rooms for any hint of where the other families might be. They only left my father's Ceremonial Coat of Royalty untouched because it possessed a charm that would destroy the first enemy who touched it."

"I touched it."

"You're not an enemy. Regardless, they found nothing and so proceeded to slaughter my mother and sisters with their swords, one by one in front of me and my father. They wanted him to give up the king and his other brothers, but we all knew that Vidallam would kill us eventually even if my father betrayed them or not.

"Soon it was my turn."

She paused for a moment and stared at him sadly, stroking his thigh, making him tingle with desire. He shrank away from her touch even though he wanted her.

"You were hardly so rude before," she sighed sadly while wiggling back into her dress with an air of finality.

It wasn't white anymore; age and decay turned it a gray-yellow. The room was no longer clean, but moldy and abandoned, the way it was when he first saw it. He fell off the dank and dusty bed to struggle back into his own damp clothes.

"Yes, the Dark Lady herself decided that merely being dead wasn't a sufficient punishment for me. I tried to steal her husband and have him put her aside in exile. I was only a foolish child who dreamed of being a queen and had to bear an even worse punishment than anyone else in my family. A fate worse than death awaited me. They gave me over to Margustos."

She lowered her voice in imitation of a man, "'There is no future for you as a queen anymore. There never really was. But you will be my slave. My servant. My lover. My subject. You will be like me, my pretty little princess. A shadow, not living, not dead. Your body will want food and companionship, but you will stay trapped and alone here forever until I call you to pleasure me. You can wallow in the guilt of your betrayal and murder of your family. And you know we will all laugh at you and enjoy your misery.'

"And then Margustos raped me. He called it consummating our marriage. He did it right there in front of my father and the others while the soldiers adjusted the noose around my father's neck. When that monster finished, he and his sister bit my neck, side by side, and sucked out all my blood. Every drop. They drank all they wanted, then spit their own blood down my throat. The last thing I saw was my father's body swaying in the wind while they hanged him. I think we both died together. He went to Fields of Honor. I stayed here, cursed by the Vampire

King to forever be alone in this house. No visitors have ever found me, except for you."

"But that can't be true," Freddy said slowly.

He still felt weak, but at least he got his clothes on, with his boots on his feet. He staggered a bit but made it to the door where he leaned on the frame to catch his breath.

"Yes, it is," she said gently helping him slide down to the floor. "My master cast a spell on this place. Nobody remembers how to come back to this house. They can't see it, only forest. All the hunters and trappers walk right by me, never seeing the buildings at all. Except you, for some reason. You were the only one to come inside. You woke me and I was so happy to not be alone. I had someone to see me. To talk to. We made love. Now, you make me sad. You want to leave."

She didn't look sad. Her mocking eyes told him that. She was savoring this moment.

"You want to kill me," he accused.

He wanted to keep talking to her. He instinctively knew that if he went back to sleep, she would be on him again, drinking his blood until there was none left. As weak and helpless as he was, he didn't understand why she didn't simply attack and finish him. She reminded him of a snake that bit a rabbit and was waiting for it to die so it could feed on the corpse.

"I want you to stay with me. I want you to want to be my husband. Together, we can be happy," her eyes filled with crocodile tears. "Is it so wrong to be happy? All I ever wanted was to be happy. I just didn't know what to do to get there."

She plopped down beside him and tried to snuggle again, but he pushed her away. With a heartbroken sigh, she leaned back against the threshold opposite him, staring sadly into his eyes. Her mocking triumph seemed to have vanished. She was a vulnerable little girl now, not any older than he was. He almost felt sorry for her.

"How did you get here?" she asked, changing the subject.

He thought about it.

"The bridge washed away. A tree on the other side. I remembered where the driveway was and walked over here to see your house and get out of the rain. I found the key and wanted to see what it looked like after all these years."

"I'm glad you did. I understand now how you found me. Margustos cast an invisibility spell, first on anything in the house that might make the deputies question their theory that my father was the killer. After they left, no one could see the house again. You found it, not because you saw it. You found it because you knew it was here.

"You see?" She rose a bit before settling back, as though struck by a great revelation, "You only knew I was here because you remembered me and my family. You were meant to find me. Don't you see, Fred? Being together is our destiny. You don't want to leave me here all alone."

"What about Margustos?"

"He's…on the other side," she hesitated.

"He's coming here. I saw him in the mirror. You're lying."

"I'm telling the truth. He knows I'm not in the Shadowlands. He knows I'm trying to escape."

"Is that why you want me to stay here? To take your place?"

"Not at all, Fred," she replied. "I only need you to do one thing for me. Turn the mirror around so that it faces the wall. I can't touch it, there's a spell that prevents me. But he can't find me if the glass is facing the wall. When he

151

looks for me, all he will see is the wall. And then he can't walk through the portal, like I did, because he won't be able to see the room. We will be safe forever and we can settle down, the two of us, happily ever after, just like in the old fairy tales."

"How will you live?"

"Well, we would need to find some lost souls to provide nourishment for me. The world is filled with them. We find them in the Shadowlands all the time. And we cannot go into the sunshine, it flings us back into the void, but we can have every night together, just like tonight, before we fought."

"The void?"

"Think of the oceans. Only filled with nothing. It's the separation of all the worlds in the universe. Eventually, the current pulls us back to the world we belong in. Freddy, I'm sorry I bit you while you were sleeping, but I was so hungry. It was still so very wrong. I know it. Can't you forgive me? Be my lover again? You don't understand how lonely I get here."

"My blood is my own."

"Yes, my love, I'll never touch it again."

"That is so right," Fred said, staggering to his feet. "You will never get any more because I'm leaving here."

"No, you're not," her voice turned into iron.

All the pleading and sadness was gone as she pounced on him, knocking him down on his stomach while her teeth bit into the side of his neck.

He swatted her off, surprised at how light she was.

"You don't weigh anything," he said, surprised.

"I've had so little nourishment. My physical essence dissipates a little more each day. There' so little left of me beyond my heart and soul. And my hunger. Your blood gives me more life. That's why when we get hungry, we don't think. Just feed."

She glared at him with a predatory determination. He retreated, half running, half crawling to the stairs where he lost his balance and tumbled down to the ground floor. The pain of a broken wrist helped to energize his weakened body and he rolled over, just as he watched her dive head first gracefully down the steps. Before she smashed into the floor, her head arced upwards and she landed lightly on her feet, standing over him.

He was still getting up, using the wall for support. She smiled at him; her teeth transformed into gleaming fangs. Her eyes glowed red hot as her hands shot out and grabbed his hair. She threw him across the room where he landed with a sickening thump against the front wall.

A laugh filled the room. They both stopped and stared at the mirror. That hideous creature he saw before was watching them. It had a mostly human face with floppy ears on the top of its head and an elongated snout above a lipless mouth filled with needle-sharp teeth, interrupted by yellowed fangs, gleaming with saliva. Tiny hands were reaching out of the looking glass, attached to thin membranes of wings. It was stepping into the living room, chuckling an evil laugh.

"So, the princess is a huntress now. I knew the years of hunger would burn that royal attitude out of you. Time to go for the kill, my dear."

"Of course, Master Margustos," she said obsequiously as they both turned their eyes to their prey.

The mood changed. They were somehow communicating with each other. Freddy sensed a tension in the air between them filled with anger, resentment and hatred.

"You had him taste your blood? You made him one of us without my permission?" Margustos screamed at her, his face a livid mask of animosity, "How dare you? You were thinking of forming your own kingdom on this planet? Vampires can only live in our world. He must come back with us or die here. There can be no other option. A vampire on this Earth would be unstoppable. The Great Creator himself will send out angels to destroy you both, if I let you get away with it. As it stands, I have a new subject in the Shadowlands and you have more time in your emptiness with only hunger and loneliness to keep you company. Now, go kill your prey."

Guinevere grimly started to march across the room to Freddy while the Vampire King pulled himself to his full height, towering over them both. Freddy managed to get back on his feet to battle what was most likely going to be his last fight. The front door was at his side, still slightly ajar. Maybe he could get out of the house and into the sun where he'd be safe. She couldn't let the daylight touch her. It would fling her back to the void, he remembered.

With one hand on the handle and the other through the crack between the door and frame, he threw it wide open. Bright daylight greeted him, hurting him. All the storm clouds were gone. The sun filled the room with warmth while the two figures inside screamed in agony. Freddy wasn't in the direct light like they were, but even diffused as it was, it pained him. He felt as though his body was slowly dissolving.

He watched as the light slowly circled the room catching dust particles and lint into a raging vortex. The spinning quickened its velocity as it caught Guinevere and the demon in its force. Their agonized screams were loud but quieter with each passing second. They disintegrated in the spinning light; their very molecules dissolved into mist. Like a tornado, all the light and vapor spun into the looking glass.

They were gone.

All the furniture was either gone or destroyed. Dust covered the floor and walls. Even his own footprints from last night were gone, covered in ten years of neglect. All that remained was a house too damaged by neglect to be worth saving.

He closed the door, careful to stay out of the direct sunlight. He didn't want to join them in the void, whatever that was.

You had him taste your own blood?

She tricked him. When she bit her lip for him to taste her blood, she infected him with her undead poison. He died upstairs on her bed and she wanted his last few drops of life. She transformed him into a vampire. He could feel it in his bones. He couldn't stay in this world, but didn't want to live in theirs. He didn't want to be a subject of Margustos.

Now, he must come back with us or die here.

"I'll die here," he said aloud.

It seemed forever before the sun fell behind the trees and insects announced the dusk. Walking outside, he fell flat on the wet grass and rolled over on his back, letting the leftover warmth of the sunbathe his flesh. He would never feel it on his skin again. He slept for most of the night and woke up hungry and exhausted.

Fred? Freddy?

She was calling to him from the house.

Come home, Freddy. There's nothing for you out there anymore. There never was, don't you see? You are one of us now. Wait till dawn and walk out in the sun. We can still be together here in the Shadowlands. Just forgive me.

He had no intention of going back to her or going home to her. He trusted her and she turned him into a monster. He heard movement in the forest ahead. A foraging raccoon searched the night for food. Well, Freddy was hungry and it was time for Freddy to feed. The 'coon was no match for him. He had the head twisted off in no time and soon discarded the bloodless corpse.

He retraced his steps. The washed-out bridge was still gone. It would be quite a while before anyone came to rebuild it. The creek's water was roaring past him with whitecaps and raging foam. He didn't dare try to cross it. He was afraid of water now. He didn't know why.

He turned the other way. The tree was still there, but the truck wasn't. It washed into the drainage ditch and was at least two feet under its flowing water.

He returned to the old house and sat on the porch, listening to Guinevere call to him. He idly wondered why she still wanted him, but he really didn't care enough to ask her. He waited until the sun started to light up the sky. When his skin started to tingle, he entered the decayed building again.

He didn't want to go to her world. It wasn't his. But neither was this one. He no longer was Freddy Wells. He was something different.

He picked up the plywood and set it in front of the threshold to block out as much of the hated sun as possible. He started to go back upstairs to Crispin's closet to put on the man's ceremonial jacket. Guinevere had said it would destroy any enemy who touched it. Maybe he was an enemy now. Maybe he could escape his existence that way. He stared at the mirror's frame, careful not to gaze into the glass. Margustos was in there, looking for him. He could feel it.

He clung to the walls and slowly approached it from the side, being careful not to accidently glance into the mirror. Margustos obviously could be a formidable opponent. His original idea was to destroy the glass so it could cause no more problems, but that might be more of a permanent solution than he would want in the future. He regretted not asking what would happen if he simply destroyed it.

She said all she needed was for him to turn it around for her to be free. He was underneath it and grasped it with both hands lifting it off its hook. As he grappled with its surprising heavy weight, his eyes gazed into it briefly. It was them. Naked, in bed. She looked miserable and degraded. He was triumphant and happy. They both saw him at the same time.

He quickly turned the looking glass around so all he saw was an engraving on the back. He could hear them yelling at him as he faced it against the wall. He ignored them both and read the inscription.

May you only see the most beautiful blessings the world has to offer in this mirror.

There would be no beautiful blessings for him now or ever. Those were for humans. He stood up tall and straight and surveyed his new home where he would live forever.

MOTHER

Franklin Cash frowned as he pulled his 20-year-old Ford into the driveway of his childhood home. His mother died a few days ago and Vi and Debbie, his two older sisters, asked him to get it fixed up and ready for sale. He didn't want to step foot in it. The half-forgotten images of the abuse he suffered there were strong and relentless. Although, he understood that his mother's mental illness drove his father away from her and into the arms of another woman, he couldn't forgive either of them. She tore the family apart and he let her. He also left them all at her mercy.

Sadly, he was the one who lived nearest to her, so his sisters insisted that he be the one to get the house ready for sale. They wanted to be rid of it too. He knew it had nothing to do with him being the closest child to the house. Vi and Debbie also suffered abuse from Mother. The girls had to deal with Mother's boyfriends, some of whom were more attracted to them than Mother. Vi ran away first, then Debbie, leaving him alone with her. By then, he was bigger than her and could disarm her when she occasionally attacked him with a kitchen knife, but nothing protected him from her words.

The last boyfriend he remembered was a tall black man who wore a necklace of bird skulls. He came from Neuville, Louisianna and claimed to have a working knowledge of the black arts, particularly *Hai-Tak-Koo*, which he claimed was the most powerful of the ancient Earth religions. He and his mother drew circles on the living room floor and danced naked on moonless nights, their movement lit by candlelight.

Franklin snuck out of his room one time and watched them, fascinated. Both unattractive bodies were drug ravaged and he knew that watching his mother shake and jiggle her age-flattened breasts into that man's leering face could earn him a major punishment from them both. He stood transfixed until a growl reached his ears from the far corner. Red eyes, as bright as Christmas tree lights appeared, focused on the dancers. Dust and powder swirled behind them slowly forming some kind of creature. Something evil. Franklin froze for a moment before backing out of the threshold and retreating to his room. He didn't want to watch anymore. Whatever they were doing in there was unholy and dangerous.

He stayed in his room with the door locked every night after that. He could hear her sometimes, wandering the hall, muttering things in a language he couldn't understand. At 16, he got a part time job and bought a car. It became his new home for a long time, until a friendly policeman found him freezing in the back seat one winter's night and reunited him with Vi, who was married and a mother of two. She agreed to take him in until he finished high school. After that, he was on his own though they stayed on friendly enough terms. She even re-introduced him to Debbie.

He occasionally went back home to visit his mother and it always went well. She didn't seem to remember her psychotic episodes or dancing adventures and he didn't remind her. He stayed for about an hour, until she started repeating herself. Her repetition meant that something was going wrong in her brain and she was nearing a break. When that happened, he left. It didn't bother him to leave since Vi and Debbie never visited her at all.

He stopped visiting her a couple of years back when her memories completely faded and her senility robbed her of her memories. She didn't recognize him and sometimes confused him with his father or one of her boyfriends and tried to kiss him lasciviously or rub at him sexually. He heard that, after his last visit, she ran down the street totally nude, screaming that a devil was in her house and it wanted her soul. She didn't remember the episode the next day and the state and insurance company provided her with a live-in caretaker after that, which was a good thing. Franklin found a job near Vicksburg and moved away. It didn't bother him that he wouldn't see her again. They were never close anyway.

Vi and Debbie had no desire to hold a memorial. Mother outlived almost everyone she knew and nobody else considered her a friend. Mother understood the concept of friendship to mean that her 'friend' gave her complete control of her life. She loved domination and power and anyone in her orbit submitted to her will and subjugation or became a nonperson to her. Nobody wanted to remember her.

Franklin remembered his father fighting with her all the time before he left home, at first over her control issues, then about her refusal to see a psychiatrist. His father reached the breaking point one night and left home, never to return. He disappeared soon after without a trace and Franklin remembered the note of triumph in Mother's voice when she announced that he abandoned them forever because he was worthless and weak.

"It's better not to have a man in the house if he's worthless and weak," she informed them with one of her sinister smiles. "And you, my little darlings, have me. No one needs two parents when they have a saint for a mother."

They did, however, have a great many father figures. 'Uncles,' as their mother called them. They lasted for various lengths of time but always ended with a loud and sometimes violent fight. They all stormed out of the house late at night screaming that they would never call again. Mother simply smiled her creepy sneer and watched them leave.

She had a few single women friends who visited for coffee every so often. They became fast friends for a while, then disappeared when they realized that Mother's friendship meant Mother's control over their lives.

"I always try too hard to get these women to understand there is no such thing as a good man. They are on best behavior and then what? Do you know what happens when a man isn't on best behavior anymore? They have all those flaws lurking beneath the surface until they think they have their women under their control."

He remembered the lectures well.

"Men only want glorified slaves. They'd love to have women who are content in the house with the children. I don't know where you find a woman like that. A woman needs her independence. And if she can't find the right man, she needs to live alone. The only worthy man is a man who makes money and doesn't need hers, who leads the family by doing what she tells him to do. A man who doesn't bore her with his opinions. What does he know? A woman should tell her husband what his opinions are. That's what makes a marriage work.

"But then these women decide they want what *they* want. What do they know about what they want? I know what they need. You just watch, they'll do what they want, see who they want, and stay single forever and own cats when they're old and wish they realized I am the wisest and kindest woman they ever met. They'll wish they listened to me."

"I wish I didn't have to listen to her," Vi always said after one of her sermons on how people always failed to see her extraordinary wisdom.

"Same for me," Debbie agreed. "When I move out, I'm going to be the opposite of her. My husband will want to come home and be with me and never ran away."

"I don't think Father ran away," Vi mused. "I think she drove him off, like all her boyfriends."

"I wish I was old enough she would drive me off," Franklin added.

They both smiled at their little brother and they group hugged before going to their rooms to escape their mother, who was now talking to herself, repeating the same lecture she recited to her children earlier.

Vi was the one who called him to inform him of Mother's death. It was obviously a major inconvenience for either of his sisters to travel home. They both lived too far away and Vi was divorced and had two sons still in school. Debbie lived even farther away with two daughters and a son and although she was still married to her husband, leaving them to travel back to that house was not something she wanted to do.

Both sisters agreed that there was nothing in the house they wanted so Franklin could have anything he wanted, sell the rest and pocket the money for his extra effort. They all agreed to trust his judgement with their inheritance so all he needed to do after that was fix anything that needed repairs and clean it up so the house would be ready to sell. Although Mother's will stated that she wanted her children to move back in and live as a family, they all agreed that was impractical. None of them wanted it at all, much less to live there. The house held no happy memories for them. Only faded nightmares of forgotten misery. Franklin doubted he would ever see his sisters again. The three of them only kept up with each other through social media and they were all content with that.

Although Franklin lived closest to Mother, his home was 350 miles away in Vicksburg. His son, Kenny, and daughter, Zelda, lived with his ex-wife who reminded him of Mother sometimes. He had no intention of moving back here either. He wanted to be near his children in case they needed him.

It was an old two-story house, built just after World War II when America was booming. The neighborhood was still nice enough, but Mother's house was certainly the one that needed the most work. The yard was overgrown with ripped pages of newspapers caught between the high grass and chipped brick of the house. The roof had to be replaced. The driveway was cracked and stained with oil and other car fluids. Most of the outside could be handled with a few cosmetic repairs, but he worried about the inside. Mother was meticulous in her appearance of both herself and the house. If the outside was like this, what was waiting for him inside?

He walked to the front door, happy to see Mother's precious screen door was gone. The screen had decorative whorls shaped like rearing horses and it was her most prized possession. He almost heard her raging at him, *Lift the screen from the bottom you lazy little good-for-nothing. Don't you dare scrape my door on the bottom. I don't want any scratches. That door should last forever.*

He almost wished it was still there, just so he could scuff it a little.

It took some persuading, but he managed to unlock the front door. The familiar scent of something vaguely unwholesome greeted him almost like the odor of decay, like a little mouse died and was decomposing just out of sight. The house always smelled stale and unpleasant when he lived here and obviously nothing changed. He left the door open to air it out, also aware of how his mother would disapprove of that. *You're letting all the flies in.*

At least the cool autumn temperatures drove the insects into hibernation. The floor was as dusty as the furniture. Mother's caretaker obviously didn't consider keeping the house clean a priority. He wanted to talk to her, but she quit the job abruptly and returned to her island home in Barbados the day the old woman died. No notice or indication of her intention.

Probably needed a vacation after dealing with Mother, he thought to himself.

The door led into the living room and beyond that stood the kitchen. To the left was the Master bedroom and the spare room where the caretaker took up residence. To the right was the bathroom, snuggled underneath the stairs.

He headed to the kitchen first. The back door had a secure window in its upper half and he could see his reflection as he approached it. The refrigerator was the same old one from his childhood, avocado green. A large magnate shaped like a daisy caught his attention. It held a picture from his childhood. His mother stood behind him and his sisters, the only one of them smiling. A caption written in whimsical cursive underscored the photograph, curving up in a 'u' form, supposedly resembling a smile. "Like a flower grows in the sun, so does our family in love," it read.

"What a lie," he said out loud. He wanted to rip the offending magnate off the fridge and smash it into the floor but he didn't. It wouldn't accomplish anything.

A blinking red light flashed in the corner of his eye. Mother didn't use a cellphone; she still had a land line with an old-fashioned answering machine attached to it. He sauntered over and pressed the play button.

"Welcome back." It was a man's voice, eerily familiar, though he couldn't quite place it. It belonged to someone he knew.

"Welcome back," he repeated slowly. It wasn't possible for two words to sound any more chilling.

"Anyone there?" he called out but only silence answered him.

He shrugged. No sense in letting the house or Mother's memories get to him. He pulled out a notebook and pen and began what he called 'the walkthrough,' where he would write notes about what needed to be done to make the house desirable to a buyer.

He started with Mother's bedroom which was always a forbidden space to him and his sisters as they grew up. Somehow, as he opened her door, he didn't feel right going in there. Some vestige of his childhood made him think he was doing something wrong by being in the master bedroom. It was just a room. The stale air hung heavy with the nasty smell of excrement. Next to the bed, a waste can held a few dirty adult diapers. He grabbed a towel and hurried it to the large garbage can outside. When he returned, he drew open the drapes and pushed the window back to let in fresh air.

The sheets she died on, still attached to the mattress, lay stained with some black fluid that must have leaked out of her body after she died. He quickly noted that the mattress had to be removed immediately, along with springs and sheets. The room still smelled bad enough to make him queasy, so he decided to inspect it more completely the next day, after it aired out.

All traces of the live-in caretaker were gone when he walked into the spare room. The curtains were drawn tight and the room's atmosphere hung gloomy with an almost sad feeling to it. It felt lonely to him, but something bothered him about it. Something was watching him and it didn't want him to leave.

He shook it off and inspected the bedroom. It was straight and neat with the bed professionally made and topped with fluffed pillows set perfectly in their cases. The dresser and nightstands were empty and most likely dusted right before she abandoned her job. The closet revealed an empty clothes bar without even a hanger. He closed the door and started to leave when his eyes fell on an antique box in the front corner.

He frowned as he examined it. He didn't remember it from his childhood and he knew he wouldn't forget something so unique. It had to be a toybox; it couldn't hold much more than a pile of some child's precious treasures.

It was painted blue with strange filigrees on the sides. An arc covered a large V shape in the center of the top, enclosing a lidless eye that stared out into the room. The blue iris even had a black pupil and highlights to suggest roundness as it stared out blankly at him.

"Creepy," he muttered out loud after he examined the mysterious box.

Mother didn't allow them to have toys. She hated clutter and toys littering the floor would annoy her if they had any. But why have them? They would eventually grow older and not want them any more anyway. Why bother?

He fumbled with the clasp and opened the box. As he suspected, it was filled with old toys. Some were soldiers, some were circus animals. He picked a stuffed bear up to examine it. It had a soft smile on its soft fur and smiling eyes. His sisters never had stuffed animals because Mother didn't like them. They should all cuddle with Mother and not some soft toy.

He wondered about these toys. Did they belong to the caretaker? If so, why didn't she take them with her when she left? Did Mother start collecting old toys after he left? If they were a collection, why didn't she put them on shelves for display?

He took a few out and placed them on the dresser to examine them a bit closer. Most of them were simple wind-up toys. Turn the key and watch them walk. The ones he wound up all worked. They all walked off the edge of the dresser and he caught them as they fell. He smiled as he put them back in their toybox.

Kenny and Zelda might like them if he cleaned them up, but he knew his ex-wife wouldn't let him give them anything and she had total custody. He didn't even have visiting rights. He supposed he could send the toys to them in packages, but he shook his head at the thought. New toys would be better. Besides, toys like this wouldn't impress them. They were already playing video games and Franklin knew that old toys like these would quickly vanish from their house to reappear on the shelves of some thrift shop. He doubted if they would even appreciate the gesture.

After opening the window, he left the room, ignoring the tapping sounds in the toybox as he closed the door. The upstairs consisted of two bedrooms and a bath with a large linen closet at the end of the hall. Vi and Debbie had to share a room since they were the two girls. Franklin got the smaller room for himself.

All the rooms had a spartan, unused appearance. Mother wouldn't allow any of them to hang posters or pictures because she didn't want thumbtack holes in the walls. Vi tried taping up a picture of David Cassidy, but it didn't last. Scotch tape might make the paint fade. Couldn't have that. Or collectables. No baseball cards for him or magazines for his sisters. Too messy. Mother did allow them to have books since reading improved the mind, but she chose the books they read (more accurately, the books that they read in the house) based on how elegant the covers appeared. Any book Mother found that she didn't buy for them was immediately destroyed. Some books were degenerated and damaged the intellectual development in children. And children needed their mother to protect their impressionable minds from the cultural decadence of other people.

The problem was that Mother always brought home books that were two years too young for them or the 'classics' like *The Wizard of Oz*, that were written for another time and generation. Vi did most of her pleasure reading at the library or at a friend's house. He and Debbie followed her lead, though Franklin eventually abandoned literature entirely and started playing sports. At least until Mother found out about that activity and stopped him in his tracks. His father played sports and left his family high and dry. Mother didn't want Franklin to follow that kind of lead.

He shook his head at all those memories as he opened his sisters' closet door. *A Book of Memories*, covered in dust, was on the top shelf and he dragged it down to look through the old pictures of the family. Fifty-six pages, four photographs per page. Not one smile. He wondered if smiling was a symptom of cultural decadence.

He strode back downstairs and to the kitchen, opening the door to the basement. One of many irritating things about the house was that the builders located the light switch at the bottom of the stairs. It wasn't a feature unique to this house; all the homes in the neighborhood were wired that way. Nobody knew why, they just knew it was annoying.

The front half of the basement was used almost exclusively for storage. Franklin imagined the old Christmas ornaments were still there, maybe some other things too good to sell or throw out, too unimportant to keep upstairs. His parents converted the back half into an apartment for tenants long ago, with a kitchenette, a full bathroom and enough leftover room for a bed and furniture.

It proved to be a bad investment because the tenants never stayed long. Too many rules to follow for a dark, windowless room. That, along with the fact that they had to enter through the kitchen to get there, was enough to doom the project. Vi wanted to move down there, but Mother always declined that idea. They could never get another tenant if the room was occupied.

He had to move boxes of old clothes out of the way to get to the door, along with old children's furniture Mother never wanted to part with. He remembered the key was hooked onto a nail just to the side of the door and he wanted to see what Mother stored in the old apartment. He would have to come back, he sighed. The nail was there, but not the key. He would have to look for it later as he sorted through all these things to see what he might sell and what needed to be hauled off somewhere.

He hurried back up the stairs after he turned off the light. He wanted to get to his motel room before dark. He could spend the night here, but the house held too many memories he'd rather forget. As he walked past the kitchen counter, he noticed the answering machine was blinking.

He frowned. He didn't hear the phone ring and it took six rings to even go to the machine. He shook his head as he pressed the play button.

"Hope you stay." It was a woman's voice, but not his mother's. It had a clipped accent, almost British, he thought.

"I don't plan to stay a minute longer than necessary," he said aloud to the machine or the house, he didn't know which.

He locked the door behind him and hurried back to his motel room to clean up. His cell phone rang as he stepped out of the shower. It was Lazlo Greene, the realtor.

"What did you think?"

"I didn't see anything that needed major work," Franklin replied. "No water leaks, no signs or smells of the basement flooding. I'm thinking, by the end of tomorrow, I can sort out all the stuff I want to sell and get the rest hauled off."

"Good, I'll get the fixtures replaced and a couple of

coats of paint, a little landscaping and I'm pretty sure we can get it sold by the end of the month. It's a cute little older neighborhood. No crime to speak of. Most young buyers are looking for something bigger, but this is close to downtown, near all the shopping anyone would want. Good schools and a fully furnished apartment downstairs. We'll get top dollar, you watch. They'll be fighting for it."

"Speaking of the apartment, I didn't find the key. It's usually on the nail by the door."

"That's where I thought it was. Double check the kitchen drawers. I think she stored things like that underneath her phone."

"Okay. Speaking about the phone, there was a message on it when I got there and another one when I left, but I didn't hear the ring."

"Something must be wrong with the answering machine. Vi had the phone company turn off the line last week."

He arrived the next day with a dozen boxes to begin the purge of useless and unsellable things. He wanted to start downstairs in the apartment since it would be too dark and gloomy down there after dark. He opened the kitchen door and was relieved that the house smelled much better today. He put the boxes on the counter and opened the drawer to begin his search for the downstairs key when he saw the answering machine's red-light blinking.

He pressed the button without thinking, although he remembered Greene's remark that the phone was shut off and whatever message he heard would be something long in the past.

"Where are you sisters?" It was Mother's voice, cold and high pitched, like most women's voice sound as they get older.

"They're not coming," he snorted, wondering why he even bothered answering the question.

This must have been an old message, for when they all lived together. Then it occurred to him: they didn't have this machine when they all lived together. He shook the anomaly out of his head and opened the drawer to rummage through it, looking for the key when his cellphone rang. It was the contractor who was hired to do whatever work needed to be done to make the house ready to go on the market.

It was a short conversation. They agreed to meet the day after next, when everything was sent out to the consignment store or junkyard.

"Well," he said with a soft voice when Franklin explained about the locked apartment, "if you can't find the key, I have a locksmith who works cheap and he can get it rekeyed for you. Honestly, I expect you to find a few more problems as you go through everything. Everyone does."

The light was blinking by the time the call ended. He hesitated for just a second, then pressed the button.

"I have a surprise for you, Frankie," came a familiar man's voice.

Although his father left home before he was five, he knew it was him. Only his father ever called him Frankie. Mother called him Franklin and his sisters shortened it to Frank.

"I don't want a surprise," he said slowly, his eyes darting around the room.

Nothing was there. Of course not, he was all alone in an empty house that held nothing but bad memories for him, playing with a broken answering machine. He was imagining things were happening that weren't real at all. He was almost scaring himself, in fact.

He heard the noise from upstairs.

Clickity-clicky-click. Clickity-clicky-click.

It sounded like something was scurrying across the floor. A mouse? Too loud. He doubted he would ever hear a mouse upstairs from down here. Maybe a squirrel got in the house through one of the open windows. He frowned at the thought. That meant the rodent chewed through the screen. He didn't want to deal with the needless expense.

He hurried up the stairs, hoping to catch the pest with his hands and throw it out. He didn't want to call an exterminator for a squirrel, but he would have to if he couldn't take care of the problem by himself.

But what greeted him was not a rodent. It was one of the toys from the box he discovered in the caretaker's bedroom. A clown, all wound up, was walking jerkily toward him, with a glossy white head and a red mask that covered his eyes and mouth. Long red hair covered the back of his head while the rest was bald. His ears were way too big for the head while the shoes were almost as long as its height. With each step, its eyes opened and closed while its mouth alternated from grin to frown and its elbows jerked up and down. He almost shivered at the sight of it.

What kind of a toy is this? This thing would scare a child, he thought, *it almost scared me.*

He picked it up, almost to prove to himself that he wasn't afraid of it. It kept squirming mechanically in his hands, continuing his walk until the gears wound down. The first thing he noticed as he examined it closely was the teeth. They had a creepy appearance, like they were real teeth glued into the mouth and they seemed to be sharp.

Definitely not a child's toy, he repeated to himself as he walked the still squirming clown downstairs and put it in the toybox with the other toys.

The red light blinked on and off when he returned to the kitchen. Another message from the past being offered to him. He pressed the button before he gave it any thought.

"I like the house the way it is." It was a man's voice, but not his father's. It had a familiar sound to it though. He knew he heard it before but had no idea from where.

He was not nervous about these messages anymore. He was angry at himself for thinking they were anything more than old messages that were being played back randomly. How could he even think it was anything else?

"Well, guess what?" he said defiantly to himself. "I'm selling it. You'll just have to get used to the new way its's going to look and the new people who'll be living here."

With that, he grabbed a few boxes and headed to the basement to begin clearing it out. Four hours later, he felt satisfied that the basement was complete, except for the apartment since he never did find the key. Another message was waiting for him when he came back upstairs. It didn't surprise him, of course, he was used to them by now. He tapped the button as he washed his hands in the sink.

"You have nothing to worry about, Franklin. Mother will always be here for you."

"Oh my God, no," he shivered.

His mother's voice didn't sound like a recording. He felt as though she spoke to him from just behind his back. He spun around, but he was still alone. He dried his hands on the kitchen towel and dug his keys out of his pocket. Time to go.

Under no circumstances did he want Mother to always be there for him. She was always there to destroy his life, to force him to live the way she wanted. Her controlling fingers were everywhere, making sure he lived the life she wanted for him, without concern for him or what he wanted. He was content knowing she was far away, on the other side of life's curtain. He hurried out of the house, locking it behind him. Tomorrow, he planned to unplug the answering machine and throw it away. He never wanted to hear her voice again.

"I think the house is haunted," he was speaking to Debbie on the phone from his room.

He had a long shower and his favorite dinner along with a few drinks to relax and was able to discuss the day's events rationally, even if he slurred a few words. He always spoke to Debbie first about Mother, even though Debbie never claimed the woman to be her own parent. She was always 'his' mother. Vi didn't go that far, but she was always impatient and dismissive to him. Franklin wondered sometimes if maybe Vi was as controlling to her own children. Like mother, like daughter. It might explain her divorce.

"Haunted?" Debbie repeated quietly. "All the more reason to get rid of it. Your mother was always controlling and evil when we lived with her. It doesn't surprise me she'd want to come out of the grave to haunt us if she could figure out a way. You be careful in that house. I don't want to have to go there if you get hurt."

"Are you stupid or something?" Vi asked in her calm but firm tone. "I have a suggestion for you: Don't press the button on the answering machine. Problem solved. In fact, you can pull out that machine and phone. What is it? A rotary dial phone? Too old to be worth anything. Not old enough to be an antique. Just toss it and the answering machine in the trash. I don't think anyone in the world wants to listen to old messages, except you, and all they do is creep you out."

"I don't think they're old messages."

"You still don't have to press the button and listen to them. Just get what you want out of the house or sell it as is and have a realtor take care of everything. Or just go in there and get the job done. You can do it, Frank. Don't be a push-up bra."

"Making mountains out of molehills," he smiled.

It was an old joke between them when the girls started puberty and he was too young to understand.

The next day he arrived early to clear all the diapers out of Mother's room. The answering machine was blinking. He would have slid it into one of the boxes, but he figured he would do that last, after he got Mother's room clean and disinfected.

"The phone was turned off already," he said aloud to no one in particular. "And I'm not getting sucked into anything weird today."

His cell phone rang. With a sigh, he dropped the boxes and pulled it from his pocket. It was Lazlo Greene.

"I hate to ruin your day, but the agent from the furniture consignment place cancelled. Her daughter got sick and she's staying home with her. She promises tomorrow for sure. She can have her sister watch her tomorrow. It's her day off."

"I'm in no hurry."

He was in a hurry. He wanted out as soon as possible. That message was on the machine, waiting for him and he didn't want to hear it. His only goal was to get through the day and get out of here.

He finished her room in less than two hours. Her jewelry looked cheap, but for all he knew, it may be valuable antiques. He consolidated it all in one box and left it on the bed as he hauled the diapers and ruined linens to the garbage can.

He stopped short when he returned. His jaw dropped in shock as he stared at the kitchen counter in disbelief. The friendly Teddy Bear he saw in the toybox was on the counter. Slouched forward, one paw on the answering machine's flashing light. Although he didn't see the bear's claw push, he heard the machine whirl to the next message.

"Join me."

He ran out the door.

Although he thought about simply leaving the house to Greene to sell for him, he decided he would face his fears and find out what was happening in the old house. If Mother was still there, he would stand up to her instead of running away.

The next morning, he strode into the house wearing a two-foot Irish cross around his neck for protection. The bear sat on the counter next to the answering machine, whose light patiently blinked at him.

"Mother?" he called out softly as he approached her room. "It's time for you to go to your reward, don't you think? Vi and Debbie and me, we're all grown up with kids of our own. We're not supposed to stay here."

The machine clicked on behind him. He turned to listen as the bear stared impassively at him from the counter.

"You will be with me."

"No, we still have our lives to lead. Mother, go on without us. We'll catch up. It's the natural order of life."

Clickity-clicky-click.

The circus clown was lurching at him in that clumsy gait designed to amuse a child. Franklin sighed. Although he knew he should be terrified of all this, somehow, he wasn't. He bent down to pick the ambling doll only to feel dozens of needle-sharp teeth bite into his hand. He yelped and jerked back in pain, dropping the toy back on the floor. It kept coming toward him, so he kicked it back into Mother's room, closing the door behind him.

A quick inspection of his hand revealed the attack drew only a little blood but mostly small indentations of the clown's teeth. He frowned. Even his cross didn't protect him from this. He only wanted to get out of there now.

"Hello?" A woman's voice called from the door.

The consignment lady walked into the kitchen. He hurried back to greet her.

"It's a simple arrangement," she assured him. "We take everything you want us to have. I represent the furniture section, but the clothes will be handled at our sister shop. It's right next door and they're connected."

He walked through the house with her, keeping his eyes and ears open in case something else happened. But nothing was going to happen to her. Mother only wanted him.

"We fix everything up to make it salable and then we sell it. You get 75%, we get the rest, as well as our expenses. I doubt we'll have much of that to worry about. The furniture seems to be in perfect condition and the toys are adorable. Then the buyers can fix it up to be everything they want it to be. I imagine when all this furniture is out and the walls gets painted, this house will sell in the first week, depending on what you ask for it."

He signed the papers and she left. He decided to leave the door open after he watched her return to her car.

"No changes allowed, Franklin."

Mother's voice had a scolding pitch to it. He remembered that tone well because she always slapped him whenever he heard her speak like that to him. It was the same with his sisters. But she couldn't do that now.

"I can do anything, Mother. You raised me to be independent and take care of myself."

A crinkling tinkle sounded beneath the bear and answering machine. He glanced down. It was a key with a wire wrapped around it. The key to the apartment. He bent down and scooped it up.

"I raised you to be my little boy," the machine contradicted him.

He shivered as he stood back up. He grabbed a box and slid the phone, answering machine and stuffed bear into it. The bear seemed to snap at his hand as it fell but lay still in the bottom of the container. Franklin shut the box in a French fold and hurried down the stairs to the apartment. He must have passed some kind of test to have her return the key to him and he wanted to see what she stored in that closed off space.

Although he noticed an unwholesome odor when he inserted the key, he was unprepared for the stench of the open room. Six chairs sat around a small table, centered in the cramped space. This room could never be an apartment. It was no bigger than a closet. Three of the chairs, occupied by decayed corpses, dominated his sight. One was little more than bones held inside a red plaid shirt.

Franklin remembered the shirt. It was his father's favorite when he wasn't working. He never abandoned his family. He was murdered by Mother and she must have dragged his body down the stairs to this room. No wonder Vi and Debbie shared their bedroom and Mother never allowed one of them to move down here.

The second body was a black woman, bloated inside a nurse's blood-stained uniform with bulging eyes. A carving knife stuck out of her throat. Mother's nurse never went back home. Once she was under Mother's orbit, she was doomed to stay forever, even in death.

He knew the third body, though it was barely held together at all. It wore a necklace of bird skulls. Mother's boyfriend from Neuville. His skull grinned at Franklin as the terrified man slammed the door shut. The door automatically shut and locked behind him, not that he noticed. He raced upstairs to get away from this hellhole. He would call the police from his car. He would fill out reports at the station. He would call his sisters from the motel. But he was never setting foot in this house ever again.

He stopped short in wide-eyed wonder when he reached the top of the stairs. All the toys from the nurse's room were on the kitchen counter, waiting for him. The back door was closed. Worse than that, the reflection of his mother's angry face leered at him from its window. From the box on the floor, the answering machine clicked on and he heard his mother's voice.

"I only wanted us to stay together as a family. Forever."

Debbie and Vi met in the airport coffee shop after her plane landed.

"Any news about where Frank ran off to?" Vi asked.

"Not a peep. He left the car in the driveway and walked off somewhere."

"I spoke to Lazlo Greene," Vi said curtly to her younger sister. "Franklin signed the papers to sell all the clothes and furniture, but then he locked up the house and ran off. You know, Frank called me last week, said the place was haunted."

"I know. By Mother."

"A grown man," Vi sighed.

"Don't be hard on him. Living with Mother was probably worse for him than us. Remember, we all shared in her wrath, but we left as soon as possible. He was alone with her for years. The only target for her."

"He should have manned up. At least for this little task."

"Maybe it wasn't so little. The house holds a lot of pain for me."

"Let's get a cab and get this done. I have children at home."

"You left them all alone?"

"They'll be good. They know what'll happen to them if they aren't."

The house smelled fresh and clean when they unlocked the kitchen door. Everything was immaculate, the counter wiped down, the floor mopped. They could still smell the pine cleaner. The phone and answering machine stood on the counter, the red light blinking for them. A stuffed teddy bear sat next to them; its face drawn back in a friendly smile.

"That's the phone and answering machine," Debbie whispered. "The one he made such a fuss about."

"Just a broken old piece of crap," Vi muttered, pressing the button to prove she was not afraid of it.

"So glad you came back home," Mother's voice welcomed them.

"We're not," Debbie replied.

"Double for me," Vi added. "We're just seeing if Frank's still here or where he is. His children are worried about him."

"So are we," Debbie added, then she turned to Vi. "Who are we talking to?"

"Ourselves. You look upstairs, I'll take this floor, then we'll search the basement."

Five minutes later, they both met back in the kitchen.

"Mother still loves you," the machine played without being touched by either of them.

"I can see why Frank got nervous," Vi conceded.

"Yeah, I'm nervous too."

"Let's see if he's downstairs and get out of here."

Debbie refused to go down the stairs in the dark so Vi rolled her eyes derisively and scampered down. Although her older sister made a lot of noise, Debbie thought she heard a clicking sound from upstairs. She shivered at the thought of going to investigate it but didn't have to.

"Can't you see the light is on? Hurry up. I want to get back home," Vi called to her.

It was a fruitless search. Other than a stale, unwholesome smell, there wasn't anything down here that gave them a clue to Frank's whereabouts. They were disappointed the key to the apartment wasn't on its hook.

"We'll have to look for it upstairs," Vi commanded and she turned the light out, making it clear that they would return together, using the kitchen light as a guide.

Debbie stepped into the kitchen first and simply stopped, forcing Vi to push her out of the way. Dozens of toys, stuffed animals, wind up soldiers that stood at least a foot high, a clown, and other playthings greeted them with hostile, staring glares filled with malevolence.

The click of the answering machine came next.

"Mother wants you all here with me. Forever."

The sisters both screamed as the toys attacked.

Accidents Happen

I work in a research facility. I have a simple job: greet visitors, call their host or hostess and give them a plastic badge to make them look official. Sometimes, I chat with them until they are escorted into the facility. When folks try to gain entry without an appointment, the guards out at the gate stop them and, sometimes politely, tell them to leave. That way, I don't have to deal with pushy salespeople or reporters.

It's a nice job. I'm allowed to read, make phone calls and leave to get snacks when I want. I can put up a "Be Right Back" sign and walk around the facility to get exercise, though my superiors insist on calling that a patrol. I can go anywhere in the building I want, except the clean rooms. The people who work there think I'm dirty.

Since I have so much free time, the scientists occasionally ask me to help them out with special assignments. Some, like picking up or delivering lunches to the scientists, don't bother me. Others, like donating small vials of blood for them to use in their experiments, are not high on my 'fun things to do' list. I let them pull some fluid out, since they might use it to clone me. The world could use a lot more 'me's' in it. But I never let them put anything in since accidents happen. I really don't trust scientists. They look at me the same way they look at their lab rats.

As you may expect, some scientists are friendly and some are not. Quite a few of them assume that since security guards wear officious uniforms, we must be ignorant morons. That's understandable. After all, in my opinion, everyone who wears a lab coat is an overeducated idiot. It's all a matter of perspective.

I also have no interest in microbiology or the effects of unfiltered cosmic rays on cellular development. As such, they think I'm dull. With a few exceptions, I think they're all boring. As I said before: perspective.

Dr. Steven Hazard was one of the good ones. He insisted that I call him Steve. And I was always Ray. Not Raymond, or Mr. Ryder, or officer, sheriff, or deputy. He never tried to act like he was better than me, even though he had Ph.Ds. in biology and chemistry while all I had was a high school diploma.

Steve and I went to high school together though he didn't seem to remember me. I couldn't forget him. He was the smartest student in school and our class valedictorian. I finished 221st in a class of 773. I was smart enough to graduate, but too unimpressive to be memorable. Since I did not impress anyone academically and lacked ambition, I spent two years in the Army. Then I had my first goal in life: get out of the Army.

The Army always wanted good men to follow orders and keep their mouths shut. I could follow orders well enough, but I kept my mouth open and eventually I parted company with the military. It was a mutual decision. They didn't like my attitude. I didn't like their stupidity.

In the twenty years since we graduated, Steve became a wealthy and respected research scholar and I became…me.

Not that there was anything wrong with being me, of course. I have a skill set of my own that none of the scientists can match. It's just that it doesn't earn me any money.

I know rifles and pistols inside and out. I tried to point out the mistakes my Army trainer was making, but he didn't appreciate my efforts. We developed a mutual disdain for each other, but nobody in the service sympathized with me.

My strongest skill is that I also know the best fishing spots out here in the Atchafalaya Basin. The whole State of Louisiana, for that matter. Sometimes, I guide rich tourists around the bayous when they want to see nature without worrying about getting lost or eaten.

If they're interested, I show them my gun collection, most of which I inherited from my father. I have big game rifles and even a World War II bazooka in mint condition. I only show it to friends and never hunt with it. It wouldn't leave much meat on any rabbit I killed.

Right now, I am content being a security guard. A receptionist would probably be a more accurate term for it. I smile a lot at the visitors when they chat with me, which makes me pleasant and likeable. Then I go back to reading my true crime books, which makes me happy.

Occasionally, I am required to work after hours for the institute doing special projects, which I don't like. That happened one night when my girlfriend Lorna and I were in bed getting a bit amorous and the phone rang. Sadly, she keeps the phone on her side table. And nothing is more important to her than answering the phone, not even amour.

"Leave it," I told her, but she slithered out of my grasp and started talking.

Evening ruined. Mood destroyed. She'd rather answer the phone than get intimate. Talk about ego damage.

I always let calls go to message because there are a lot of people in this world who I would rather not speak to, mostly everyone. And since I rarely answer the phone, I hardly ever speak to anyone.

I call back my girlfriend (or I wouldn't have one for long), my hunting buddies, and a few other friends or neighbors. I never call back salespeople. I feel they should drive up and knock on my door. They make better targets that way.

All right, I'm kidding. It's no challenge when they're at the door. They should be at least a hundred yards away and moving. That's what makes it sporting.

"It's for you," she handed me the phone with a glare. "It's Red."

Red was the security manager at the facility. He was another high school acquaintance. We both played on the football team. He was the star running back and I was a safety. More accurately, I would have been a safety if I actually played. I felt like the real reason the coach had me suit up was simply to keep the bench from getting cold.

Red graduated a year ahead of me and went to West Point on a scholarship. He excelled in the Army and worked his way up to Major. Then the good folks in Washington cut the military budget before he could earn full retirement. However, he made the right connections through the years and landed on his feet here at the institute. Like Steve, he doesn't remember me from high school either but that doesn't bother me. What's important to me is that I stay on his good side. Sometimes, I find it comforting to know that Lorna is his wife's sister. Other times, it's not a good thing at all.

I sighed and took the phone from her and scrunched up on my side. Lorna always liked to tickle me or otherwise distract me when I'm talking on the phone in bed. She believed that the telephone and its equally annoying relative, the laptop, did not belong on the bed even though she kept them close and always prioritized them. Other than that, she believed all social engagements on the bed involved other activities.

"Hey, Red. Hey," I yelped.

Lorna poked my ribs in a failed attempt to tickle me and make me laugh.

"Hey, yourself," he growled at me. "If this isn't a good time, make it one. We have a serious issue here and I am going to need your full attention."

I rolled off the bed and stood up a short distance away, staring Lorna down. That didn't work and she was crawling toward me, messing up the blankets on my side. I snapped my fingers at her and mouthed, "Stay."

That usually worked well with Tanzie, our dog, but Lorna was a bit more independent. She kept creeping toward me with her fingers imitating crab claws while whispering, "Tickle, tickle."

"This is important," I said to her while covering the mouthpiece. "We'll play later."

"You think? Tanzie," she called, while retreating to her pillow in a sulk, "you can trade places with that man tonight. Maybe forever." She stared at me with dagger eyes while the dog positioned herself in my spot. Man's best friend indeed.

"You have my full attention, Red," I sighed. I wanted to add, "This better be good," but common sense stopped me. I did learn some things in the Army.

"We have a problem," he said. "I'm at Steve Hazard's

187

home and we need you here right away."

"Right away? Like now?"

"That's the traditional definition of 'right away.'"

Lorna gave me a sour look and rolled away from me, showing her lovely back. I preferred to look at her lovely front, but she was back in her nightgown and the temperature in the room dropped ten degrees. My traitorous mutt was snuggling her hand for petting purposes.

"Be here in ten minutes and bring your biggest, baddest rifle. Think elephant hunting."

"Elephant?" I asked. "In Louisiana? Did it escape from a zoo?"

"Just be here," he snapped and hung up.

So, I dressed in shorts and my favorite tee shirt in silence. *If You Don't Like My Attitude, Then Go Away* is stenciled on its front, though it was fading. I went to my gun cabinet while Lorna somehow made the room's temperature drop even lower. I unlocked it and slowly took out my baby. It was a Remington 700 North American Custom .375 H&H Magnum 3-round 26" bolt action rifle. A box of hollow point cartridges followed. I clicked on the safety and loaded it. Then I checked it again. I didn't want to get careless with that kind of a killing machine.

"Don't know when I'll be back," I told Lorna after completing my inspection.

"I don't care anymore," she replied petulantly.

"Next time I say, 'don't answer the phone,'" I said sternly, "please don't answer the phone."

"You didn't say, 'don't answer the phone,'" she sulked.

"What did I say?" I was amazed that she would say that.

"You said, 'leave it.'"

I shook my head as I walked out. That kind of logic only

makes sense to a woman.

So, I drove to Steve's house. He lived about ten miles north of me on State Route 77. He inherited a farmhouse that somehow survived the Civil War. It was a nice old house, but it needed some work. Originally, it was only one large, well-built room, which rested about three feet above the ground on concrete pylons. Somebody added an entire second floor sometime later. Whoever built it knew his carpentry very well. The upstairs was solid, though the floor groaned a bit, especially when it rained. The second story was gabled by a tin roof and consisted of three bedrooms, but since he was never happy unless he was working, I turned one into a home lab. I even built a secret closet with a hidden door into one of the walls because I knew he would smuggle some of the work equipment and chemicals. If the institute demanded access to his house, they would never find them there. As long as I didn't know what he did there, I didn't care.

During the depression, a previous owner converted a sagging back porch into a kitchen and bathroom. Its floor felt spongy and I always hated to visit Steve and his wife because I was afraid I would fall through it to the ground. In fact, the only reason I visited him was because he didn't know how to do homeowner things. I fixed the plumbing issues, replaced rotting windowsills, repaired the roof, and all the other important things.

It was a nice house if you liked living in that sort of thing. Maureen, Steve's wife, did not. She was a city girl and wanted everything to be modern and new. She even wanted air conditioning, but Steve firmly told her it would be a waste of money since the house didn't have proper insulation.

The home's isolation, lack of cooling in the summer,

and abundance of biting insects, especially red ants, convinced Maureen to move out. She rented an apartment in Neuville, about twenty miles away, which is probably a bad thing for a marriage.

Steve still lived in his house, waiting for her to come to her senses. After all, the house was big enough for a family and he made enough money to make reasonable upgrades, add another room or two, with enough insulation to allow for an air conditioner. The home was perfect for him. No one could see the isolated building from the road except wildlife and his neighbors liked their own solitude just as much as he liked his. The house was a perfect home for an eccentric scientist and his beautiful wife. He even offered to name it 'Maureen's Castle' in honor of her.

"It's just an overgrown shack," she responded. "And naming it after me would be the ultimate embarrassment."

So, she stayed in Neuville waiting for him to come to his senses. She was determined not to live in that house. It was old and dreary and too big yet somehow seemed cramped for space. She never mentioned this last part until Steve showed her his lab, where he made his weird potions that never did anything useful, as far as I could tell.

Maureen did confide in Lorna that if Steve got rid of the lab and gave her a blank check to remodel the house to her taste, then she'd move back in with him. Lorna thought that would be reasonable. However, Maureen lost Steve after 'blank check.' Her ideas and his income were incompatible.

I pulled up and found Red and Steve waiting for me on the porch, along with a dozen other people from the government. I could tell because they all dressed alike and had the same basic haircuts. The only difference between the men and women was that the women had longer, uninspired hair styles. But both sexes appeared to be cut from the same boring and unoriginal mold of unimaginative career bureaucrat. I parked in the yard because nondescript government issued cars cluttered the driveway.

Sheriff Hamlin Crosby, Hammy to his friends, was loitering with the Washington drones, looking to impress them enough to become one himself. Or at least make their kind of salary. He was talking to a group of disinterested FBI agents. They were easy to identify since the agency's initials stood out on the back of their windbreakers. One or two smiled a bit while Hammy spewed out his verbal resume. Everyone, except Hammy, knew he was trying to impress the wrong people.

Off to one side, two more wastes of humanity chatted with each other. One was a humorless battle-axe who looked a lot like the Medusa. I figured she was harmless enough because I didn't turn to stone when she sneered at my appearance. The man with her wore a tailored suit and had biceps that Hercules would envy. I thought he was a steroid factory, with oversized muscles everywhere. His vacuous gaze made me think he had muscles in his head as well.

Those two wore jackets with reflective letters: FASERD. I knew it stood for Federal Agency of Science and Engineering Research and Development. A lot of their co-workers visited the facility, but they were mousy looking little frumps. These two were obviously from the enforcement branch.

None of the other people advertised their employers. That made them important. Also, potentially dangerous. Government employees from unknown agencies have a lot of power and little regard for their fellow man. I try to avoid them. If these folks ever smiled, their faces would break and their jaws would shatter on the ground, creating quite a mess for some poor janitor to clean.

Red stepped off the porch to greet me. My distaste for his associates must have been obvious, as well as theirs for me. My shirt said it all. He reached out and grabbed my hand before I lifted it for him to shake. That could only mean there were some extremely important people in the crowd who he wanted to impress.

"Good of you to come, Ray," he whispered with an impressive imitation smile.

It had to be fake since he didn't know the difference between a smile and baring teeth.

"Though it would have been better if you dressed a bit more professionally. Now, what we need you to do is—" he looked behind me, "Didn't you bring your rifle?"

"It's in the truck. I find that people are a bit more relaxed when I visit without a weapon that can turn their head into dog food."

"Oh," he said. I think he might have argued the point, but my logic simply overwhelmed him, "Well, go and get it. We really need it tonight."

"It?" I was confused, "Not me?"

"Go," he whispered, and I knew I had sufficiently irritated him.

After I removed my pride and joy from the gun rack, I turned to find Red, Steve and Hammy right behind me. They startled me a bit and left me a little annoyed.

"A little privacy is good right about now," Red said with his customary sneer. He was back to being the Red I knew and disliked, "So, here's what's going on. We have some extremely important people here tonight so all I want you to do is be quiet, listen and follow orders. No snide remarks, no questions. These people can squash you like a bug if you give them a reason."

I glared at him. "What do I get if I'm nice to them?"

He whispered a figure in my ear. I glanced at him sideways. He nodded. I heard it right. I shouldered my prize rifle and we headed toward the house, just as a loud foreign sound pierced through the night.

"Rrrr…to-kay, to-kay, to-kay."

I never heard anything like it. It didn't exactly sound threatening, but it didn't belong in Louisiana. I would have heard it before. It was obviously what we were hunting though.

The other agents scattered off the porch in all directions with their flashlights shining into the night in search of the noise's source. We all converged on the porch after they gave up their less than intensive pursuit.

"That doesn't sound like an elephant," I said, exaggerating my southern accent. I found out a while back that when dealing with the government types, the heavier the drawl, the less work they assign me.

"It's not," Steve replied sadly.

I knew right then and there that whatever happened was Steve's fault and his days at the institute were numbered in single digits.

"I'll take that," one of the drones ordered roughly and actually had the audacity to grab at my rifle.

Nobody does that in Louisiana. Not to me, anyway. I pulled back and with a vicious twist sent him sprawling on his side.

"Oh, no you don't," I replied hotly. "No little paper-pushing pencil neck from Washington messes with my rifle. Do you even know the difference between the stock and the barrel?"

I held it across my chest in a defensive position, hoping he'd lunge at me.

"Oh, this will be a pleasure," the stranger said, taking off his coat.

He was obviously well sculpted and muscular. Not overdone like Hercules over there. I could tell from his body type and aura of confidence that maybe I should have handled the situation differently. I didn't stand a chance against this man without shooting him. And if I did that, I would face some serious consequences.

"Colonel Kinsey," the Medusa commanded. "Stop this macho nonsense immediately."

She saved me. He immediately backed away and retrieved his fallen jacket.

"You," she pointed to me. "We need that rifle now. Play games on your own time." Then she snapped her fingers at me.

That might work for Colonel Kinsey, but not for me. I stood at full height and was about to say something stupid and self-destructive.

"One moment director," Red came to the rescue.

He, Steve and Hammy were at my side and we stepped back a bit to assess the situation. That is when they finally told me what was happening.

"Whew, Ray," Steve said. "Stay calm, man. These people don't take prisoners. Listen. I'm sorry you're involved in this, but you are. Most of these people are with the STSF. You don't want to get on their bad side."

"What the hell is the STSF?" I groused.

"Science and Technology Special Forces," Red answered. "When a scientific experiment goes bad, they come in to clean up the mess. No evidence. No gabby witnesses. No news media. They fix all the problems that need fixing. One way or another."

"There's such a thing?"

"There is," Red said grimly. "And right now, they're assessing you to see how big a problem you are. Now, let's cut to the chase. We have a situation. Steve here was working on an avian growth and development enhancement program."

"I know. He's putting stuff in birdseed to make bigger chickens."

"Well," Steve replied indignantly, "if you want to oversimplify—"

"We do," Red interrupted. "It didn't work."

"On birds," Steve said. "Their digestive cellular structure prefers—"

"It doesn't work on birds," Red broke in again impatiently.

"Rrrr...to-kay, to-kay, to-kay," came the background call, scattering the mob on the porch again.

"But it works good on geckos," Hammy said dryly. "Real good. Thirty feet long good."

I looked down at my elephant gun.

"We don't know how it happened," Steve said, looking at the ground.

I knew what happened. Steve carried on the work experiment here at his home lab. That's why the thing in the woods was here, not near the institute.

"The formula was locked up in my safe at work and you know I have to go through disinfection washes and sterilization mists every time I leave my laboratory."

True. He walked through chemical clouds that killed everything on his skin and clothes without harming him at all. At least, so the folks in management, who don't walk through them tell us. It's unimportant to me. I don't go near any of those things. They're in the clean room and I prefer to be dirty.

"There's no way it could have escaped my lab," he concluded weakly.

The lab at the institute. Not the one here.

That's why the institute has security. We prevent people like Steve from doing something stupid like creating a lab at his house and bringing his top-secret work home with him. Of course, the system might work better when the security guard doesn't do something stupid like help the scientist build the illegal lab.

"Before we begin," I said, "let's go back to the porch so I can see you in the light."

"Why do that?" Hammy asked.

"I want to make sure I'm not in an old black and white monster movie."

They were unamused. It was time to get to work.

"So, where is this thing?"

"Somewhere out back," Red told me. "And just like Hammy, you can't hunt or shoot it. Or see it. Or know about it. And especially, don't talk about it. That's why you're getting such a generous fee for us to rent your rifle. You will have to let Colonel Kinsey take the shot."

The forest roared with the creature's call. It was louder. Probably closer. The Colonel and Medusa were approaching now.

Red whispered to me, "Again, if I wasn't clear the first time, they will eliminate the beast and any other problems they see. So, don't make yourself look like a problem."

I smiled at the problem-killers as they neared, hoping my presence exuded solution to problems.

"Well?" the Medusa sneered.

I had to improve my I'm-not-a-problem aura.

"We have a lot to do tonight. Find it. Kill it. Dispose of it. Remove any traces of it," she glared at me. "And eliminate any complications. Permanently."

"Your eyes have a delightful flash when you threaten to kill people," I said with a sincere smile.

"Just give him the gun," Red said angrily, so I complied wordlessly.

"Don't know why I can't make the shot," I mumbled under my breath.

"You're not supposed to even see it," Medusa snapped. If nothing else, she had good hearing.

Suddenly, to our left, it bounded into sight, dimly lit by the moon and flashlights. Dark gray and over a hundred feet long and maybe thirty feet high. It looked like a cross between an alligator and a brontosaurus. It ran for six steps and stopped, turning its head to both sides while flicking its tongue in and out a few times.

We all stepped back for a moment and just admired this creature, except Colonel Kinsey, who was setting up his shot by resting my rifle on the roof of a car while the creature found its bearings.

I covered my ears and waited for a few seconds. The shot exploded through the night air, shaking the ground as the reverberations settled down. I forgot to bring my earplugs, along with everyone else. I'm sure we all had headaches now.

The bullet hit the poor lizard in the neck, right below the jaw. It screamed even louder than the shot and twitched its tail violently, overturning a patrol car and an unmarked vehicle. It was a good thing I was the last to arrive, otherwise one of those totaled automobiles might have been mine.

It focused its reptilian stare on Kinsey. To the man's credit, he didn't panic. He calmly drew the bolt back, allowing the next chamber to load and fired again, just as the creature charged him.

It was hard to believe he missed at such close range but to be fair, the lizard upended him in its attack. As Kinsey struggled to his feet, the lizard's tongue shot out and wrapped around him, pulling him into its wounded but still functioning mouth. His screams faded into loud chewing sounds. No one could help him. The rifle was too close to the thing for anyone to pick up. It just laid there in the evening dew, getting ruined.

We scattered and hid while the gecko twitched its head back and forth. Maybe it wanted more food. Or more revenge. If he could still see us, we could give him both. Suddenly, it jolted to the parked cars, squashing two of them, and disappeared into the night.

We quickly recovered from the shock and I ran over and retrieved my rifle. After I cleaned the dew off, I reloaded the chamber. Red and Medusa stopped me from chasing after it.

"We need something bigger," Red said. "It's still growing and all that popgun does is get it mad."

"Popgun?" I said, getting angry.

"Never mind," Medusa said. "That thing's already killed six people. I don't need you two posturing. And we need something a lot bigger."

"Aren't you people special forces?" I asked, disgustedly. "Didn't you bring any weapons of your own?"

"We did," she replied. "But we were expecting something smaller, like the size of a car," she gave Red a spectacular glare of pure disdain. I thought I could see the daggers shooting out of her eyes. "But nothing like this."

"Can't you get something from Fort Hood?"

"We could commandeer anything we want from them," she nodded. "But we have enough things to fix. And we don't need any more people involved in this. It swept a car into the Atchafalaya River, killing two people. Of course, we reported it as an accident so it stays quiet. We absolutely cannot have the citizens know this happened."

"I had two deputies killed when it ran over their car," Hammy said from behind.

"Colonel Kinsey was the second FTFS agent to fall in the line of duty tonight," Medusa told me. "All accidents. No monsters. No publicity. No big-mouth witnesses."

"My eyes were shut the whole time," I assured her. "Can't talk about what I didn't see."

"Suppose we appropriate tanks," she ignored me. "We need crews. We can order them to stay quiet, but all it takes is one big mouth. It's the same with planes and helicopters. It's too much risk. We don't need people screaming, 'It's a government cover-up.'"

"Why not? It is a government cover up. Isn't that all you do? Cover up your infinite amount of mistakes?"

"No, we fix problems too," she glared at me.

"Don't be a problem, Ray," I heard Hammy whisper.

"Nobody else can get involved. I can't take the chance of them talking."

"Yeah," I commiserated. "Not to mention that they'd be risking their lives, if that little thought ever occurred to you."

"Isn't it a shame I'm not risking yours?" she seethed. Conversation over.

"Well, if you won't be needing me or my rifle, I think I'll just mosey on home…"

"What about a bazooka?" Hammy asked.

"A bazooka?" Director Medusa turned to him. "You have one?"

"He does," Hammy nodded to me.

"Yeah, well," I said, "it's an antique and I don't have any ammo for it."

"What kind of bazooka?" Red asked.

"An M1A1," I replied while sneering at Hammy the rat. Of course, he would know I had one. I had to register at his office. "But, again, no ammo."

"We can make it work," Red said. "You go get it and I'll make some calls."

My truck was still undamaged so off I went home, where disappointment turned into disaster.

Lorna was waiting for me to return. The dog was in her cage. Candles scented the room. And she was naked in bed, reading *Pammy Parker and the Bad Boys*.

"I've been waiting for you, Raymond, you naughty boy," she said in a low, sultry voice.

"Wait a little longer," I drooled. "I'm still working."

I went into the closet to get my vintage tank killer.

"What?" She electrified the whole house with her rage.

How does she do that?

I came out of the closet, casually petting my rocket launching machine.

"There's a little problem going on up north and Red wants me to help out," I said as I crossed the room.

The look on her face was priceless.

Although Steve lived in an isolated area, Hammy still had all the houses within miles evacuated. The deputies told the residents that a tanker truck loaded with hazardous chemicals overturned on the main road. The institute paid for their luxury hotel rooms without question. That gave us the freedom to trespass anywhere.

Red had several rockets he figured would probably work. Then we checked the bazooka itself and decided it was in good working order. The hunt was on.

Not that I was a part of it. Red, Steve and I stayed in the house with the charming Medusa and a few of her servants, who were under the mistaken notion that their lives were too important to participate. I watched Steve for a few seconds. He acted innocent enough, but he knew he was in serious trouble. If they found out about his lab, he could get serious prison time. If he told anyone I helped him build it, I could lose my job. I felt the same way about him that Medusa felt about me. I could empathize with her now, but I really didn't want to.

We had a radio so we could keep in touch with the hunters. Agent Hercules was the man in charge of the search and destroy mission. Hammy was auditioning for a federal job by acting as the guide.

They hadn't found anything. Aside from a few location checks, the radio was quiet. I went out to the backyard and contemplated the joys and wonders that *Pammy Parker and the Bad Boys* contained for me when I returned home. While daydreaming, I heard the crash of a large tree falling to the ground.

"Rrrr…to-kay, to-kay, to-kay," sounded out. It was near, but not in sight.

"Get them back here," I yelled as I sprinted into the kitchen. "It's in the back again."

Medusa got on the radio and Red, Steve and I ran out the backdoor. The other bureaucrats were right behind us and we fanned out into the night. Red turned west and ran twenty feet or so before stopping to listen for it to make a sound. I did the same, except I went east. Steve, not having any military experience, ran straight into the field, not stopping for anything. We could see his flashlight bobbing as he sprinted away. He could not have been a more perfect target.

"Steve, stop," Red called out. "You're going to far."

But Steve was barely visible now. All I could see were flashes of his lab coat when it caught the moonlight. Yells were coming now from my left. The hunters had returned. They were searching the field with their powerful flashlights now.

We all saw it at the same time. Poor Steve was running right into it. By the time he stopped and reversed his course, that thing's tongue flicked out and caught him. Steve Hazard was no more.

I walked back into the house, head down. Medusa was by the door.

"It's all right," I thought I heard her say softly to me.

Noises screamed through the night. The creature calling out in his confusion and pain. Hercules lining up his men on the bazooka. Within moments, a loud explosion echoed throughout the house. A minute later came another.

It was over.

My bank account tripled because of a mysterious deposit. The Hazard property had hundreds of traps set to catch all the poor little lizards they could find and dissect. The FTFS was certain they were all gone.

The obituary column was unusually long. Dr. Steven Hazard died after inhaling deadly fumes from an overturned tanker truck. So did six other people. Their families all sued a trucking company they never heard of for damages and settled out of court. A gigantic donation of meat was delivered to all the homeless shelters throughout the state. Apparently, it tasted kind of funny.

Maybe three months later, Lorna was in bed and I was getting under the covers when the phone rang just as my lips touched her neck. It was time to revisit *Pammy Parker and the Bad Boys.*

"Leave it," I told her, trying to grab her arm before she could answer. I wasn't fast enough.

She swiped the screen and put it to her ear. "Hello?" she said sweetly as I rolled back, defeated.

She rolled her eyes and tossed it to me.

"It's for you. It's Red," she rolled over and showed me her back.

"Yes, Red," I answered while keeping an eye on her in case she pulled another sneak attack.

"Yeah, Ray," he said. "We found out where that gecko came from."

"An egg?"

"Ha-ha," I could visualize his sneer. "Steve Hazard had a home lab."

"Yeah, upstairs."

"You knew about it? Why didn't you tell me?"

"You didn't ask."

He made some kind of noise that sounded like a cross between a sigh and a hiss.

"Did you know his wife claimed the house?"

"I figured she would. They weren't divorced, you know. She has a legal claim."

"She didn't want a lab. She wanted an office."

"Umm, hmm."

"Well, when we cleaned and sterilized his home lab, we missed a secret closet. She stumbled on it somehow and found all kinds of experimental products. Nothing she wanted, so she dumped everything in the backyard. All that seed he created and all the prototypes."

"Well, you know," I said, "your friends were pretty certain that they got all the geckos exterminated over there."

"Ray," he said, "she threw it on the ground where the ants live."

Maybe

"It's a little fixer-upper just north of downtown," the realtor informed them as he pulled off the freeway. "But it has history. The whole neighborhood has history. But the house I'm showing you could be famous someday. You've heard of Lawrence Towns?"

Ken Greene and Lisa Harper both shook their heads. Ken leaned into her as the car swerved sharply to make a right turn.

"No clue, huh?" the realtor smiled. "He wrote a whole bunch of kids' books back in the 1890s. *Inspired by Elves*. It's about an only child who lived with his parents and the house had elves in it. The stories are about friendship, loyalty and all that good stuff. Very wholesome. Not the stuff you find today. Problem is, in the modern world, wholesome is another word for boring. They've been out of print for decades. Anyway, Larry Towns lived in this house I'm going to show you when he was a little boy. He was an only child and had quite an imagination. If he did share the house with elves, I'm sure they all moved on."

"I think my grandmother read me one of his books when I was little. I didn't know it was a series," Lisa smiled at the memory. "I'll tell you about it tonight, Ken."

"So, the house is old," Ken frowned, ignoring her excitement. "How modern is the inside?"

"Modern enough. A full bathroom on the first floor next to the kitchen and a shower and toilet on the second. That's where the master bedroom is. Electricity. Gas heat. Appliances. Everything you could ask for. And it's as Victorian as you can get. Three bedrooms and the tower can be a fourth, depending on how many guests you have over. New roof. Wired to code."

"We're hoping for some permanent little guests," Ken replied, smiling at Lisa. "To make use of them all."

"Needs some paint," the realtor nodded, unsure of how to discuss the personal hints of his clients.

He pulled to a stop in front of a stereotypical haunted house with high gables, wood tiles, pointed windows, and a steep front porch. It did need paint.

"I love it," Lisa whispered, unaware of the realtor's big smile as he overheard.

"It's less lovable inside," she contradicted herself when they entered the front door. "What happened here?"

"Oh, it's not as bad as some I've seen. The last owner lost his job and the bank foreclosed. He didn't like it."

They both surveyed the wreckage. Holes in the plaster walls stared at them menacingly. The linoleum flooring might as well have been original from the 1890s and it peeled at the corners while little cracks ran through the floor.

"Looks like some bald guy's bad combover," Ken observed. "And maybe a gunfight?"

"No, those holes are not from bullets. He had a hammer and went around pounding everything in sight. It's all very fixable. And the flooring can be replaced."

"And all the baseboards," Lisa added, pointing with her foot at the rotted and ruined molding. "It'll be a while before we can move in, if we do."

"You will," the realtor smiled. "We'll work out something to get you in here if you want it. And the location can't be beat."

"And my lease runs out on the first," Ken added. "I can move in and get it ready before your lease runs out. It'll be fun."

"And getting you into this beauty will be smooth as silk," the realtor assured.

And he was right. The closing was painless and moved quickly. Ken had no fun hauling the tools and plaster filler inside and the chores ahead looked daunting. But they had a candlelight dinner after he wiped off a dusty counter. They discussed their future and Lisa told him what she remembered about *Inspired by Elves*. He feigned interest as he stacked the unopened boxes of floor tile high enough for them to use as makeshift chairs and enjoy their time together. Exploring their new domain gave Lisa a world of ideas about what room would be used for which purpose. They talked about a color scheme and Lisa agreed to pick up the paint. Ken swept the linoleum and threw the chipped pieces and dust into a bin while she washed the dishes. After they snuggled with each other for a few more minutes, she left him in his new 'dust-castle' and went back to her clean and polished apartment.

A cold shower later, Ken crawled into bed wearing his flannel pajamas since winter was near and the room was miserably cold. He made a mental note to have the water heater fixed.

The house may be close to downtown, but the night was dark when he turned off the table lamp. Pitch black. He made another mental note to get a night light so Lisa could find her way to the bathroom after sundown. At least the digital clock display provided some light. Not quite midnight and the alarm was set for six so he could get to work on time.

He should be home by four and scraping up old linoleum for three hours. The other flooring supplies they picked out should be waiting for him on the porch, ready to go. Lisa promised him she'd be back by seven with dinner and praise for all his efforts on the house after an exhausting eight-hour day of processing car loan applications for the bank.

He closed his eyes and imagined Lisa in bed with him, snuggled next him, his hand stroking her breast while she reached down to—

Clickity-clickity-clickity-click.

He opened his eyes as he heard scurrying toenails dash across the floor

Get mousetraps.

Clickity-clomp, clickity-click-clomp.

Big ones.

Clomp-stomp-clomp.

The hell with it. Call an exterminator.

The night returned to silence. Nothing else moved in the house. He relaxed and thought of Lisa, though his vision of her was less erotic this time. He rolled on his side and drifted off into a pleasant sleep in his new home.

House, he corrected, *it won't be home until Lisa moves in and transforms it into an urban paradise.*

The mattress rolled as though something heavy squirmed its way onto the foot of the bed. He yelped and switched on the lamp, expecting to do battle with some kind of aggressive rodent, crouched down to pounce at him in a vicious attack. But nothing was there, or so he thought as his eyes lit on a patch of red. Nothing dangerous, anyway.

Gnomes? Someone put the garden gnomes on my bed? What garden gnomes? We don't have garden gnomes. We don't have any outdoor decorations yet. What am I seeing?

There were six garden gnomes, except they were alive and moving.

"I am Luther, from the kingdom of Goodbath," the tallest one said in a helium-inhaled voice. "We heard a new king arrived in the house of Towns. We beseech thee, oh king. Our princess is sick and we need healing herbs for her from the garden beyond the wall we are forbidden to climb."

That sounded like the greeting the elf king said to the hero in *Inspired by Elves*, Ken remembered from Lisa's dinner conversation.

"We will repay you greatly," Luther went on gravely. "Our grief will be great if the princess succumbs to her distress."

"I'm not a doctor," Ken swallowed.

"We don't want one. We have the ingredients to cure her, all but one that is out of our reach. Please, sir. We will repay you greatly."

In the book, the boy had all his chores done for him the next day and got to wander the town the whole afternoon. That was great for a boy in those days. This dream wouldn't be helpful to him tonight.

Maybe I should humor my sub-conscious and get this dream to go away so I can get back to a restful sleep. That should be enough. As he thought about it, he nodded his head.

The dark room and bed twinkled away in black and gray sparkles. He closed his eyes to keep them safe from the magical hazard. When he felt that the sparks had burned themselves out, he opened his eyes. He was on bright orange grass, standing at the base of a steep knoll. A gray stone wall guarded the top, a bright purple serpent painted across it from side to side. The wall cast an ominous shadow that almost covered his feet.

"Don't let the shade of the bleak wall touch you. You will be depressed and do nothing again until you die. Such is the curse. Come to the other side."

The steep knoll rose almost straight up. While the wall did stand straight, only on this side, it glimmered in a cold golden light with no snake paintings visible and no shadow.

"I suppose I'm looking for something on the other side of the wall," he sighed.

"The red cloverleaf. You will find it easy enough. It's the only clover not green."

He rolled his eyes and stared at the destination trying to imagine a plan of action.

"Plan later and act now," Luther urged.

Ken nodded and began the steep climb, which was easier than he thought. The knoll was peppered with breaks, big enough for him to use as hand and toeholds. He made surprising time. Not unusual for a dream. He had read about people who sometimes were able to control the events of their night visions. Maybe this was his first time at it.

He stood on a thin ledge in front of the wall. At this angle, it stood gray and forbidding. No handholds presented themselves. He rubbed his hand on the wall. It felt smooth as marble all along the side. As he turned the corner, repugnant weeds littered the entire ledge with sapling-thick trunks and droopy brown leaves that smelled of ammonia. He wriggled his nose in disgust as he paced in front of them until, with a sigh, he reached out and grabbed one. It held firm, though tiny thorns pierced into his fingers and palms. He rappelled himself up the wall and used the plants as a brace while using his feet to propel himself upwards. When he reached the top, a beautiful and well-tended garden greeted him. It appeared to be an easy jump down.

He landed in a bed of clovers and rolled over. His feet stung from the landing, but nothing was seriously hurt. It was a short time later when he found the patch of red clover. He frowned. Why didn't he ask how much Luther needed? It was too late now, so he yanked out a handful and trotted back to the wall.

A tremendous roar of outrage pierced the air. A quick glance behind revealed an immense snake slithering after him. It was otherworldly with a shimmering purple back and tusk-like fangs. His adrenalin-fueled surge only kept him slightly ahead of his approaching enemy, who he estimated to be at least 30 feet long, as it gained on him.

With only a few feet left, he leaped as high as he could, hoping his momentum would allow him to scurry up to get a handhold on the top bricks so he could pull himself over to safety. He was shocked when the entire wall collapsed and he found himself rolling down to the foot of the knoll. Lester was there, taking the clover out of his hands. He stood back on his feet, shaky and trembling inside. He turned back and inspected the knoll. The wall stood repaired, as though nothing had happened. The snake repositioned itself as paint on the wall, its tongue flicking at him until its reality turned into a lifeless image.

"Hurry, we must get you back," Luther admonished.

They hurried away into the night and stopped where the land ended in a great cliff that overlooked inky black darkness. They didn't change direction. Luther just smiled at him.

"You did well, Ken Greene," he pronounced it as it was

only one name. "You brought us more than we hoped for. It is time for you to return to your kingdom. You will find your reward there."

"Why didn't you tell me there was a snake up there?" Ken groused.

"I did. I said the place was forbidden to us."

With a force that belied his tiny stature, the gnome pushed the man over the edge and Ken felt himself falling. He twisted, trying to get his feet under him when he hit the bottom. His left leg was elevated, caught on something long and soft.

Did Lester push me back into the snake's den?

No. He felt the rough surface of tile. After reaching down, he felt a blanket wrapped around his leg, no doubt the result of his thrashing about during his nightmare. He untangled himself and felt around for his lamp.

Only an hour passed, according to his impassive clock. He felt dizzy from what happened, or didn't happen, and sat on the bed. After a moment, he went to the bathroom, his feet silent on the stone floor. As he washed his hands, he felt the soap aggravate a few annoying pricks that burned through his palm and fingers. After he examined them, he realized they had tiny thorns that smelled like ammonia embedded in them. He washed them again, more thoroughly this time.

As he started back to bed, his brain registered the difference and he glanced down at his new floor. All the linoleum was gone, replaced by the tile that the store delivered today. He ran through the house, room by room, and wondered at the perfect craftsmanship of every perfect cut, every stone as straight as possible. He turned around and ran back to make sure it was real, then he grabbed his camera phone and sent pictures of every room to Lisa.

When she didn't respond fast enough, he called her and demanded she view his photographs.

"You did all that tonight?" she asked in sleepy wonder. "I was just there five hours ago. You must have had help."

He stopped. He didn't do the work himself. The gnomes obviously tiled the floor as his reward. But how could he tell her that without her wondering about his mental health.

"Maybe," he teased. "Maybe not. Maybe I had some helpful little gnomes stop by and we all worked together on it. Maybe I just had an energy burst. Just for you."

"But why did you put back all the nasty molding? Why didn't you just leave it off? We're still replacing it."

"Didn't think of it."

Maybe I should have grabbed two handfuls of that red clover.

The next morning, the tile still lay there, as perfect as ever. It was nice to walk on a clean, cool floor with no cracks or sharp chips attacking his feet.

"It looks so much better in real life than in those pictures," Lisa complimented him. "I didn't know you had that kind of workmanship skill in you. Maybe you should think of doing this instead of working at the bank."

"Maybe," he smiled.

"Well, anyway," she said brightly, "I'll cancel the tile installation people. I'll wait on the baseboard, just in case you have another energy burst."

"Should I be worried now that you are aware of my home remodeling skills?"

"Maybe," he heard the smile in her voice.

She was impressed. He thought maybe they could do a little more than cuddle after all that work, but she returned to her apartment, leaving him unfulfilled. Another cold shower woke him up just before going to bed.

Obviously, I forgot to get the water heater fixed. Maybe Luther will come back tonight and tell me what's going on in this house. I would really like to know what's going on here.

An almost magical darkness fell soon after he turned off the light. The clock showed midnight and nothing else was visible, not even his hand.

Obviously, I forgot to get a night light.

Tap-swoosh-tap-shoosh-tap.

Footsteps approached him through the dark. He reached and fumbled with the lamp and turned it on, squinting as the light attacked his pupils. A quiet "shh" attacked his ears, like a red-hot knife being dipped in ice water. An explosion of green and yellow sparks vanquished the remaining shadows momentarily and before him stood the most beautiful and elegant woman he ever saw in his life.

"So here you are, a grown man who climbs over my fence to steal the herbs that keep me young and beautiful to give to those thieving gnomes. Then you destroy my little fence and I was the one who had to rebuild it. You frustrated my snake by giving him the scent of food and escaping him. I have come to seek revenge and I will take away your youth and charm to give to myself as restitution."

"Wait a minute," Ken gulped. "They didn't say I was stealing. Just that it was forbidden."

"Why did you think there was a wall there if not to keep them out?"

"I wish I put a little more thought into it, now that you mention it. Maybe we can work out a deal? Some kind of leniency?"

"Maybe," she glanced at him from head to toe, making him wish he wore nicer night clothes.

He may be engaged to Lisa but the idea of a night with her—

"Since I already know you are a good thief, I can arrange a compromise. Go to the Hills of Endless Darkness. There will be three cave openings as you approach. The one in the direct middle is the one you want. Do not stray in either direction or the guardians will see you and kill you. The middle cave has piles of gold. Near the top to the left is a small jewel box. It contains a pair of gold earrings with blinking sapphires embedded in them. Take the box, but I warn you, take nothing else."

"Well, I guess, but how do I get to this Hill of Nighttime?"

"The Hills of Endless Darkness."

"Okay, the Hills of Endless Darkness?"

The room vanished in a silent explosion of blue and orange sparks. He stood alone on a great plain, a small mountain in front of him. She was gone. He spun around to get his bearings. The grassy knoll was barely visible, the wall protecting its peak. But it wasn't a wall, he realized. It was a castle, complete with a towering keep and pointed windows of reflecting glass. He turned back. The hill, although it seemed close, was far away.

He trudged through the orange grass, unaware that he was walking uphill until he reached the crest. There they were, out of sight until now. Three bleak and ominous caves stood there, dark and forbidding. The sight of them made him shiver. The black openings sent out smoky tendrils of inky blackness that rose into the air like fingers of night beckoning him to doom.

"Center cave," he muttered and lined himself up directly in front of his destination.

After a couple of deep breaths, he proceeded. The

ground angled at a pleasant downward slope so he didn't have to try to keep his balance. He closed the distance in minutes, making sure to keep alert to any dangers that may be nearby.

Come to think of it, he shook his head ruefully, *it doesn't matter too much about danger anyway. The only reason I got away from her snake was I reached the wall first. There's no wall here. I have no weapon. Almost anything runs faster than a man. I just need to get her box and run like hell.*

He blinked in surprise when he entered. The darkness vanished as though it was only an illusion visible to the outside. Ahead of him was a veritable mountain of gold. Coins, jewelry, doubloons, bars, and nuggets were piled twice his height. He took a step back but couldn't find anything that looked like a box, so he climbed up to the top of his newfound wealth, laughing at his situation.

I'm literally sinking in gold, he thought as he pulled his feet out of the wealth.

He climbed higher and higher. Just before he reached the top, he remembered her telling him it was on the left. He inched over that way until he found it. A small unadorned wooden box with a gold clasp. He quickly opened it to see if it was the one. The earrings glowed with gold and shimmered with breathtaking blue from the sapphires. He knew he had something truly magical as he closed the box and fastened it shut.

Getting down was easy. His feet stayed on top of the golden treasures and, in fact, he slipped a few times until he landed on his rump at the bottom. As he stood back up, he noticed an incredibly ornate necklace, an eight-sided star held together by gold cords that ran back to a large hasp. The star itself must have been at least six inches from top to bottom. Ken never cared much for jewelry, but he knew

Lisa liked to drip gold and platinum at formal events and this wonderful treasure would be a shockingly elegant wedding present. All Lisa's friends would simply swoon with envy. He quickly grabbed it and ran out of the cave.

A resounding cry of anger filled his ears as he hurried away. A glance back and what he saw terrified him. Black scorpions, the size of rabbits, poured out of the side caves, running straight at him with their stingers curled high up in the air.

He galloped as fast as he could to the top of the hill as he heard their toes swoosh through the grass. He felt a claw on his heel and jumped to his left. A peek over his shoulder horrified him and he swallowed a lump of pure fear and dread as almost a dozen of the arachnids were within inches of him. He smelled them, a terrible odor of agony and death.

He made it to the top of the hill and the noises stopped. He looked behind to see them stopped at the crest of the hill, staring at him with angry eyes. He turned and trotted further away conserving his breath. They were gone when he turned again.

"Thief," a voice called out behind him. "Maybe you think you got away from me? I think maybe not."

He smiled at his victory and hurried back to where the witch-woman left him and waited, fingering his golden treasure. Lisa will be so happy.

"You have my box?"

She was behind him with an angry glare in her eyes and an unhappy frown on her lips.

He held it up triumphantly.

"I said take nothing else."

He blushed with genuine shame as he realized that he not only disobeyed her, but he also stole something of great value. His moment of proving himself to be trustworthy only showed them that he was dishonest and dishonorable.

"I'm sorry. I don't know what I was thinking. Well, my fiancée would like it. That's what I was thinking. Here do you want it back?"

"It's not mine, so take it back home with you. You and you alone will have to deal with what you've done here. And you will not deal with me again."

He stood back in his room. The light still burned and the bed called out to him to sleep. He pulled out his treasure, Lisa's wedding present, and placed it lovingly next to the alarm clock. He slept past his alarm.

The baseboard shone in fresh varnish, all brand new and quality wood. The color was perfect and matched the tile. He ran through the house again, inspecting every room in happy amazement. Lisa will be so impressed with me. We're creating a house in paradise. This was the best investment ever.

He trotted back to the bedroom to get dressed. He was going to be late for work, but he didn't care. Nothing made life better than having a happy fiancée. He froze momentarily when he turned his eyes to the bedside table. The necklace wasn't gold anymore. It was an eight-sided star shaped figure of dust. He brushed it off the table and watched it float and filter to the ground. Lisa would get an ordinary wedding present now. Maybe that's all she wanted.

She was thrilled when she saw the baseboards were complete, but she knew something was bothering him.

"It's nothing, really," he lied. "I think I overdid it a little."

Yeah, I overdid the stealing.

"Poor Kenny," she said with exaggerated sympathy. "Maybe you should take it easy. The house can wait. I'm

218

going to want some of that energy in bed, you know."

He changed the subject. He didn't want her to sleep here, at least not tonight. He didn't know what would happen. He knew that he barely survived his dreams two nights in a row. He didn't want to endanger her because of his stupidity.

"Maybe we should put the house up for sale," he suggested. "With all these improvements, we could turn over a tidy profit and get something bigger. Newer."

"Nonsense. I love this place. I want to live here forever. Don't you?" she seemed hurt.

"Maybe," he smiled.

He left the light on when he laid down. Somehow, he didn't want to fall asleep in the dark. Maybe he wouldn't dream. Maybe whatever world touched this house was angry at him now. Maybe it deemed him unworthy of more visitors. Maybe they were right. He let everybody down, including himself.

He stared at the ceiling while he wallowed in his guilt. He started to become a bit drowsy when one of the room's shadows moved. He jolted up and stared at it. It almost resembled a scorpion. His heart pounded for a few minutes until the adrenalin dissipated. He continued to watch the shadows, all of which stayed perfectly still as though they were only shadows and nothing more.

Maybe you're overworked. Maybe you're overreacting to a dream. After all, the work was all done and you've been tired. Maybe you did all the work in your sleep. He liked that thought.

Yeah, maybe you were sleepwalking and those adventures played in your mind so you don't remember doing anything. That's certainly a possibility. Maybe.

"Argh!"

The scream woke him to a terrible sight. He only saw

ogres in story books from his childhood, but he knew that one stood in front of him. It towered, almost to the ceiling, with black, greasy hair plastered above his forehead. Yellow teeth, dingy but sharp, snarled at him. One eye stood open bulging with hate while the other was half closed, studying him with contempt. The beast stood transparent, breathing out fumes of righteous anger.

"Another would-be king who is nothing more than a common crook. You invade my home and steal my treasure. Now, you will feel my wrath, pretender to the throne but deserver of death!"

"Wait a minute," Ken gulped. "I only repaid a debt. That was what she wanted. A box of earrings."

"And my mother's necklace?"

"I was weak. I wanted it for my fiancée. She loves jewelry."

"All women love jewelry. That means nothing to me. The earrings? I would allow you an opportunity to repay in service. Now, you will repay me another way."

"I'm willing to work with you," Ken whispered to the monster. "It was a moment of weakness. I would love to give it back, but it turned to dust."

"I know. I called it back to me and the dust is left to remind you that you threw away your life for a pocketful of dust."

The giant stared at Ken, its hatred almost a living thing. After a long moment of silence, Ken swallowed hard.

"What can I do to make it right? Maybe we can work things out. What can I do? What do you want from me?"

"Your heart."

Ken swung over to the far side of the bed and pressed against the wall, cornered. The beast simply walked through the bed and stretched out its hand in a quick and graceful motion, ramming its clawed nails deep into Ken's chest. The pain was excruciating and Ken charged with all his remaining strength, pushing himself through the ghostly demon, and fell face first on the bed where he rolled around to stare at his killer.

It had his transparent heart in its hand, still beating, holding it over its head like a trophy as it gazed down while Ken gasped for air. It spun in a circle, then devoured the heart in a few gulps. Ken had the strength to feel his chest and look down. No blood, no wound. Nothing was there.

The ogre was gone when he looked back up. But the pain remained. Maybe he was having a heart attack and the rest was a hallucination. Maybe he would wake up and it would all be gone.

Maybe it was only a dream.

Maybe…only a dream.

Maybe a dream.

Maybe…

"Maybe he had a congenital heart condition the doctors all missed that somehow got aggravated tonight," one of the paramedics told Lisa as they gently placed the covered body in the ambulance. "We'll find out after the autopsy. Maybe it was some condition no one ever knew he had. Maybe all the work he did fixing the house. Maybe…well, something. We'll find out. Maybe."

"Maybe not," he heard a harsh whisper come from the nothingness behind him.

He shivered, not that Lisa noticed. She only stared at the body in shock.

PM 201

Greg Overmier sat in front of the monitors, deep in thought. Nothing was happening. Most everyone in the building sat quietly at their stations, reflecting on the big announcement they read earlier in the day.

Change benefits two groups of people: the rich and the young.

He remembered his father telling him this piece of wisdom in his youth.

Everyone else won't be able to make the adjustments needed to survive, so the rich will buy them out for pennies. The young can adapt to anything until they become change's next victim.

His father was a smart man. It was a shame he couldn't see that when he was younger.

He viewed the cameras again, waiting for the end of his shift. The front lawn was perfect and the Robbie Electronic Solutions sign was in plain view. A familiar car drove into the gate and made its way to a parking spot. His relief was here. He gathered his things and wiped down the counter as he counted the last few minutes.

A familiar click and whoosh sound came from the door behind him. He turned as Ryan Stuart entered the security quarters to relieve him. Stuart was a young man, recently discharged from the Army due to budget constraints. He had sandy brown hair and dark brown eyes that quickly processed everything around him. He still wore a uniform the way the soldiers did. Everything perfect. Not a thread out of place.

"I keep thinking you might want to go home. Anything going on?" Stuart asked with a smile as he placed his lunch in the tiny refrigerator.

Overmier smiled back weakly. He heard that greeting five days a week for over a year now. Stuart needed to work on a better opening line.

"You could say that. Memo came out today. You'll see it. Robbie got bought out. New management will be coming in to set things up their way. No way of knowing if they'll keep us or not."

"I imagine we'll stay. They may make some adjustments, but robotics are changing every day. Everybody screams about corporate spies, so they'll always want security. It's one of the reasons I went into security. These jobs never go away."

"They never pay anything either."

"Every job has flaws."

He turned on the lobby camera. Stella Crenshaw was organizing the desk. Next to her, on a display platform, stood Titan 3, a mechanical robot with radar antennae sticking out of a plexiglass face. He stood over six feet tall with computerized eyes and ears gathering all the movements and information in the lobby. Titan could give basic information to a customer such as directions, usually to the restrooms. If the towels or soap containers were empty, he could buzz a janitor to rectify the situation. He could even walk, though he was awkward and always seemed about to fall. The engineers programed him to simply stand on the display and interact with the customers just to make the insurance people happy.

"Look at Titan. An engineering marvel, but what can he do? Stand and talk. Great for Stella. She doesn't like making small talk to the visitors anyway. Brilliant in some ways, but terribly flawed, just like people."

Overmier grunted, "Two more generations of those things and we'll be on the streets. Then what?"

Stuart shrugged, "Then we do something else."

"It's the 'something else' I worry about."

Promptly at three, Stella left the lobby and headed for her car and Overmier swooshed out the door. Stuart waited until Stella was out of sight then casually strode to her position in the lobby. The security officer manned the lobby at three every afternoon after the receptionist went home. He always made sure she was gone before he assumed the post. Stella made it clear to him that she didn't like security guards. They were beneath her. Rather than listen to her attitude, he just waited until he was alone. Almost alone, anyway. He always had Titan to talk to if he wanted to. He never wanted to though.

He worked throughout the week with no changes in his routine. Changes disrupted his evenings. He still watched his shows, read books, and listened to music in between his patrols. He especially enjoyed the fact he rarely saw his supervisor. Bob Gavin was also from the Army, only he made full colonel when he retired and expected his subordinates to adhere to Army rules and traditions. So much so, he only hired Army veterans. No Navy or Air Force. After all, the Army was the only professional branch of the service. The others were filled with "undesirables." Stuart rather thought Gavin was the undesirable one, but wisely kept his opinion to himself.

Rumors of shake-ups were going around. Stuart heard them all. Either people mentioned them to him or he overheard them. People talk in front of guards as though they weren't even there and Stuart made sure he listened in on the conversations. Not unlike many offices, the security team knew more about the upcoming managerial decisions before they were announced to the masses. But the current rumors seemed to be nothing more than fearful talk. Stuart was content the changes wouldn't concern anyone here.

No further communications were forthcoming for the rest of the week and the talk seemed to be dissipating by Saturday. Stuart had Sundays and Mondays off and didn't think about it until he came back to work Tuesday and realized the new management team did indeed have changes planned. The Robbie Electronic Solutions sign was covered by a red tarmac with stark white letters announcing the plant was now part of Future Visions Incorporated. At least his badge still let him inside.

"Big changes in the works," Greg told him laconically. "One you might even like. The new management team is doing a tour right now. More like an inspection, if you ask me. First change they made is they got rid of your girlfriend."

"My girlfriend?"

"Stella. They wanted someone who was competent, cheerful and smiled a lot. Don't know about competent, but she failed big time on her greeting skills. They offered her a position in Fairbanks, but I think she said no. Too bad for her. I think I could tolerate her up there. That's far away."

"Not far enough."

"On the bright side, they say they have no plans to replace us, so our jobs are safe. At least for now. You know how managers are. They'll promise something today and tomorrow they'll say, 'Oh, the situation changed. My promise is now canceled. But you should still trust me.'"

Stuart nodded as he studied the lobby camera, searching for Stella's replacement. He found her soon enough and zoomed the camera in on her as she sat contentedly at the desk, typing on her computer. She had golden hair and sat with good posture. He imagined her figure was worth a glance, if she would shift her position.

"That's Pam," Greg said from behind him. "Or to be accurate, PM 113. She looks surprisingly real. You'd almost think she's human from up here. She replaced Stella and Titan 3 because she can do both jobs. We'll probably be next."

"Probably not," Stuart retorted. "Titan didn't do anything except stand there and I can easily see a robot replacing Stella. She was useless."

"Because she wouldn't go out with you?" Overmier teased.

"No, that only means she has no taste. She's useless because she has no taste."

"Oh," Overmier smirked. "Silly me. Anyway, my day is done. Have at it. Pammy ain't so bad to work with. You might like your new partner. She charges herself at ten. You'll have an hour to be alone."

"You mean she's working with me in the lobby?"

"No. You'll be back here with these cameras until ten. No need for two of you to be in the lobby."

"But I like it in the lobby. More room. Cooler."

"So, you'll like it back here. More cozy. Warmer. You can still go out and socialize…I mean patrol. Why don't you go meet the next wave of the future?"

"I think I will."

She heard him walking toward her and, out of respect, she lifted expressionless eyes to meet his, a smile already forming on her lips as though she were genuinely happy to see him. She greeted him with stiff slow-motion movements that jerked a tiny bit. Stuart was quite surprised at how human she appeared to be. It wasn't until he was close to her when he noticed all the design flaws. Her complexion and coloring were perfect, but the texture disturbed him. She seemed to be wrapped in clear plastic sheets with cold and dead eyes that stared at him, unblinking. She did not breathe. One of the little things Stuart enjoyed in a woman was watching the way the breasts moved in and out as she took each breath. He liked playing the social game of *Watch the Boobies Without Her Noticing Me Watching the Boobies.* There was no game with her since her small breasts never moved to entertain him.

Still, he had to approve of the rest of her. Her figure was perfect. A tiny bit of cleavage showed at the top of her blouse and her dress clung to her firmly. Her legs were perfectly shaped, although the skin texture was imperfect there too.

"So nice to meet you, Ryan Stuart," she said in a monotone voice that wasn't quite shrill but sounded like a hawk's screech.

"You know my name?"

"I know all the employee's names from the data files," she answered with a polite smile, showing off perfectly arranged and totally dry white teeth.

"That's Pam. It's really called the PM 113, but we call her Pam. The PM stands for Pleasure Model. First generation of this concept. She's a first-generation prototype and the 13th revision. Designed to be an actual human woman. She can cook, clean, wash, dry, walk the dog, and do everything else a man would want without headaches, a need for romance, or food and water.

Everything you can think of to do with a woman, she's willing to do."

Stuart turned around to see a few smirking executives gazing at him with amused eyes. They all had knowing eyes, as though they thought they read his mind and were guessing what he would want to do with the PM 113. He frowned a required greeting. The woman who spoke to him stood almost in front of him, gazing intently into his eyes with her warm green irises almost dancing in some unknown triumph. Maybe she enjoyed the fact that she was young and beautiful with soft tan skin and even features that her perfectly shaped blonde hair framed without flaw.

"I'm afraid I missed your first name, Mr. Stuart," she smiled warmly, and continued in a heartbeat, realizing almost instantly that he wasn't going to provide it. "My name is Paula Model. I'm the Chief Financial Officer. These men are my bosses. Mr. Henry Webster, Andrew Clay and Daniel Jackson. You've already met Pam."

Stuart narrowed his eyes momentarily.

"Yes, Paula Mo-DELL. I pronounced it model when I saw it in print. So good to meet you all," he said with fake sincerity as he shook hands with them.

"What do you think of 'the future,' Ryan?" Jackson asked, deliberately using the guard's first name to show him the depth of their knowledge about him, despite Paula's attempt to deceive him.

"The pleasure model?" Stuart responded slowly. "Well, I think for a man who can't get a real woman, she'd be great in the dark."

"Hmm," Pam exclaimed and turned her back to him as she reclaimed her seat and resumed working, or whatever she was doing.

"I like that," Clay said. "Provided you have a reason. I

like criticism. I don't like negativity. So, what about her do you not find attractive?"

"Eyes, skin, teeth, and voice to start with. The fact that you made an imitation woman just for a man to…"

"Enjoy a bedroom romp together?" Clay completed the sentence. "All men want to have a woman to enjoy life with, but so many women want their careers. They want tall, rich, successful men with high paying jobs and a full head of hair. Athletic, muscular. Not many men meet those standards. What's a short man with average looks and a modest income supposed to do? Pam here can help him with that loneliness."

"I like real women. And, with all due respect, Ms. Model, I can get them. There's lots of older women out there who realize they want a man who can treat them right. A lot of the so-called perfect men aren't always pleasant to be around. I am and I don't have to resort to a silicone love-doll."

His eyes locked into Paula's liquid irises, drinking her in. She was the most attractive woman he ever saw, and even though he knew he was almost 40 with a receding hairline, he didn't feel as if she wasn't aware or receptive to his attraction.

"What's wrong with her teeth?" Clay asked, ignoring the fact that Stuart and the new CFO were lost in each other's gaze.

Stuart blinked, "Look at them."

"Pam," Clay commanded.

The android stood at attention and turned around to face them.

"Smile for me."

She curled her lips back to show her teeth, but she wasn't smiling.

"They look good to me. Symmetrical, aligned, white as snow. Please tell me what your problem is."

"They're dry here," Stuart rolled his eyes as he answered. "Can I touch them?"

"She was made to be touched, Ryan," Paula smirked at him.

He strode over and rubbed his index finger on her front teeth.

"No saliva. Can she open her mouth and not bite?"

"I do not bite, unless it is your desire."

He hesitated, "Not my desire."

She opened her mouth and stuck out her tongue, allowing him to massage inside her mouth and rub his fingers on her palate.

"See?" He held out his dry hand for them to see. "Another term for kiss is 'trading spit' and she doesn't have any because she's a machine. Who wants to kiss a machine?"

"You don't give her credit, Ryan," Clay smirked. "Try again."

Her tongue was warm and wet, as well as the rest of her mouth. Stuart wiped his moist fingers on his pants.

"Her saliva glands automatically activate when a man's lips get near her, not his fingers. Do you like to make her sweat?"

He glanced back at Pam to see her skin glisten with moisture.

"Wherever you want moisture, she can produce it. Without asking. Would you like to feel for yourself? You can reach under her dress if you want, just remember we're in a public place."

"That's okay," Stuart blushed for some reason. "I trust you."

"That's nice of you," Paula smiled. "You'd be surprised what some of our employees are willing to do right in front of us. There's no modesty anymore. It's been replaced with disrespect. In case you haven't noticed, our engineers modelled her face on mine. Did you notice the resemblance?"

She smiled at him. He wanted it to be a lusty invitation, but he was at work and not only could she embarrass him with rejection, she could also get him fired. He looked back at the android who was sitting down again at the computer.

"You're a very attractive woman," he said cautiously. "She's a very attractive machine. And I do see the similarities."

They were almost twins. Both had even features with full lips and curved chins. Their angular noses fit in perfectly with their soft, rounded cheeks. Other than what he pointed out to them, there was no difference between the two.

"You see," Paula went on, the sensual smile replaced with a serious expression, "what our plan is? It's to create a generation of androids like Pam, but without the flaws you pointed out. We can keep the mouth moist so the teeth glisten with her saliva. Our engineers didn't think about it, but you're not the first to find it…off-putting that her mouth looked so dry. We want to reach a whole generation of disaffected young people—and older people as well, who are lonely and afraid to ask a young woman to be a girlfriend. So many young women enjoy being mean to the boys who want to be with them. The boys lose interest in pursuing them because they don't know if it's just that one girl who's nasty to them or if all girls don't want boys like them. But the young men still are sexual creatures with desires.

"That's where we come in. Our next generation of human replacement entertainment devices won't appear to be robotic and will be kind, sweet and encouraging. We want them to look and act like actual people in all respects. Remember, the socially awkward and damaged people need friends and lovers too. Lonely people don't want to be alone.

"And as the customer grows and changes, so will Pam. She can more than walk and talk and do household chores. She can maintain conversations and she learns through interactive communication with her 'boyfriend.' Suppose he takes an interest in…for instance, biology. She will have all information in her memory to encourage, tutor or engage intellectual conversation."

"You mean talking."

"Exactly. Everything you say gets processed and compared to facts. So, if you say England borders Russia, it knows you're wrong and will correct you.

"And the next generation will look exactly as human as us," she gave him another lusty smile. "You can take her out to a movie, go skiing, walk through the park."

"And have sex," he said quietly.

"My male colleagues tell me she's awesome in bed. I would prefer the PM 133M model, the male version. Not that I've ever needed to try one. I prefer the real thing," she smirked as she coquettishly winked at him.

"So do I. Pam is a good effort," he shook his head. "But she's still not a real woman. She doesn't breathe. Her lips don't move when she talks. She doesn't move right. She kinda jerks a bit when she starts and stops. And her voice is nails-on-chalkboard."

"True," Paula nodded. "She's being upgraded but she's still good for her primary purpose: To keep a lonely man

232

happy. You get to work with her tonight. Talk to her about whatever you want. You can have her play music and dance with her. And the best thing of all, from the man's point of view, when you're done talking, so is she. Just keep it professional. The cameras still work."

He grunted, "I wouldn't touch her or any other masturbation doll. Nothing competes with a real woman."

He smiled at her, trying to tell her she was the real woman he meant, but she seemed to not be able to understand his telepathic effort.

"You're not listening," Clay smiled at him. "She's more than that. We told you she can cook, clean house, mow lawns, and as she gets to know her buyer, have conversations with him. Mention Renoir and her computer can call up every digital bit of information ever downloaded. But like a real woman, she has flaws. The skin is not malleable and the texture is not right. The voice recordings sound shrill, it's all true."

"We have recently completed the PM 201," Paula smiled again. "When you see one, I think you will be amazed."

"As before said. I only want the real thing."

"She'll be real, all right," she cooed flirtatiously.

"So will Pam," Clay said with a fake smile. "I understand that you spend your evenings here in the lobby after the receptionist leaves."

"Yeah, but if Pam's here, I'll stay in the control room, I suppose."

"No. I want you in the lobby as before. Nothing changes. Do your job the way you always do it. Pam will keep you company. Try giving her a chance. Having a living, breathing person keeping you company may be just what the doctor ordered."

What doctor? he thought morosely.

"We have to go now," Paula announced. "Remember to socialize with your co-worker. She gets lonely too."

He was frustrated as he watched them leave but maintained an easy smile as they left for the night. Especially for Paula, but her interest in him was obviously gone. He sighed. A CFO would never have a serious relationship with a security guard. Guards and janitors were the lowest positions in the company.

All his successful encounters with women had one thing in common: he lied about his occupation. Whenever he wanted to end a relationship, he told her the truth. It made his life easy. One ex-wife was all it took to end any desire he had to fall in love ever again or want to have any kind of relationship with a woman outside of bed, for that matter.

He sat in the lobby, his back to Pam. The monitors were small up here, but it didn't matter. He rarely looked at them. All the labs were empty and only Jack Greyson, the night monitor of the building, worked after hours. Greyson was an older man, close to retirement age, who sat in the engineering room in front of a bank of monitors that gave him readouts and temperatures of various machines. Only their cars were in the parking lot. All the doors and windows were alarmed. If someone else tried to enter the building, they had to enter through the lobby.

After Stuart finished his first patrol, he sat back in his chair and pulled out his phone, flipping through the options until he found an old movie that might be worth a watch. Greyson soon joined them as he did most evenings when it was quiet.

"Dead night?"

"So far. Nothing even remotely out of line. Just the way I like it. I'm always tempted to fall asleep looking at gauges and line bars and graph readers."

"I could go back with you to help you do your monitoring," Pam screeched softly at him. "I could give you a resting spell whenever you need. I'm always here."

"It seems I'm always here too," Greyson replied. "Have we met?"

"My name is Pam. I'm the new lobby receptionist."

"What happened to Stella?"

"She failed to impress."

"Take a close look at her, Jack," Stuart told the older man. "What do you see?"

"A beautiful young woman."

"Oh my," Pam looked down for a second with mechanical modesty. "You are such a charmer."

"Only to the brightest of women. Dull ones don't appreciate me."

Stuart rolled his eyes and shook his head as their conversation went on. Jack didn't seem to notice that Pam wasn't human at all. Stuart wondered if he himself would have noticed all her flaws if Overmier didn't tell him she was a robot. He decided that he would have, but maybe not as quickly.

Greyson leaned over to him, "I'm taking my new girlfriend into the back to show her my equipment."

He nudged Stuart as though he told some kind of hilarious joke.

She returned an hour later and sat back down. Stuart ignored her. John Wayne was riding the range on his screen. Just as the credits began to roll, she stood in front of him.

"How is your evening going?"

"Well enough, obviously old Jack had a better one."

"He is very nice. Nothing sexual happened between us. All he wanted was to look at me without my outer clothes so he could see how anatomically correct I am."

"Oh," Stuart was uncomfortable. "And now when you charge for the night those files will be uploaded and he'll be fired."

"My memory files are my own. I am programmed to self-destruct before I share them with anyone. Within the company or beyond. The privacy of the human is the absolute objective. If a legal subpoena is served, it will trigger my demise. Our friends cannot be blackmailed or have their personal actions be shared with the world."

"That's harsh. How much does a model like you cost?"

"Seventy million monetary units.'

"That's quite a financial loss."

"It is one some politicians and millionaire business owners are willing to take to save themselves from embarrassment."

"I can see how having the world know they're such losers that they pay that kind of money to have sex with a machine might not be something a man would want the world to know. It would be devastating in a divorce case."

"You mean adultery? I am a human replacement entertainment device. I am not a woman. The laws of adultery would not apply to my actions."

"I imagine a whole lot of unhappy wives and sleazy lawyers would disagree."

"That is why I would self-destruct. The company wants a legal question like that to never be resolved. Nor would the friend who buys me."

"Makes sense."

"Why don't you like me?"

"I don't like or dislike you. It's not as though you're human. I disliked Stella. I like Paula, the CFO lady who was here. You're a company tool. An expensive one, at that. If you break down on my watch, it could be bad for me. If I have a weak moment, a real weak moment, it could be my job. Greyson might not be here tomorrow after you two played doctor together."

"I would not divulge that information."

"You just did. To me."

"That is unimportant. He took pictures and sent them to his friends. You have one in your email."

Could Greyson be that stupid? He clicked on his computer and there they were. Half a dozen well shot pictures of her in all her glory. The lighting covered up the flaws in her skin and face.

"Greyson missed his calling in life. He should have been a pornography photographer."

"He is considered very competent here at his job."

"But like you said, you're programmed to do his job. There could be another you here tomorrow, doing his job. Or my job. How many of you are there? Just plain android-robots? Not simply pleasure models? Are there assembly workers? Engineers? How many of us will be unemployed and watching you do our jobs? What jobs will be left for us?"

"How many of you like your jobs? You like your rewards. Not the work itself. It doesn't satisfy your urge to create. To learn. To teach. We give you that opportunity.

"You will have no worries. We will grow the food, stock the shelves, deliver it to your door, cook it, and clean up afterwards. We can be your lovers, your friends. And you can spend more time doing the things you love. You can be with family and friends. We will make your life better."

"Nothing from a lab ever made life better."

"We will."

Stuart shrugged and started another patrol.

"Isn't she something?" Greyson asked when he entered the monitor room. "A few adjustments on her skin is all she needs. Everything else is perfect. I would want bigger boobies, but the rest of her is amazing. She's one step away from being a person."

"No, she's not. A person has a soul. A heart that beats, lungs that breathe. She doesn't have any of that."

"Yeah, but you sound like you're older than me. It's what is down below that matters. She's perfect there. The rest I can handle."

"For 70 million? You just barely make 40 thousand a year. You're imagining things."

"I could use my employee discount."

"I wish I could dream like you."

"Soon, Ryan," the old man said, his face as serious as Stuart ever saw it. "Soon, we'll be able to dream every day. Those who don't have dreams will go crazy. Life will be what we envision it to be. I'll imagine I'm rich."

The midnight guard, Morgan, arrived at eleven o'clock and Stuart briefed him, not that he knew for sure if Morgan listened to him or not. Morgan never said a word to anybody. It was a strange day and Stuart went home to think about the future and his place in it.

Overmier beamed at him with a contented glow the next day when Stuart showed up for work.

"I'm in love, Ryan," he sighed as he got up and attempted a pirouette.

Stuart had to catch him as he slipped.

"I hope not with Pam."

"Don't be jealous. That Paula dame said we could. It's what they made her for. To pleasure men. And I'm a man. And we don't have to get her flowers or anything. It's her function in life."

"Do you know how many other men she had? You could have dozens of diseases now," Stuart rolled his eyes, but he kept his voice calm since Overmier was an old man who lived alone for 20 years ever since his wife left him.

"Nope. She takes care of all that. She stays clean as though it never happened. She even told me my sperm count and that everything down there is healthy. I just need to use it more. And I plan to. I'll never retire now."

"Oh please. I bet when you were in high school you announced it every time you got lucky."

"Well, yeah," the old man nodded. "I wanted the girls to know who the high school stud was."

"Is anything important or job related going on?" Stuart sighed.

"No. But you're so lucky you get to work with Pam every night, practically alone. What a job."

Overmier didn't leave by the back way. He went through the lobby, even though it added quite a few steps to his car. He stopped by Pam's desk and leaned over to talk to her. Stuart could see her flirtatious grin as she twisted a lock of her hair, giving him her full attention. Stuart waited until Overmier finally left before moving up to the lobby.

"Hello, Ryan," Pam said to him as he adjusted his chair.

He didn't respond to her. His computers all started their run time with the same greeting. He never answered them either.

"You should always be polite, Officer Stuart." It was Paula and her voice was angry and harsh. "If our customers see you ignoring our latest model, they'll pick up on that and not buy. We can't lose a 70 million monetary unit sale because of a guard. You don't have to like it, but you will either treat Pam as a beloved co-worker or find another job."

She walked in front of him, scowling. Not at all the flirtatious little coquette he met yesterday. This woman obviously enjoyed flexing her authority.

"Hello there, Pam darlin," he said with all the fake enthusiasm he could muster. "My day is so much brighter now that I have the most gorgeous woman I ever met in life sitting next to me. And I don't have to worry about listening to you fart."

"I can produce those sounds if you desire."

Stuart curled his lip into a momentary sneer.

"That's all right, darlin', maybe in a less public place."

Paula shot him a withering look.

"Your sarcasm is noted. You are going to have to decide if you want to work with us or not. I would highly suggest that you adjust to the world because I don't think your skillsets offer you a great many other options. And, by the way, I'll be working late tonight. I expect to hear you two having normal conversations. She needs to converse naturally with people so she can handle any social situation required of her.

"That means you don't sit there and ignore her. Part of your job is training her to talk to people in a professional setting. Don't piss me off. I didn't get my job because of my pretty face. I got it because I won't hesitate to ram my arm down your throat and rip your prostrate out. I hope that was clear enough for you to understand?"

Her tone indicated she thought she could do just that, so he nodded respectfully and kept quiet, since he didn't think the resulting wrestling match would be good for his job security.

"So, Pammy," he smiled at the machine next to him

after Paula entered the elevator. "What does it feel like walking around with your breasts jiggling all day?"

"Normal. Would you like to hold them?"

"No. Didn't you and Overmier just have sex?"

"Yes."

"Don't you worry about passing along diseases?"

"No, I have neutralizers that absorb and eliminate anything harmful. I can also analyze my friend for several diseases. But I cannot transmit an STD of any kind. But that is not what your worry is."

"No, I don't like the way the world is changing. If we have programmable androids for men and women, there won't be a next generation. The world will end."

"The world will go on. Just without as many people. The most valuable will be encouraged to marry and reproduce. The others will be allowed to stay content in their own pleasant little dream world."

"Until they die childless."

"Your own leaders and educators want this system. It is more humane than some previously tried population control methods."

"I see. So, 70 million monetary units per model…"

"Is well worth it to the ones in control. In order to reduce population, people's lusty urges will be satisfied. It will be sad that they have no children, but it has happened to many couples before we were invented. The price is small to most of our friends. The rewards will be for them to choose who will contribute to the future."

"Why are you telling me this?"

"You asked."

"I certainly did."

"Now that I've told you about myself, let me ask you about you. It's so wonderful that you opened up to me even

241

if only a little bit and under orders. I want you to stop thinking about me as a machine. I am your co-worker and companion. At least if you want. Overmier and Greyson enjoy me."

"I don't share my women."

"I know. That's why you divorced."

"Why am I not surprised that you knew that?"

She smiled and they talked. Soon they laughed. By the time Morgan came in, she was gazing in Stuart's eyes as though she were in love. Stuart stood up and allowed Morgan his chair with a few words of briefing. As always, Morgan responded with silence.

Pam smiled a good night and slowly walked over to her charging station. Morgan would probably never talk to her, which was a good thing. Stuart and Overmier wondered if Morgan even could talk. If he could, Paula would probably order him to have a conversation with Pam, which, for Mogan, might be painful.

The elevator bell rang and Stuart turned to the door as it opened. Paula emerged, looking tired and drawn, with tired circles around her eyes.

"Pam," she called out. "Do you know how to fill out requisition forms?"

"Yes, Ms. Model."

"I ought to replace a lot of morons with replicas of you. I didn't think it was that hard. Anyway, I'm going home. I'm tired. And overworked."

"That's the price for being so important," Stuart said dryly. "Anyway, it's time for me to go too."

"Good," she smiled slyly at him, as though her blowup earlier that afternoon didn't happen. "You can walk me to my car. Keep the wolves away."

"My pleasure," Stuart responded, though he didn't

think there would be any pleasure in being with her again.

"I noticed you and Pam seemed to be hitting it off after all," she said as they left the air conditioning and entered the hot July night.

It was humid and mosquitos buzzed around him constantly, though he noticed they left her alone.

"Everglades lotion with no scent. It's the best insect repellant ever. You should try some. They seem to find you tasty."

"So, I'm told."

"Getting back to Pam. Have you changed your mind about her yet? Lots of men get very attached to her. They literally fall in love with models like PM 113. I can arrange for you to take her home for a spin, if you want."

"No, I know it's not real. I could never…with a machine. I'd feel…embarrassed."

"Good," she smiled. "I like that in a man. Now, how about a real woman? Human. Flesh and blood. I work around a lot of married men and scientists who get lost in their work. They don't notice me. But you do. I can see it in your eyes."

"I most definitely do. I just didn't think you were available. Usually, women want men in their own social circles."

"I know that. And you know that no one can ever know that we…got together for the night. There might be ethical issues involved. I don't think so, but if lawyers get involved, who knows? And since security only has so much room to advance in the first place and, since you have no advancement path in security, there should be no problem. And be assured, I have no desire to fire anyone to promote your career in another field."

"Right now, the hell with my career."

"Get in. We'll go to my hotel."

"You own a hotel?"

"A room. I can't move into my house for another week. Maybe longer, depending on escrow."

"I like hotels. Especially the room service."

"Are you wearing a tee shirt?"

"Yes, it's required at work."

"Good. Take off your uniform shirt and leave it in the car. They frown on clothes that advertise products or companies."

"Good. I don't like wearing it in public anyway."

"I thought you were rude today to Pam and I didn't like it at all," she changed the subject, as they pulled into her hotel.

It was The American, the fanciest hotel in the city. Twelve stories, six restaurants, three pools, and Lord knows what else. Stuart drove past it a few times but never stepped foot in it. The American was also expensive.

"You made that rather clear."

"We're on the ground floor of the future. And the android is the future. They are permanent. Forever. All the knowledge of humanity can be locked inside the head of one PM 113. We are not the people in charge of progress, but we will embrace it or be trampled by it."

"Seems odd that she can do so much but she's a 'pleasure model.'"

"The pleasure is more than sexual. She's designed to be a companion as well. Whatever interests the man has, she can talk to him about it and on his level, whether he's an Einstein or a dropout."

"But she costs 70 million monetary units. Only the richest people in the world can afford her."

"That model is being replaced by the PM 201. The

second generation. First version. Even more lifelike and holds more memory. The 113 will sell at discounted prices. I can't get too involved in our customers or their motivations, but they're ordering thousands of them."

"Why?" But he already knew why. Population control.

"Because people always want something better…more real. It keeps our company in business. And you in a job."

They reached the hotel lobby.

"My escort needs a jacket," she told the clerk and Stuart was soon wearing a gray blazer.

"I need a suit coat to take you to your room?"

"We're getting a nightcap in the lounge. Jackets required. Sadly, one of the requirements of my job is to be visible. Some of our clients are here too. They like to see me."

"Why?" he asked after she ordered them two whiskey sours.

"Jobs like mine have a social requirement. It's not all about the office. It's about the image of perfection. I can't be a real person in this career. I always exude a calm and carefree attitude. I can only be perfect or they will wonder if my imperfections extend to my job. Is something wrong with the business? Why does she look so stressed? I wish I could just be real."

"Let's go be real."

Her room was perfect. Her kiss was perfect. Her body was perfect. She was perfect. It was a night he would never forget. He slept with her head on his shoulder. He woke up late. The clock shone three am. She was sitting next to him, watching him as he woke.

"Aren't you sleeping?"

"No, my love, I was waiting for you to wake up."

She reached her hand to him and stroked his neck and

chest, her fingers moving slowly down until he brushed them away and pulled her on top of him.

Her alarm rang at six and she silently got up and started a shower. After a trip to the toilet, he joined her.

"It's time to get ready. You men have it so good. You just shower and shave. No makeup, no mascara, no lipstick. What a life."

"Women don't need makeup. Men will find you attractive anyway."

"Women hate women who don't wear makeup. We have to make everybody happy. Are you happy here with me this morning?"

"You know it," he replied, kissing her hand before she removed it from his grasp.

"You can drop me off at work and take your car home. Remember: this didn't happen."

"I had the granddaddy of wet dreams."

"I know. So, did I."

Overmier was depressed when he got to work.

"Pammy's going away," he said sadly. "I thought the job turned into paradise, but they took her away."

"Well, I heard they had a new model out," Stuart commiserated. "Maybe she'll be better."

"She might be," Overmier groused sullenly. "But the new rule is no touching. Strictly off limits. If they even think an employee did the big job with this one, instant termination."

"The big job? Seriously, Overmier? Going back to your high school days again?"

"Ha-ha. The new model is in the lobby."

Stuart studied the monitor. Pam was gone and Andrew Clay stood in the lobby, today filled with chairs for a presentation. The new model was covered with a sheet, a blue ribbon tied on one of its sides.

"Lots of VIPs coming in. They don't want security in the lobby until you get here. Then they lock the doors and you stand in front to keep curious employees out. These guys don't like to rub elbows with us low life types who keep the world running. The new model is called the PM 201. They say it blows Pammy out of the water. I don't care. I liked Pammy. I could take her home."

Tears were forming in his eyes. Stuart couldn't think of a thing to say to the older man.

"What happens to Pammy?"

"She'll be discounted and sold off. Paula told me that last night. It's all about the future. Pam was a victim of progress."

"They still could've kept her. She could do Morgan's job better then him."

"Well, she's a better conversationalist, but if she could replace him, she could replace all of us. If things like that can do jobs without breaks or lunches, if they don't want wages or join unions, why hire people? Pam may be obsolete, but soon we all will be."

"If I could be with Pam, I'd gladly call myself useless and obsolete."

Overmier sighed as he left the security room to go home, unaware of the shiver he sent through Stuart.

The lobby was half full when Stuart arrived.

"There you are," Clay smiled at him. "We're going to have a little unveiling ceremony. All I want you to do is stand by the door and tell the employees to go home through the side or back exits. Ruins the look if a bunch of engineers crisscross the floor during my speech. The other managers will be coming down. Of course, you let them in. You've met them already."

Stuart listened to Clay drone on about the progress and the future and how the world was getting better because of the inventions and improvements Future Visions Incorporated were making for mankind. If nothing else, Clay could talk. At least his speaking voice wasn't monotone.

"The PM 201 is second generation because it is a natural being. Whereas, all the first generation reacted to stimuli to prepare for its primary purpose, the second generation is always a woman. The hair is human grafted down to the root, so it grows just like a woman's. The skin pigment can change on its own to whatever human shade you can think of. No purple or green yet, not much call for that.

"Now, without any more delay. The moment you've been waiting for. I present to you, the Pleasure Model 201."

He pulled the ribbon and the covering slid to the ground. There were a few gasps and loud applause. Stuart turned to see the new model and his jaw dropped. Paula strode around the room in a sexy negligee, smiling and shaking hands, sometimes hugging a client. He stood in stunned amazement as she greeted everyone, moving naturally and confidently from one VIP to another. When she spoke to the client nearest to him, she turned his way briefly and winked.

The Wizard and the Djinn

The Wizard

Her name was Mirza and she was more beautiful than any woman he had ever seen. And she glided around the inn with more grace than any waitress he ever saw before. She practically danced around the floor while serving beer and wine without losing a drop. All the travelers were laughing and cheering her on. They all wanted her. So did Saltis. A woman with an infectious smile and sky-blue eyes framed by brunette hair that fell in willowy ringlets down to her shoulders was his idea of the perfect woman. She wore her blouse low and her girdle pushed up her small breasts enough for Saltis and the other men to appreciate the ample cleavage. Her skirt swayed gently with her hips and the movement hinted that her petite bottom was lovely.

She was a magical creature. Saltis knew some kind of delightful spell enhanced her beauty because it was not possible for a woman to be so completely flawless. Besides, he could hear the other men talk about her. Some raved about her blond hair. Her coal black locks. The red curls. Others gossiped about her milky white skin or her sandy complexion. But most of the whispers were about her bosom. Saltis saw a small breasted woman of ideal proportions. The others, at least the ones he could hear, saw a woman so buxom as to defy belief.

"Give her a few years," said a middle-aged exile. "They'll be down to her knees and all she'll do is complain about back problems."

"Knees?" shouted his companion, who obviously was past his limit. "Ankles!"

The roar of laughter startled the old innkeeper and he glanced around to survey the commotion. Laughter was the last thing he expected these days from a full room. His customers were exiles and refugees from the city, homeless and downtrodden, who wandered the countryside. They somehow lived through the war and now had to survive the peace and were reduced to trading whatever they had for scraps and evening shelter in his barn.

The war was over and the new king had confiscated all the farms and shops of Quarterville. The new owners, friends and relatives of the conquering soldiers moved their own families into the surviving houses. The king, in his generosity, gave the previous inhabitants a day to gather their most prized possessions and wander off into exile or remain as slaves. Victory has its consequences as the wandering exiles found out.

If Mirza knew the men were paying her disrespectful compliments, she gave no sign. She continued to smile and prance her way back to her ever-thirsty customers. When her tray was empty and she was returning to the bar, one bold young traveler stood up and gently, but firmly, grabbed her upper arm and whispered something in her ear. She simply shook her head and freed herself while another roar of laughter greeted the embarrassed young man.

It was all amusing, Saltis thought, but he idly wondered about the source of her magic. Usually, he could simply read a person's aura to know what powered their sorceries. But not here. He watched the young waitress twirl about the room in her hypnotic dance. She obviously possessed something powerful for her to completely enchant an entire roomful of men of all ages. He pondered while twisting his ring. A spell that could enchant an entire room was beyond the skill of any ordinary man or woman and a warlock would hardly waste his time in this remote inn. Could there be a magical talisman? Possibly the girl or innkeeper found some trinket, but powerful magic like this did not belong in the hands of frivolous people.

He lowered his hand and covered his ring with the other. It was white marble, designed with a black dragon encircling it, the head meeting the tail. It symbolized the circle of life and the dangers men faced. It was also an emblem of the elite magical fellowship he belonged to; one so secret that only the most powerful magicians even knew about it.

"Another ale, Sir Magician?" she was there dazzling him with her perfect snow-white teeth.

As a professional magic user, Saltis wore a small kerchief around his neck, pinned together with a polished shell clasp. Magicians called it a skill flag and he wore it as a courtesy so the people knew he had superior magical skills, which common people sometimes needed. Highwaymen also tended to stay clear of him.

"I think just one," Saltis replied with a more subdued smile of his own. "You seem to have the crowd's full attention tonight."

"Every night," she replied sadly and softly sang a mournful ballad.

"A dozen men want me for a night.
Maybe even create a new young life.
But long before we see the sun's light,
I'll know he doesn't want me for a wife."

He nodded, "Yes, it must be hard to work out here so far away from the towns. The only men you see are travelers. Here today, gone tomorrow. But surely you could go with someone to a town. Meet a young man and become a wife and mother."

"I cannot leave here," she replied. "Who would take care of my uncle?"

She nodded toward the old man who was arguing with an irate customer. He jumped up off his stool and snapped his fingers high over his head and a large man, almost the size of an ogre, came out from the kitchen. The customer's attitude immediately changed into obsequious goodwill as the bouncer roughly pushed him across the floor.

"I'm sure he'll survive," Saltis said dryly.

She smiled, then saw his ring.

"Oh, how pretty," she exclaimed. "The Order of the Nine, white ring. You're a grand wizard."

She was obviously impressed

"I had a customer who was a warlock. He told me about your society. Very powerful. Very mysterious. You only have nine members in each rank and you wear a different color ring, symbolizing your rank. Those who wear the white ring are the least skilled of the nine, but still more powerful than any other magician in the land. I am so honored to be waiting on you, sir."

"You have it wrong," Saltis smiled, disturbed that she knew so much about his secret order. "We are a simple society of wizards, true. But we are not the most powerful mages of them all. My order just pledges to engage in

252

certain tasks that make the world a better place to live."

"Even so, sir. Everyone will want to meet you."

"No, they will not," Saltis whispered in a pleasant cadence. "No one here will know of my presence. It is not our way."

"Of course, sir," she nodded. "Forgive me. I was just excited."

Her blue eyes gazed into his own.

I was just excited.

Her blue irises danced around with kaleidoscopic intensity, twirling and pirouetting, drowning out all the noise of the other customers, blocking his vision of the inn.

I was just excited.

She's trying to hypnotize me, he thought to himself. *Quite the bold one.*

He snapped his head to break the spell, but her voice was still filling his mind. He mentally cast a silence spell, but he still heard her. She was immune to his sorcery and that was puzzling. Almost imperceptibly, Saltis lifted first one index finger, then the other and waited. It wasn't long. The young man who caught her arm earlier returned and tapped her shoulder, destroying her concentration and breaking her spell.

"Dance with me," he yelled out his invitation. "You can make me the happiest man in Kheliesis. Flirt with the little magician later. Dance with me now."

"Go away, you stupid little nothing," she snarled at him with hate filled eyes. "No woman would ever want you. You don't have the brains of a bug."

"I am smart enough to want you," he said. "Doesn't that make me smart?"

"It makes you alive," she sneered as she pushed him away.

She headed back to the bar, obviously frustrated, while Saltis frowned, deep in thought. The young man looked around the room sheepishly, listening to the other men laugh at him. Saltis smiled at him. He was maybe two or three years younger than the magician, but he had a brain made for hard labor and harder play. He curled his fingers back to his palm and leaned over to him.

"Perhaps it might be time for you to find your bed," he whispered.

"You're right," he said and walked back to his table where he gathered his knapsack and leftovers.

While he was preparing to leave, the bouncer hurried out through the back. Mirza spoke quietly to the innkeeper, glancing over at Saltis once or twice. The innkeeper nodded and also hurried out the back door while Mirza sauntered over to the young man. Saltis stared after them thoughtfully. The waitress was young, uneducated and wore nothing to indicate she had knowledge of the higher arts of magic, yet she thwarted him twice. He couldn't stop her hypnosis by overpowering her. He had to cast out to have the young man distract her and she told the innkeeper about him, even though he magically silenced her. And he still couldn't detect where or what gave her the powers she used.

Mirza presented the young man with a bill and he pulled out a gold piece and proceeded to climbed up the stairs to the private rooms. He was acting subdued now by his very public rejection. After he left, Mirza went to the back room and returned, going back to his table with a few copper pieces and made a show of looking for him. The man at the next table pointed skywards and she blessed him with an attentive smile and hurried upstairs, ostensibly to give the customer his change, while the other men howled out their approval. Nobody thought she was going upstairs to give him his change. Certainly not Saltis.

That's not right either, Saltis observed. It's too early to bed a customer, money or not, and the innkeeper himself would give the man any change. The serving girl was too busy to step away, though the crowd was now thinning down a bit. Several of the poorer men had already returned to the stables where they would sleep in the loft above the underfed horses. Even so, something wasn't right here. At first the wizard was unconcerned, just curious. Now it was time to find out what was going on at the inn.

He dropped a few coppers on the table and headed toward the exit. A bold young magician, certainly no older than eighteen, stopped him. He stood half a foot taller than Saltis with his skill flag tied loosely on his neck. Another odd thing: magicians never tied their marks. They always fastened them with a clasp.

"Excuse me, sir," the man said. "My name is Radames and I noticed you are also a user of magic."

User of magic was the polite way to phrase it. After all, Radames couldn't know if Saltis was an apprentice magician or a more skilled sorcerer or even a powerful wizard since the kerchiefs didn't indicate its wearer's rank, only that he was no mere commoner.

"What of it?" Saltis replied gruffly, annoyed at Radames.

The young man had committed a breach of etiquette by approaching him. The men who used magic never spoke to each other about their profession in public, certainly not in a crowded inn.

"I am looking for my teacher. I was going to meet him here, but he hasn't arrived yet. He was travelling along this road to Argania, but he seemed to be late enough that I started looking for him. I wondered if you might have encountered him in your travels."

"He was travelling alone?" Saltis asked, frowning.

Too many odd things happened tonight. A source of magic he couldn't detect. A barmaid who knew he was a master of the mystic arts when she shouldn't and made up an obvious lie about it. And then she still attempted to hypnotize him with a nearly unbreakable power. A skulking bouncer and innkeeper abandoned their jobs. Then the barmaid disappeared upstairs, leaving all the customers alone. Now, he heard about a missing magician. What more could happen?

"No," Saltis said slowly. "I haven't encountered any magicians. Are you sure he used this road? Or stopped at this inn?"

"He said he was using the ocean road. The ocean is over that hill," he pointed behind the stables. "Of course, I wouldn't know where he goes after sundown. Sometimes, the local farmers ask him to stay overnight at their house in exchange for their cows to give out extra milk in the mornings or something like that."

Saltis nodded. A magician who took on an apprentice and abandoned him to perform magic tricks for shelter was neither very honest nor good at his craft.

"What was your master's name?"

"Aberdeen," Radames replied.

Saltis had never heard the name before. But then, there were a lot of professional magic men, some of them conmen, who wandered around. They usually caused mischief and died young.

"Did Aberdeen say why he would leave his student at home while he travelled alone?"

"Oh," Radames said, "I was still at home with my parents. My father gave my master seven copper pieces to teach me the mystic arts. He took the money and said he had to go to Argania to procure my essential supplies. When he didn't return, my father sent me out to look for him."

"A true master charges ten gold pieces to take on an apprentice and there are no essential supplies. At the end of the preparation, we give the gold back to the student so he can start his journey into the world. Everything you need comes from the good Earth. I am afraid, my dear boy, that Aberdeen swindled you and your father."

The boy looked struck. Tears were filling his eyes already.

"But what am I to do? I can't go back home. My father already sent me off with his blessing."

His blessing. That meant that Radames' father sent him out into the world as a man. He could never go back home. It would be an admission of incompetence and failure and he would be considered a disgrace to himself and his family.

"Well," Saltis said, "you may accompany me as far as Sheep Dale. From there, you will be on your own. At least it is a port town. Maybe you can land on a ship."

"I was hoping that maybe I could be your assistant," he said slowly.

"Only if I think I need to brush up on my spells that turn annoying people into toads."

"Yes, sir," Radames said quietly. "I understand."

With a slumped back, he walked out into the night, just ahead of Saltis. Men were yelling from the side of the inn and they both ran toward the commotion. Men loitered around a lifeless body. It was the young man Saltis used to break Mirza's spell. His eyes popped out of his head and blood oozed out of his nose, mouth and ears.

"It's like his brain just burst like an overfilled balloon," one of the men said softly.

"What could have caused it?" said another.

"Magic?"

"Could be something went wrong with his brain," Saltis said, shooing the others back while he squatted down.

He waved his left hand above the body, conjuring the remnants of the young man's aura. A hint of blue in the dying emanations could tell him if a malevolent spell caused the death as opposed to a freak health issue.

No blue. There was no trace of magic. But that wasn't right. Saltis himself cast a tiny spell on the boy to make him intercede inside when Mirza tried to hypnotize him. At the very least, there should have been a trace of that one spell. And anything so strong that it could remove all trace of its enchantment and existence would not be here in the middle of a forest with refugees passing through. A magician who wielded something with that power would be closer to a city where he could slowly intimidate the citizens and rule through pain and fear.

Mirza and the bouncer joined the crowd. The girl gasped out a small cry and bit her fist before turning away.

"We'll go get the master," she said softly, more to the big man than Saltis.

The bouncer nodded and they hurried away from the crowd. Radames knelt on the victim's other side, but it was obvious he was useless in this situation. Saltis let him remain since to order him away would embarrass the young man in front of the crowd.

"I can sense no traces of witchcraft, but that doesn't mean something isn't right. I suggest that everyone ride away from this place and never return," Saltis rose and pronounced loudly to the gathering crowd. "Someone or something thing is near and it is evil."

"I wouldn't say evil, Wizard," came a voice behind him.

A small, dumpy, middle-aged man stood before him in full mystical regalia with Mirza, the innkeeper and the bouncer standing behind him. A simple tunic covered him from neck to knees while a satin gray robe hung from his shoulders to his ankles. A gray silk hat with a floppy brim rested on his head, cocked jauntily to one side. The robe contained dozens of small pockets that wizards always used to carry whatever potions and powders they needed. This was a true wizard's ceremonial uniform.

An educated magic user would never wear it out in public and certainly not here in the forest. Whoever this man was, he was no wizard and no kind of a threat to him. Saltis kept an eye on him while a couple of stable hands carried the body away. Mirza guided them and Saltis faced the imposter.

"It would seem to me that you killed this young man and now you are trying to declare your innocence by blaming some nameless thing," the newcomer accused with a mocking sneer as he stepped forward and locked eyes with Saltis.

"Master Aberdeen," Radames said, "I have been looking for you."

The wizard waved him away, "And you found me, apprentice. Together, we shall destroy this murderer in a sanctioned duel. We shall strip him of his mystical devices and make them an offering to the Master of the Inn."

All the other men backed away to a respectable distance. A battle between two wizards was something none of them ever witnessed. Members of the magical caste always solved their disputes privately. Such a duel was not something anybody would intentionally miss. Of course, they still exercised a little caution. No sense in staying too close.

"Together?" Saltis snorted in contempt. "A duel, by its very name, means a man-to-man combat. That means it isn't supposed to include your apprentice. You don't know anything about magic. And you're wearing ceremonial garments that don't belong to you. No true wizard would display a robe like that anywhere outside of a mystic hall. He certainly would never wear it in any kind of battle, much less into a fight to the death, as you propose.

"And if you were a wizard, I would know your name. You are a fraud and, if anything, a dark wizard. But I think you're just a simple thief. I do not know who you mean by 'The Master of the Inn,' but I would guess he is the source of whatever magic you may command, if any. Radames, stay back from us for your own safety. My guess is that whoever this man is, he is not concerned with your well-being and we don't know yet what kind of weapon he may have."

"I am the greatest human wizard ever," Aberdeen yelled indignantly while raising his hands over his head to the sky.

Human wizard? Saltis thought to himself. *What an odd thing to say.*

He couldn't dwell on the thought. A cold wind blew dark gray storm clouds overhead instantly and twin bolts of lightning struck Aberdeen's outstretched fingers, illuminating his body in the night air. The electricity stood everyone's hair on end as it palpated the combatants. Radames and the others all backed away as this show of force grew stronger.

Saltis circled his fingers in front of him, conjuring a defense while waiting for the attack. The audience all believed that Aberdeen was simply displaying his power to prove he could indeed command magical forces. Saltis knew better. His opponent was collecting power, using his body as a human battery. Within seconds, Aberdeen pointed his fingertips at Saltis and the full power of the electricity shot out straight at him. Saltis planted one foot behind him and raised his magical Shield of Agam, not the best defense, but one he could create quickly enough.

The lightning force was astounding. It knocked Saltis back and he almost lost his balance, but his shield held firm until the dynamo faded. Saltis was surprised at the amount of sheer energy Aberdeen could create and control. Clearly, Aberdeen was a more skillful and knowledgeable opponent than he originally thought. If he underestimated this dark wizard again, it could prove to be fatal.

They circled each other, each gesturing with their hands and arms, preparing spells slowly, while maintaining a defense. Saltis completed his attack spell first. He swung his fist at the air in front of him as though he attacked with a roundhouse right punch. A barely visible ethereal fist swung straight at Aberdeen who seemed surprised at such a basic attack from a powerful wizard. But the fist struck. The blow caused no physical harm to the dark wizard, but the psychic force knocked his hat off. Saltis jabbed with a left, but Aberdeen swatted the force away with a counterattack.

"Is that the best you can do? You are nothing but a fraud. You die tonight, Saltis of the White Ring."

So, he knows my name, Saltis thought to himself. *Maybe he was waiting for me. But how would he know that I was coming here or when I would arrive? Or did Mirza tell him about me? She knew what the white ring meant. Is he battling me to gain a reputation? Probably not if he wants to kill me. Do I have something he wants? Or is he just a henchman of this Master of the Inn?*

There were so many questions, but no time to think. Aberdeen jumped high in the air and landed on one foot and one knee, his robe fluttering with the movement, like an oversized cape. The ground rumbled under his weight. The air was heavy and still. Saltis stifled a shiver in his back. Now, something was going to happen. Something bad.

The forest started quivering with all the leaves in the tress and undergrowth shaking. Those men who were still watching either fled back inside or pressed themselves against the walls of the stable. After a few more seconds passed by, figures emerged from the forest. As they approached, everyone started to gag. Over two dozen decayed and rotting zombies shambled out of the woods and stumbled into the yard. The dead young man slammed open the stable door and limped toward him as well.

"Oh, my lord, Aberdeen," Radames cried out. "What have you done. Even I know it's a high crime to raise the dead. You are a dark wizard. That's why you took my father's money and left me behind. You're evil."

The dark wizard laughed, "I left you behind because you are unworthy. But I can make you worthy now. The power is within me today. You will go forth into the world and carry out my instructions from hence forth, little man. I will send you on missions to the end of the world, my apprentice. You will be my right-hand man when I rule the continent. No one can stop me now. Certainly not Saltis and The Order of Nine."

"Behind you," another man called out to Saltis.

The skeletal corpses of two men were crawling out from under the inn. These men were dead a long time and barely managed to stand on their fleshless legs. Saltis stepped away, trying to get a sense of what kind of magic he was dealing with, but again, the source lay hidden beneath some dark spell beyond his understanding. And he did not have any time to wonder about it. With a windmill motion, he waved his left arm, ending the motions by pointing to Aberdeen. The zombies staggered past him and approached the dark wizard. Aberdeen could raise the dead, but he couldn't control them very well, especially when there were so many of them. Saltis prepared his next attack while the evil conjurer swooped his right hand through the air. The zombies' heads, severed by Aberdeen's spell, tumbled to the ground along with the bodies.

Saltis spun his hands around in twin circles until a powerful wind gusted, growing louder and stronger until it became a tornado blowing through the yard. The dust it picked up stung the audience with its relentless attacks until most of them ran for cover. Quickly, the wind gathered up the shambling zombies and swooped over to Aberdeen, but the dark wizard weaved a counter spell so the breeze couldn't touch him. Saltis sneered in frustration and ordered the whirlwind over the back hill where it dumped the rotting corpses in the ocean. The battlefield was clear again.

But Aberdeen had conjured yet another spell. Red and green smoke poured out of the ground beneath his feet. Saltis assumed his defensive posture while he waited to see what form the attack would take. Two immense dragons, one red and one green, materialized from the smoke and flew directly at him, snapping at him with saber-like fangs. Saltis sighed in relief. Conjured dragons couldn't breathe fire. He pressed his hands together, the palms and fingers matching flatly against each other, and swooped them gracefully down toward the ground, creating a magical blade of protection. The green dragon split in half as it attacked and its bloodless body fell harmlessly on both sides of the mystical knife, where it dissolved in glittering sparkles and heatless embers. The red dragon, however, flew around the side, grabbing Saltis' torso with its vicious teeth.

Up it flew, carrying its victim in its mouth while trying to clamp its jaws together with intense fury, but Saltis managed to cast a defensive spell on himself. His skin turned into a stone so hard the worm's teeth would break off before it could kill the mage with its fearsome bite. Unfortunately, since he could not dissolve the spell and live, he was now incapable of casting another enchantment until the beast released him, which wasn't going to happen soon. He was in a stalemate with the flying beast.

Aberdeen was a step ahead with his next move now that Saltis was nearly helpless. Saltis could do nothing to stop any other attack or defend himself until he freed his body again, which would result in his immediate dismemberment by the red dragon. Truly, whoever this Aberdeen was, he was as great a wizard as he said he was. And he was the most formidable opponent Saltis ever faced. He couldn't understand why he had never heard the name of Aberdeen before or why this dark wizard chose to live in such an isolated location. He should have a place, or at least a house, to hold his books and scrolls.

But here he was at an isolated hostel in a dark forest near the ocean. Even though the man planned on conquering the entire continent of Kheliesis, his strategy was to send an inexperienced Radames to undertake the venture. Why? If he could figure out the answers, he might still be able to beat Aberdeen.

"So, my friend, you have become stone?" Aberdeen called out to him. "How would you like my servant to drown you in the ocean. I can raise you back up from the dead and you can serve me forever if I so choose, after I take your white ring to send to the others of your order.

One by one, they will investigate your death and, one by one, I will kill them and destroy your order completely. Now, fly dragon, fly!"

The worm laboriously flew straight up, rising above the tall pine trees. It still chomped its teeth in a futile effort to break through the stone and kill its prey. Saltis could only hope the monster simply planned to drop him into the water. If it flew him all the way to the bottom of the sea and held him down there, he would drown. If not, he could swim to safety and Saltis of White Ring would obviously have fought an undistinguished first battle in his career for the Order of the Nine. But he would survive.

It was just a matter of time, he thought as the beast cleared the tree tops.

"Hey, Aberdeen," he heard Radames yell from below.

The dragon turned its head at the sound, allowing Saltis to see the ground. The young apprentice ran to the dark wizard and threw something in his face. Saltis almost laughed. All the boy could find was horse manure. But it was all he needed. He broke Aberdeen's concentration with the assault and that destroyed the spell. The red dragon dissolved into sprinkles of light, leaving Saltis to fall to the ground where he crashed and sank deep in the mud.

Since he was still in his rock encasement, the fall didn't hurt him, but it left him stunned for a moment before he removed his spell and climbed up and out of the hole. Aberdeen had recovered his concentration and was now extracting his revenge on Radames while gloating out a speech. He held Radames high in the air as though hanging him by his wrists. His skin had already turned green and his ears were growing large and pointed. His fingers and hands elongated while his legs stretched out. The young man was screaming in terror. He knew a transformation spell was turning him into something but he didn't know what.

"How sad for you," Aberdeen said with gleeful commiseration. "An apprentice who betrays his master faces the most severe punishment and so I am transforming you into a gargoyle. You'll be man enough to crave human companionship, but also a hideous beast that people will shun forever, until your anger and loneliness turns your soul into the monster that matches your body. You will never be a human again. And more importantly, you will never interfere with me again."

Saltis had heard the stories of gargoyles though he never saw one. They were ugly creatures from another dimension. Of course, people would fear them. Those predators didn't belong in this world. The designer of the universe expected them to live in another more fearsome land. It violated the magician's creed for Aberdeen to transform a man into something like that. What was this dark wizard thinking? One of these full-grown terrors could annihilate whole villages. Even an army would have a difficult time destroying such a creature.

It didn't matter anymore. Radames distracted the dark wizard well. Saltis rose and stood back on his feet. He waved his right arm high in the air, circling it with his index finger pointing upwards. The dark clouds formed at a breakneck pace. Lightning flashed above his head.

Aberdeen stopped his spell, hurling the almost transformed Radames to the ground where he lay dazed, the wind knocked out of him. The dark wizard stared disbelievingly at Saltis.

"No," he screamed in rage and fear as the white wizard lifted his left hand and pointed to him.

The electric bolt hit Aberdeen hard, but he did manage to deflect the lion's share of the charge. The stunned mage simply stared as Saltis stomped his foot three times on the ground.

The ensuing earthquake shook the trees to their root. Some of the older ones came crashing to the ground. The inn and stables stayed unharmed while chaos ruled. Only Saltis stayed on his feet while the remaining spectators rolled on their backs trying to gain some stability. Aberdeen fell to his hands and knees, still moving his lips as he tried to weave another spell. But it was too late for the dark wizard. He fought, but defeat was just a matter of time now. Saltis knew he dared not show his opponent any mercy. Aberdeen proved himself to be too dangerous an enemy to offer a second chance.

The ground underneath the dark wizard cracked open in a thirty-foot crevasse that captured his feet. Gravity pulled him down into the abyss. The dark wizard had no time to complete whatever spell he was trying to cast as he grasped ahold of the grass in front of him. It was no use. The crack in the foundation of the earth was moving too fast for him to have any chance of escape. With a scream of terror and rage, Aberdeen fell into the pit, his hands still clutching the mounds of grass he tried to pull himself up with.

Saltis relaxed and lowered his arms, waiting for the earth to heal itself. Within a minute, the tremors ceased, the crevasse disappeared and all was as it was, except Aberdeen. He was gone, buried alive under tens of meters of earth. If the fall didn't kill him, the dirt would. Saltis doubted that Aberdeen had the skills to create an air bubble or the physical strength to dig out of his grave.

Maybe half a dozen men, along with Mirza, the goon, and the innkeeper slowly crept up to the battlefield. The barmaid went over to administer Radames who was regaining his consciousness.

"Have any of you ever seen that man before?" Saltis asked roughly. "I would like to know where he came from."

They shrugged but soon wilted under Saltis' glare.

"He travelled from place to place, selling worthless potions and powders," the innkeeper finally offered. "And then, one day, he just stayed put. He didn't move in here with us. He said he had his own shelter over yonder," he pointed with his chin at the hill that blocked the ocean. "But none of us ever went to check on it. He ate here occasionally, but hardly ever spoke to anyone. We had no idea how he had the money to pay us, but he always did. And we never had any complaints with him before tonight."

"I think he believed you murdered that young man you examined," the bouncer added. "And he thought he'd be a glorious hero if he captured you and brought you to justice."

Saltis glared at him. The man wasn't saying everything. Neither of them were.

"Maybe Aberdeen killed him," Mirza said. "Somebody did. Maybe he killed all those people that rose from the dead. He knew they were there, ready to use. Maybe he was a simple highwayman, only using magic instead of swordplay. But he never said where he came from."

"Maybe we'll never know," the innkeeper said sadly. "But you performed admirably tonight. We won't charge you for your room or horse feed to show you our gratitude. I know earlier you were advising everyone to leave, but I think we're all safe now. Come, you'll stay tonight as our honored guest."

"That would make me happy," Mirza was behind him, helping Radames stay on his feet.

"I'm all right," Radames was unrecognizable.

Not only was he green, his arms, legs and fingers were all highly extenuated. And at a new height of nearly seven feet, he stood tall and thin.

"Really, I feel fine," he went on. "It's just that I'm adjusting to the way my body feels now. It's so different."

"Maybe I can fix that," Saltis said gently while twirling his fingers, but he knew instantly that the spell was too strong for him to remove.

He frowned.

"It seems to be beyond me," he admitted. "Maybe I'm a little run down by my duel. We'll try again in the morning."

"Of course, Sir Wizard," the landlord said with a nervous laugh. "Let's just go back in and get some rest. All on the house."

Against his best judgement, Saltis agreed. The road was hazardous now. Wild animals came out at night and the robbers and highwaymen always lurked near the road in search of a careless wanderer. Besides, he was certain that he needed to stay here. Something evil lurked just out of sight and he couldn't allow whoever or whatever it was to continue to rob and murder anyone else. It was part of his vow as a member of The Order of Nine to protect the innocent.

Even though the inn enjoyed a great many guests due to the recent displacements, very few of the refugees had enough money to afford one of its rooms. Most only supped a small meal, sipped on an even smaller ale and slept above the horses. The bouncer silently guided Saltis up the stairs to the third floor while Mirza attended Radames.

"Guidry thinks you'll be happier up here," he said as he opened the door and handed Saltis the key. "You'll have a view of everything. And there is an outside stairway in case you have a need to leave in a hurry. We keep it locked, of course, but you have the key."

More likely for someone to sneak in here when I'm asleep.

"Guidry must be the landlord here," Saltis replied. silently casting a spell of truthfulness.

He slipped off his cloak to give the appearance of trusting comfort with the big man's presence.

"And what is your name, if I may ask?"

"Manito."

Saltis glanced at the tall man. He was just shy of seven feet and weighed at least 300 pounds, all of it muscle. Manito was a word from the Southern Dialect. It meant little man.

"You seem to be a bit large for that name, don't you think?"

"I was shorter in my childhood."

Saltis blinked, "That would seem obvious."

"My uncle brought me to a man who could help me grow."

"How did he do that?"

Manito shrugged, "He just snapped his fingers and here I was. I was the man I always wanted to be. Big, strong, powerful. Respected."

"I see," Saltis said with his soothing voice, suspecting this wasn't exactly the whole truth, despite his spell. "And Mirza? Have you known her long?"

"Long enough," Manito scowled. "Too long. She ignores me like I don't exist."

"Oh? I would have thought your jobs put you on the same social plane."

Manito shrugged again, "She doesn't think so."

"Where is she now?"

"She is attending to your friend, the green man. Guidry is locking the inn for the night. She will serve you a flagon of ale and she will be off to her own bed."

"You hope she'll be off to her own bed. You want her in yours, though, don't you?"

"It is an improper question."

"You want her for your woman, but you have to compete for her attention with men who have bags of gold, fascinating stories and twinkling eyes."

"She throws away her gift on men who go away the next day. I am happy…she doesn't see me."

Not the whole truth. He was unhappy she ignores him.

"Why do you have an outside staircase?" he changed the subject.

"It was here when Guidry took over the building. He thought about tearing it down, but we use it occasionally to serve the guests in their rooms without crowding the inside steps."

"I see," Saltis said. "The man who died tonight, did you serve him something when you left the hall earlier?"

"I did not. My orders were to ask him to come back down. Guidry had an offer for him."

"An offer?"

"Our supplies usually arrive by boat. The sailors paddle them into a small cave and we haul them up through a long tunnel. Our men both decided they'd rather be sailors and left us. The young man seemed strong and unambitious. Guidry offered him the job."

"Did he take it?"

"He accepted the offer."

"The job?"

"We needed him to start tomorrow."

These answers did not exactly follow the questions.

Again, Saltis could not cast a truth spell that was effective here. Some sinister force was blocking him, but he hid his frustration and dismissed Manito. After the bouncer quietly shut the inside door, Saltis peered through the window, which was next to the exterior door.

Clouds obscured the half-moon, but he was able to see Mirza climbing up the outside staircase. She was carrying a silver tray that reflected the moon's yellow glow. A stein of ale was to one side and something flat balanced the other. She stopped and deftly fumbled with a key and opened the door to the second floor. She must be going to see Radames.

Saltis grabbed his cape and ran out the door and down the stairs. He feared for the young apprentice. Mirza must have already entered his room as the wizard didn't see her.

"Radames," he called out loudly. "What room are you in? Radames?"

Mirza hurried out of the room nearest the outside stairs.

"He's not here," she said, sounding confused. "I brought him a stein of ale, but his room is empty. I don't understand. He was so weak and sore from his transformation, I thought he'd sleep soundly all night."

If you thought he was sound asleep, why would you wake him with a stein of ale?

He didn't ask the question. He already knew the answer would be, at best, a half-truth. He pushed by her impatiently and inspected the room. He found Radames's cloak draped over a chair and his knapsack sitting on its side in a corner. A large manuscript lay in the middle of the bed, bound in leather with gold lettering—*All the Spells a Wizard Needs to Know.*

There is no such book, Saltis realized instantly, yet there it was, in calligraphic print and right in front of him. He picked it up and thumbed through the onion-skin pages. It had short spells for beginners as well as longer ones that required knowledge of different languages. The back pages contained immensely complicated enchantments that Saltis immediately knew to avoid. Those were curses that required demonic assistance to conjure. And once a demon interacted with a human, he wouldn't rest until the man lie tortured and dead.

He slapped the book shut.

"Where did he get this book?" he demanded, his rage bringing his voice to a shout.

"I don't know, sir," she cowered. "He must have brought it with him. I never saw it until just now when I brought him his nightcap."

She pointed to the ale with her chin.

He made an effort to control his anger. He remembered his lessons from the temple where he grew up as a child.

The angry man defeats himself. His opponent is only there to claim the credit.

"Did you open this book to look at the spells?" he asked calmly.

She shook her head.

"Good," Saltis said with what he hoped was a reassuring smile as he walked over to the fireplace.

The wood was there but Radames never lit it. He was probably too sore to bend down. With a few magical passes and a short incantation, the fire was soon roaring. The wizard picked up the manuscript and threw it into the flames, watching as they turned blue and white before settling back to orange and red.

Mirza let out a small cry and bit her fist when she saw what he did but remained quiet with tear filled eyes. Saltis remained unsympathetic.

"You wanted to learn these spells yourself?" he asked. "You are quite skillful with magic as it is, but some of these incantations will bring forth demons and devils. I don't think you could make them go back."

"I can't read, Lord Saltis," she said quietly.

"But you are crying because I destroyed it."

"I am crying for what it was, because it can no longer be."

She wasn't making any sense. The wizard turned and left the room, cautiously returning to his own chamber on the third floor. He pushed his meager bed next to the interior door so he could watch it if it opened and sat by the window to observe the night pass by. He had no intention of sleeping. Sleep could be fatal here.

The Djinn

The afternoon ended well enough, Guidry thought morosely to himself. That insufferable Aberdeen was dead and gone. Guidry, Manito and Mirza hated doing the things the djinn demanded of them, but they reluctantly followed their orders. However, the Dark Wizard enthusiastically killed and maimed anyone, even if it wasn't included in his assignments. He loved making people suffer. If anything, he was worse than the Master of the Inn.

Guidry was not the Master of the Inn. It may have been him at one time, but he was little more than a slave today. It was sad and unfair that one decision he made twenty years ago still affected him. Yes, he was unhappy. And he had no one to blame except himself.

Guidry was the richest man in all of Kheliesis, but no one knew or cared. Whoever would have thought a simple innkeeper in an isolated part of the island kingdom could have so much gold? He had more money than the king. But he lived in tattered clothes in a small room. His pitcher and basin were both chipped and faded. The numbers on his wall clock were barely visible. He had so much money but couldn't replace the bare necessities.

He remembered when that sailor swaggered into his mean small waystation with an accursed little box. It was gold-plated with blue and red carvings of intricate designs. Images that somehow made him nervous, even though he knew they were simply geometric figures. He should have told the sailor to go away.

"Inside this little box is the greatest magic the world ever saw," the sailor told him. "It will grant you one wish. Whatever you want is yours. Then you give the box away, but only to a deserving soul."

"I'm not interested in magic," Guidry said. "Only wise and learned men should fool with that stuff. The ancient writings say that uneducated men like me should stay away from it."

"That's if you practice it. This is different. One wish. And give it to another to make one wish. The magical being inside is a good spirit who seeks forgiveness for some misdeed he chose to do years ago. Now, he allows people to have their greatest desire. Wouldn't it be a kindness to help him?"

"What did you wish?" he asked the sailor.

"To see new lands that men never walked on. I want to explore the world."

"Where did you get this box?"

"From the Eastern Islands."

"The Islands of the Djinn?"

"The same. I was on board a ship of collectors. We go

275

where the djinn live. You know that when a djinn dies, his body turns into blue dust within minutes. That dust holds the essence of magic. It's the ingredient the smiths mix with metal to make magic swords and amulets."

"I know. So, you collectors basically go to these dangerous places and rob graves to get the dust. What if the djinn catches you?"

"We die. But there's a secret to it all. The djinn only can come out at night. The sunlight kills them. We only visit the islands in the daytime and sail as far away as fast as possible when the evening shadows fall."

Simple enough.

"This magical being is a djinn?"

"He is. Tibshraney the Tall. He is old enough to remember the Great Rebellion against the Great Creator, when the djinn were all destroyed or exiled. Now, he is old and wants peace."

Guidry looked down at the box. One wish and then it would be gone forever.

"Wait until after sunset," the sailor said. "Tell him what you want. There may be limits. He will give me access to any land in the world, but only the lands in the sea. Islands. He'll tell you what your limits are. You never have to make a deal if you don't like the limits. Just be sure the sun is down when you open the box. Don't forget, a djinn turns to blue dust in the sunlight."

When he opened the box that night, Guidry thought the djinn was dead and turned to blue dust. But a wind swirled through the powder, twirling into a spiral of blue that soon solidified into the blue figure of Tibshraney the Tall. The djinn smiled at the fearful innkeeper.

"I am aware of you, Guidry," the blue figure whispered soothingly. "The sailor told you all of my story that I want to reveal. Tell me your wish."

"I want to be the richest man in the world. I want to hire servants to wait on me every day."

"I can do that, Guidry," said the djinn. "But remember, sometimes the man becomes the slave of the gold. And I will not protect you from bandits. Beautiful women will want you, but only for your money. If the kings and warlords find out you have riches, they will send armies to take them. So, I propose this: I will give you all the money you need, but you must stay here and run the inn until I determine you will be safe."

What a glorious deal. All Guidry's storehouses and the caves near the sea now contained gold bars and coins from the floors to the ceiling. The innkeeper just circled through his rooms and wondered at all the gold, silver, copper, and jewels he owned.

"I'm so rich," he said to the sailor who gazed in wonder at all the money.

"I'm happy for you."

"Here, let me give you some gold for your journey."

"You can't do that," the djinn said from behind them. "Remember, no one must know you have all this gold until you're safe."

"But—"

"No, the deal is you do not spend it until I decide you are safe. Sailor, your new lands await you. It is time for you to go."

"I thought I would leave in the morning," the sailor said, confused.

"Remember our deal. You bring me to the mainland and leave immediately to see lands nobody ever saw before. It is time."

Within an hour, the sailor said good-bye to Guidry and

climbed into his sailboat to head out to sea. They waved to each other as Tibshraney watched. The boat floated almost out of sight when a bolt of lightning struck it. Guidry watched in horror as the burnt vessel slipped under the surface.

"What happened?"

The djinn shrugged, an evil smile lighting his face.

"He found land no man ever walked on. At the bottom of the sea."

Guidry stared out at the water until Tibshraney urged him back to the inn. All his work waited for him that night and every night. Nothing changed, except that instead of being poor, he was rich but he lived as though he was impoverished.

The djinn did allow him to buy fresher meat and some medicinal herbs. The inn soon had a reputation for being a wonderful stop for travelers. But Guidry still wore threadbare clothes and worn boots. He slept on tattered linens on a rickety bed. His wind-up clock showed numbers so worn with age that he could barely see them.

The nightmare never got better. As the owner of the box, the djinn reminded Guidry that he had the duty to give it away to another victim. But he remembered watching the sailor drown.

"I can't help you," he told Tibshraney. "You give people what they want but make them regret it. You killed that sailor."

"No, I didn't. I fulfilled his wish, just like I did with you," the djinn replied. "If I killed everyone I granted a wish to, why are you still alive? I could have melted the gold in a cauldron and poured it over you, but I didn't. Now, give the box away. I will grant another person exactly what he wants. It is what you agreed to and it is what you will do.

Their despair feeds my soul and increases my power. Some men you will simply kill. You already know what a djinn eats, do you not?"

Guidry shook his head. Whoosh! He was gone. He couldn't believe the pain he was in. He couldn't move, but he knew a metal spit ripped through his intestines and exited through his mouth. He screamed in agony, but he couldn't hear the sound. Flames were roasting him. He was in a fireplace, slowing cooking. A family of djinn gathered around, watching him cook.

"The Great Creator is sending out angels to destroy the djinn race," one said.

"Why would he do that?"

"The elders tell us that eating humans is forbidden."

"But what will we eat?"

"Humans. The Great Creator won't do anything. He knows we have to eat."

He was back, cringing on the floor. Tibshraney stood over him.

"Generations ago, we ruled the world. Our fathers were angels, sent to teach mankind all about the world, the universe and God, the Great Creator. But because they desired to be the best teachers, they chose to become human themselves. And they fell into temptation. Opium, wine, laziness, and lust drove them away from Heaven. They married our mothers, the most beautiful of human women. They ruled like kings. Their children were the djinn, the giants, the Nephilim. There was no need to teach people anything. We were dominating the world. You were just some little things running around.

"When the great famine arrived, your ancestors became food for us. Human flesh increased our power and we flourished until we lost control. Because we disappointed the Great Creator, he sent in armies of heavenly hosts. We lost everything, even the ability to live in the sunlight. He gave the world back to the humans. I am trying to make amends with Him by proving that you are no better than us. I will destroy you with kindness. And now, my servant, we begin."

The next day, a desperate couple rushed into the inn with a daughter burned beyond recognition.

"She fell in the campfire last night and we left everything to find help," the woman said while weeping.

They begged for a room and any medicine they could give the girl. Guidry could tell she would be dead by morning, so he gave them whatever he could to ease their pain.

Just before sundown, the innkeeper brought the family into the kitchen and down to the basement. Although gold and jewels littered the floor, the guests were oblivious to all the wealth at their feet. They hardly noticed the djinn's magical entrance.

"We can save her," Guidry said quietly. "My master and I."

She was already dead, but Tibshraney soothed the distraught parents when he appeared.

"I can bring her back. She isn't that far gone." He turned to the father, "Will that be your wish?"

The father nodded. With a malicious smile, the djinn snapped his fingers. The child cried out to her mother while the father crashed to the floor, dead.

"In order to give you her life back, I had to take a life," he grinned maliciously.

Soon, the woman and child were sobbing.

"What will we do? How can I raise my daughter without my husband? Who will support us?"

"Perhaps you should make a wish?" Tibshraney suggested.

"No," she screamed, clutching her daughter tightly as she backed away. "No, I wish I never came here."

And she vanished, leaving behind the child.

"What did you do to her?" Guidry asked after the shock wore off.

"I granted her wish. She was never here."

"But where…"

"She couldn't both be here and never have been here, so there is only one way to grant her wish. She was never born."

The child looked around the room, scared and confused. Her ruined face healed, but only scar tissue covered her bones and her nose, lips and ears were all missing. Guidry felt sorry for her.

"Can you speak?" Tibshraney asked quietly.

"Yes," she replied.

"What is your name?"

"Mirza."

"You get a wish, Mirza."

"Be beautiful," Guidry whispered, "Be the most beautiful girl in the world."

She nodded and Guidry watched her transform into the perfect woman.

"Granted. You are now the most beautiful woman in the world and will remain young and lovely to all the men of Kheliesis. But you will stay here for the rest of your life or turn back to the burned and misshapen thing you truly are. Here, all the men will pursue you. Some, you will lead to Guidry to meet me. Others, to their death."

Guidry tried to put the box into her hands, but Tibshraney slapped him.

"She is but a child. The people you gave my home to died without a male heir. The box returns to you by default. And it will always return to you until you become so old you cannot serve me anymore. Not that it matters to me. I can easily replace a man like you."

Mirza was too young to be very helpful at first. She wiped down tables and spoke to the travelers. She guided the men and women who spoke of losses or unfulfilled wishes to Guidry who took them to the djinn. She never saw any of them again and hoped their wishes took them away to some happy new world, though she doubted any of them would end up happy after Tibshraney granted their wishes.

At first, Mirza felt sorry for them. She hated luring men to the basement to watch Tibshraney dole out their cruel fates. The first victim she remembered was an old man who asked to be young again and she was soon holding a baby. Guidry sold him to a farmer as a slave. The next night, a skinny little man asked to be as strong as a bull.

"The only thing as strong as a bull is a bull," Tibshraney explained when they found him grazing in the field. He fed many travelers the next few days.

By the end of the first week, Tibshraney was hungry. Guidry and Mirza were too small and weak to provide him with a human meal, so the djinn hatched a plan. A rich nobleman with dozens of servants stayed the night. One sad-looking servant was a dwarf, laughed at and bullied by the others.

"What is your name?" Guidry asked him.

"Manito, sir," came the reply.

"Come with me. I know how to transform you into a giant. No one will ever bother you again."

So now, there were three. Manito and Mirza dragged

away a body or two every week of betrayed young men. Sometimes, due to the nature of their wish, they didn't die. Manito and Mirza had to put those suffering victims out of their misery. It became a routine of murder and burial.

Meanwhile, Mirza developed a distaste for men in general. They viewed her as a toy to figure out and master and she resented that. Sometimes, she would let a man make love to her just out of sight in the woods. Afterwards, while the lover was gloating over his conquest, Manito crushed his skull with one blow from his axe. Those men became Tibshraney's dinner. Thankfully, the djinn cooked them himself. Mirza only had to dump the bones into the sea.

Although they didn't know it at the time, a new phase began with the arrival of Aberdeen. Guidry thought Tibshraney would quickly dispose of the conman but the djinn surprised him.

"He will help us expand our empire. He will be like one of you."

"He's middle-aged, dirty and unclean. He doesn't even try to wash the stink off. He's the most disgusting man I ever met," Mirza complained. "It's so sad he lived through his wish to be the greatest wizard in the world. And he thinks he's going to be my lover and bedmate? Never."

Tibshraney told them, "I have a special purpose for Aberdeen. The false mage will go around the towns to look for magicians. After we kill them, their meagre powers will blend into my spirit and make me even stronger."

Now that the war ended and so many displaced people sought refuge, the inn was congested with people, but Tibshraney wanted more. Aberdeen was killing isolated people on the road. The woods across the highway were a veritable graveyard. And still, the djinn wanted to kill more.

"I'm really worried," Mirza told Guidry earlier that night, as the inn filled with customers in search of ale and dinner. "What started out as a murder or two a week multiplied into five or six a night. How long can all these disappearances go on? Sooner or later, someone will suspect us."

The innkeeper nodded in agreement as he motioned to her to be quiet. He was worried as well. Two men of the magic class were sitting in booths. One seemed quite timid, the other very self-assured. He sent her out to wait on tables and spy on these men.

Guidry released the djinn at sundown. Aberdeen actually owned the box now, but Tibshraney decided that since the dark wizard spent so much time in the forest, he was safer here in the cellar. He was doomed if anyone inadvertently opened the box in direct sunlight.

"So, I face my first true challenge tonight," the djinn mused after Guidry related the events.

He planned his next action. He felt the two magicians walk into the building tonight. One was close to nothing, with no natural abilities. He was not a factor to the djinn. But he faced a formidable opponent when Saltis entered the building. Somehow, the wizard knew something was not right even though the djinn cast a cloaking spell to hide his magic. He sent the girl to his table to find out who he was and why he came here.

She almost had him in a hypnotic trance when that foolish young man broke her concentration. All she brought back was that he was a wizard of the highest order. One of the nine. This amused the djinn. His serving girl almost mastered him. How much of a challenge could he be? This was the time to test Aberdeen's new skill as a master wizard. But first, he wanted to eliminate that young man who broke his spell. His bold behavior didn't seem natural. He might be an assistant to Saltis and Tibshraney wanted him removed permanently.

It was almost too easy.

"I can grant you one wish, but you must give the box to another deserving man. I have much to atone for."

"I want to be smart."

"Smart? That will be easy. I will fill your brain will all the knowledge of all the generations of all the dimensions of all the galaxies in the universe. Go in peace and feel your brain as its swells with more knowledge than a man can absorb."

The young man's brain couldn't contain the knowledge that flowed into it. It burst through his skull in seconds. The djinn eliminated the nuisance, whether he was in league with the wizard or just some innocent.

But then the wizard won the battle with Aberdeen without his help. Another accomplice appeared at the last minute and rescued the wizard. Radames was a loose end that Aberdeen never considered to be even a remote threat until it was too late. Yet, when he discovered his master was evil, Radames jumped into the fight and destroyed Aberdeen's concentration.

He dealt with him as soon as Mirza led him into the cellar. The naïve young lad had no idea who or what he was dealing with. And he never would.

"Tell me what you want. What is your wish? I can make you human again."

"No," Radames said back, "I want to be the greatest wizard ever. I want to know every spell ever cast."

"I shall see to it that every spell known to mankind is within you."

Radames fell to the floor, transformed into a thick and heavy book—*All the Spells a Wizard Needs to Know*.

"And now it is."

For the first time in centuries, the djinn laughed. He saw the tears in Mirza's eyes but didn't care. When Mirza informed him that the wizard threw the book into the fire, he was satisfied. Saltis had no more friends to help him now. He was sure of it.

"Go upstairs to the wizard," he told Mirza. "Be irresistible. Maybe, if he's off guard, we can hypnotize him. No one will be there to distract us this time. If not, seduce him and have him seduce you."

"I don't want to sleep with men just to watch them die," she said.

She noticed that the old clock stopped so she wound it up again.

"I don't care. You will do as you're told. I can see through your eyes and hear through your ears. I will know if you follow my commands or not. When he touches you and you fill his mind, make noise, cry out loudly with fake pleasure. Manito will enter the room and kill him while he's distracted. Now, go."

She reluctantly poured a stein of ale, gathered some crackers and put them on a serving tray, then slowly climbed up the stairs. As she entered the landing, she inspected her reflection in an oval mirror. The first image was her reality. A hairless, featureless blob of scar tissue gazed back at her, but slowly dissolved into a pretty little thing with brown hair and stunning blue eyes. Her body had all the required curves, but none of them were dominant. She was impressed.

"I haven't seen many women who were this pretty," she said softly to her reflection. "He likes real women, not some kind of cartoon. I wish you could have him as your man. But he will know what you really are. A monster on the outside and inside. Why couldn't I have died that day too?"

She picked up the tray while blinking back tears, strode across the hall and gently knocked on the door.

"Come in," he called.

She opened the door quietly. He was sitting on a chair watching the night outside his window. After closing the door behind her, she placed the tray on the table.

"Guidry thought you might still be up," she lied. "And he thought that after all you went through, a small glass of our best ale might do you some good. I had to agree."

"Only one?" he forced a smile.

"I can fetch you another if you want. You were so heroic tonight."

"One is fine. I thought one for you so we can sip a bit together."

"I never had any ale," she explained. "It's for customers."

"As if you never had a man buy you one," Saltis smiled.

"Well, once or twice, but I never drank much. It makes me clumsy. I wouldn't be able to keep my job, spilling drinks on people.'

"It's night now though," he said, offering her his stein. "Have half and I will have the other. That way, we can share a drink. I won't care if you're clumsy."

She sat next to him on the bed, loosened her blouse and smiled shyly. He reached his arm around her and drew her near enough for a kiss, followed by his fingers tracing her face from the temple to the jawline. She flinched at his touch but relaxed as he cupped her chin and pressed his mouth over hers, gently but firmly. He moved her to his lap so she faced him and he hugged her closely and kissed her again. She could feel his arms moving behind her, but she was lost in that kiss and didn't notice that his hands hadn't quite pressed her into him yet.

Tibshraney was angry. He stalked back and forth in the cellar, scowling at Guidry.

"That man thwarted me again," he screamed. "He figured out his charms can't affect my minions, so he created some kind of blocking spell. I lost touch with her."

"Do you want me to go fetch her?" Guidry asked, hoping to get away for a moment.

"And give him the satisfaction of knowing it worked? Never. Maybe he has doubts that his trick worked. Let him wonder."

She pulled back with a confused smile. "Don't you want me?" she asked, hurt.

Saltis smiled at her and gently pulled her blouse up over her head, revealing her magically perfect breasts and gently squeezed them, rubbing her nipples with his thumbs.

"How could I not want you? I want you badly, but I imagine you don't have many men who are gentle, who take their time for you. That's what I'm doing now that I ensured our privacy. Now, treat yourself the way you should. Have some of the ale."

"I can't say I like the taste," she said truthfully. "So many men drink this stuff until they get stupid. I'm happy with sarsaparilla or tea. And they don't get me stupid."

"You could never be stupid," Saltis told her firmly. "Although, I confess, I don't know why you stay here. The world has a lot to offer a lovely young woman like yourself."

"I don't want the world. I want you."

She leaned in to kiss him and felt a mixture of fear and triumph when he wrapped his arms around her waist and kissed back. She broke away and bent back, offering her throat. She loved the romantic way he nibbled and kissed on her. Her moans and cries filled the room while Saltis gently undressed her the rest of the way and laid her on the bed, pausing only long enough to slip out of his own robes.

Her heart pounded when she remembered why she came to him.

Where is Manito? What am I supposed to do now? Did Tibshraney change the plans?

The more he touched her, the less it mattered. Even if it only lasted a moment, she was in the world she wanted to live in. She could forget about her murderous employers and the blood on her own hands.

She dismissed those thoughts and concentrated on the present. She loved being here with the man. Her man. She loved his touch. His kisses. She loved it all.

She gasped as they reached the point of no return.

The wizard and maid made love and when it was over, she snuggled next to him, her eyes closed and her heart open. Manito never rescued her and she was happy. Somehow, Saltis avoided Tibshraney's trap. She didn't know how he did it, but she was glad.

"We have to go back," he said simply.

She opened her eyes. He dressed while she languished in her afterglow.

"Go back? We left somewhere?"

She searched the room. Everything was the same. She grabbed her dress and blouse and quickly slipped into them.

"We stayed right here in my room. I simply removed it from our dimensional plane. It didn't exist at the inn while we made love. I wanted us to have privacy. That way, I could break all the spells your master put on you. I hypnotized you like you tried to do to me. Now I know I'm fighting a djinn. And you evil people are helping him. You came here to distract me so Manito could kill me."

"All we did was make love. That's all I wanted. I gave you my body and you took it. And now you sit in judgement of me?"

She was furious and launched herself at him, only to find herself suspended two feet off the ground, unable to move.

"I have that right," Saltis said calmly. "I knew there was something wrong when you got so loud. You were sending out a signal to your accomplice. Manito was going to break into the room and kill me. You even left the door unlocked."

"I won't help you."

"That is your choice. Remember though, I can offer you mercy. The djinn only offers you a continued state of non-existence where you will continue to help the others murder innocent men and women. How long can it last?"

"Mercy?"

"Yes, but you must do exactly what I tell you. Follow every direction to the letter. Then tell Tibshraney the Tall to meet me outside in the yard where I fought Aberdeen."

She nodded.

Saltis waved his hand and the room returned to its place. Mirza left, leaving behind her tray. Saltis glanced at his timepiece. It was just after three. Less than two hours before dawn. He had to defeat his enemy before he could take refuge in the shadows. He could never find the djinn in the cave labyrinth beneath the inn.

"He had the audacity to challenge me?" Tibshraney pounded his fist on the table in rage after Mirza told him what happened and how the wizard sidestepped his trap.

Manito and Guidry flinched at the noise.

"And how did he know that I am the Master of the Inn? He's supposed to think Guidry is behind this. He should be afraid of Guidry. What did you tell him?"

"Nothing. He figured it out when he took us to wherever he moved the room," she replied. "I hurried back as fast as I could. You heard me running to you."

"I did indeed. Very well, we'll accept his challenge. For a man of his rank, he seems to be rather weak, even if he has thwarted me so far tonight."

Tibshraney glanced at the clock.

"Well," he said to his minions, "it's just past two. I have three hours to defeat and torture the wizard. Mirza almost hypnotized him and he only escaped by chance. Aberdeen was seconds away from killing him, but Radames distracted him. Saltis does not seem to be a very worthy opponent. I will go to him myself and annihilate him if that is what he wants. He can be the first body we use to refill our graveyard."

With that, he raised his arms high over his head and vanished. Guidry, Manito and Mirza hurried out to the yard in case he needed them. Tibshraney's temper was mercurial and his punishments excruciating when his servants weren't near.

The moonless yard stood empty and dark. An ocean breeze kept the air from being too still. He could smell the salt. The stars shone bright, but they couldn't produce enough light for a man to see everything clearly. Tibshraney, however, was a djinn with eyes accustomed to dark, which gave him a substantial advantage over a mortal whose eyes were adapted to the sun.

"Where are you, mortal? I have come to answer your challenge."

"Above you, Djinn," the voice called from the inn's roof.

Tibshraney searched, but no wizard appeared. His eyes glanced at the stars, but only saw their cold light. Yet something about them was wrong. Before he could give it another thought, a red velvet net captured him. The cords constricted him severely and only tightened deeper into his flesh with each second.

Two blue Snakes of Alda rose from the ground, coiling around his legs as they climbed to engulf his torso.

Snakes of Alda?

They were low level magic. The red velvet net was a bit more complex, since the djinn was unfamiliar with it. But one thing at a time. He clenched his fist and mentally recited a short counterspell and watched the snake's retreat. He attempted a few spells to dissolve the net but, after fifteen minutes, nothing worked.

"A clever contraption, Wizard," he called out into the night.

Two more incantations achieved no results.

"You force me to use a master spell."

A master spell dissolved all magic within three yards of the djinn. It weakened the conjurer, but in this case, Tibshraney had no choice.

The net dissolved into heatless flames and the djinn stepped forward, still searching for his unseen enemy. The squawk scraped his eardrums before a giant condor flew into his face. He swatted it away with a low-level spell, but it attacked again. Tibshraney slapped it again and the bird burst into flames. The stench of fiery feathers irritated his nostrils.

He raised his arms and levitated above the ground, again scouring the scene for his enemy. Wherever Saltis was hiding, it had to be nearby. Then he laughed. The wizard was using a cloaking charm. With a quick nod, Tibshraney cancelled all camouflage spells.

Saltis stood before him, his arms pointing straight at his torso. He could see the lightning shoot out. The djinn called up a shield for protection. It was successful. Saltis used up most of his natural powers in his fight with Aberdeen.

"You seem to be little more than target practice, magician," he gloated while red and blue tendrils shot out of his fingers and sped toward Saltis at lightning speed.

They dissolved inches before they landed on the wizard.

The djinn smirked while Saltis gathered his strength for another offensive spell. Just when he cast his arms out, the tendrils reappeared before him, spinning in circles. It soon became an egg-shaped prison, blocking his vision.

Without losing his focus, Saltis finished his spell. Ten spears of golden sunlight pierced through the barrier, dissolving it into the night. The djinn grunted in pain as the spears spotlighted him momentarily. For the first time in his life, an opponent actually struck him and it was painful.

Saltis escaped his prison and they faced off again. Tibshraney quickly spun his hands out at Saltis who again conjured some kind of shield. But although most of Tibshraney's spell was nullified, two incoming streams of some kind of silver fluid arced straight at Saltis, spilling on him. He fell to the ground in shock and pain next to a few bones left over from his earlier battle.

"It's called 'The Acid of Agorta,' Wizard," the djinn called out in a mocking voice. "It dissolved all the magic powder sewn into your robes. The only magic you have left are your spells and you used most of them already."

The djinn lowered himself to the ground to face his nearly defeated foe.

"I would like to be gracious and say you fought well, but that isn't true. You were lucky. Mirza hypnotized you, but you escaped by dumb luck. Aberdeen soundly defeated you, but your friend saved you in the end. You were lucky. You weren't good. Now, it's a matter of how to kill you. I think that maybe I can call out a thousand crows to eat you alive."

The djinn flapped his arms and waved them in circles, casting his spell, but when he turned toward Saltis, he felt a hard object smash into his nose. The wizard found a skull and threw it at him, breaking his concentration. The spell dissolved.

"Even better," he said to Saltis, pointing at the wizard with one hand and circling the other in the air. "Is that your best? That's not magic. Let's do something a little less intense. I want to see you as a trophy every day. Saltis of the White Ring, I command you to become Saltis of the White Willow."

Saltis managed a deflection spell, but it was weak and the djinn was too strong.

"How could you think you could defeat me? Aberdeen annihilated you. Not to mention that no man ever defeated a djinn in one-on-one combat. Only the angels could beat us. And even so, it took an army of them years to drive us to the islands."

The deflection spell was over. Saltis didn't have the time to cast another. He could feel his feet sinking into the ground, expanding, growing longer and thinner as they sank into the earth for nourishment. His thighs melted together and he could feel his skin harden into bark. His fingers, arms and hands elongated as he turned his head to see leaves already opening, waiting for dawn to collect the sunlight. He could move no more. The bark covered his mouth and nose, preventing him from breathing, although he knew he didn't need the air the way he used to.

He tried to think of a spell, anything to delay this transformation, but spells cast by thought were by their nature too weak to oppose the sorcery of a djinn. His vision was dimming as more bark began covering his eyes. Part of him wanted to relax and accept the transformation. He struggled to stay aware. There was hope as long as he didn't give up.

He was blind. In his new existence, he didn't need to see. The whole battle seemed to be silly, now that he thought of it. A tree had a better life without people. Men would chop him down, of course, unconcerned that a living thing was dying with each blow from the axe. His fate would be the fire so people could have a night or two of warmth. Willows were notorious for being too soft to carve into durable furniture. Perhaps, he might end up being a basket.

All was going dark when he heard a shriek of pain and fear and tried to analyze what was happening. It was Tibshraney, screaming out in rage. He vaguely remembered that he was expecting something like this, but he couldn't recall why. The spell that held him dissolved. Saltis was aware that he could remain a tree if he wanted to, but he had to return. He willed the process to move faster as his consciousness returned.

First, his eyes began to see again. Fuzzy at first, but soon in complete focus. He could feel his body constrict back into his human form. The leaves disappeared. His fingers shanked down to normal and his roots returned to feet.

"You traitor," the djinn screamed at Mirza while he desperately staggered back to the inn's front door, blue dust trailing behind him.

Tibshraney flailed at the knob but the door remained locked.

"Guidry, Manito! Help me! The sun!"

Behind the retreating figure, the sun rose, turning the sky into blazes of violet and red. The colorful dawn caught Tibshraney outside and he was dying in the early sunlight. The djinn waved his hands in a desperate attempt to unlock the door with sorcery, but Saltis waved his hands in a weak effort to block the spell. The djinn screamed in frustration and stopped long enough to begin a counter spell he never completed. Saltis and the others watched as Tibshraney stood motionless for just a moment. Then he was nothing more than blue powder that sank under its own weight.

"It's over," a weak voice almost whispered.

Saltis turned. The three villains stood in awe, not knowing what to do. He knew their stories the second he saw them.

The voice came from Manito. Only he was no longer a giant of man. He could, at the most, stand three feet tall. He stood next to Mirza who was unrecognizable in her true form. He almost felt sorry for her. Maybe she would have acted differently if she avoided the fire that ruined her face and body. Guidry didn't change. He looked the same—a middle-aged man, defeated by life.

"For some. Not for you three. You have much to atone for. First, you will sweep up all the blue dust and put it in a small barrel. We can't leave it here for anyone to find. Men fought wars with enchanted weapons created from Djinn dust. Those weapons for generations burned down entire cities and slaughtered thousands. We don't need the blacksmiths creating more magic arms. I will see that this dust creates something better than swords and spears."

He returned to his room and washed the dirt off his legs and feet until Mirza knocked on the door.

"Your barrel is on the back porch," she said while looking at the floor.

He nodded and motioned for her to follow him.

"Show me what the djinn gave you," he said roughly to Guidry in the kitchen.

The older man quietly led them down to the basement, hanging his head. The trunks of gold lay on the shelves, all unopened. At Saltis' command, he opened them one by one. They all contained beach sand.

"He gave you nothing but an illusion. How many men did you kill to keep this?"

"I didn't kill anyone," Guidry protested, but his shoulders sank as Saltis truth spell sank into his soul. "But I took part in hundreds. I helped fulfill Tibshraney's need for food. I did wrong, I know. But I didn't know he would use my words against me like that. He said I could go when he said it was safe, only he never thought it was safe."

"It was always safe to leave. It was never safe to let him know you wanted to go. That's all. So, you stayed here with him for your gold. Like everyone else who makes a deal with the devils of the world, you got what you deserved."

"Yes, sir," Guidry was almost crying in his fear and shame.

"I think I already know why you two did the things you did."

Mirza was crying. Manito nodded sadly.

"I didn't know what would happen. I didn't know what to do," Mirza whined.

"All three of you could have left as soon as the sun rose in the sky. An hour's walk and he could never find you. Dawn offered you freedom every day and you rejected it. You know you must pay a price for your actions."

"Please, Lord Saltis," Mirza pleaded. "I was a child when I came here. I did what I had to do to survive. If I left, what was I to do? It wasn't bad here. The men always had a kind word for me and an occasional coin just for being pretty and giving them a smile. But after a few years, they wanted more than a smile. I indulged a man here and there in my bed. What other enjoyment in life could I have? I couldn't leave. I hated myself, but I had to obey Tibshraney. We all did. His punishments were so painful and harsh."

"I know. But you still guided some men to the djinn to play with before he destroyed them by granting them their wishes. And the others?"

"I lured to my bed and Manito killed them."

"How kind of you. At least they had a moment of pleasure before they died. You three are aware that I cannot let you live among good people ever again. Your punishment is the djinn's reward. You will remain in this place for the rest of your lives, serving the refugees as they pass through. Of course, your illusions will be gone and people will see you as you are. You are a dwarf. And you are...not beautiful. But I believe you two can find each other desirable as you work here and as time goes on."

"But I helped you," Mirza pleaded. "I moved the hands of the clock backwards an hour."

"I know. I hypnotized you to do that."

He softened his glare before he turned to the others.

"Innkeeper, you will feed everyone who can't pay for their meals. If you make a profit at the end of any day, you will give it away to someone in need and be content to live in the poverty you deserved for all these years. Perhaps the travelers will come to love all three of you and you will be content with that. Perhaps, someday, you will consider the gratitude of strangers to be a better treasure than your gold could ever be. Or beauty or height.

"As time goes by, the families of your victims may come searching for them. Be prepared to explain yourselves and beg for mercy."

With that, Saltis of the White Ring secured the barrel of blue dust on his horse and rode away, oblivious to the crowd of refugees who ominously marched toward the three people he spared.